1

2

Flatland: A Romance of Many Dimensions

3

BOOKSFROMTHEFUTURE

The Centre is Everywhere, The Circumference Nowhere

(By way of a Foreword)

FLATLAND, SEE ANECHOIC CHAMBERS.

Circle

"An anechoic chamber (an-echoic meaning non-reflective, non-echoing or echo-free) is a room designed to completely absorb reflections of either sound or electromagnetic waves. They are also insulated from exterior sources of noise. The combination of both aspects means they simulate a quiet open-space of infinite dimension, which is useful when exterior influences would otherwise give false results." [1]

Flatland is where you find it. Wandering through Edwin A. Abbott's 'Romance of Many Dimensions' brings to mind a short story written in 1941 by Argentine author and fabulist Jorge Luis Borges—less than twenty-five years after *Flatland* is first published in 'novel format'. An unnamed man, as anonymous as the Square narrator in *Flatland*, describes his existence within a gigantic library of interconnecting hexagonal, book-lined rooms that constitutes his entire known universe. 'The idealists argue that the hexagonal rooms are a necessary form of absolute space or, at least, of our intuition of space,' he explains. 'They reason that a triangular or pentagonal room is inconceivable.' The tone and the emphasis upon geometry at the start of the story offer a clear historical echo of Flatland—both tales take place in universes that require quite specific rational explanations from their narrator in order to exist. In fact, anything outside the established visual order is treated as intrusive and suspect. 'The mystics,' according to Borges' narrator, 'claim that their ecstasy reveals to them a circular chamber containing a great circular book, whose spine is continuous and which follows the complete circle of the walls; but their testimony is suspect; their words, obscure. This cyclical book is God.'

In this respect it is interesting to note the outbreak of heretical sects in these fictional worlds as responses to the logic of both narratives. Flatland is plunged into chaos by the 'Chromatic Sedition' of the Colour Revolt and ensuing Universal Colour Bill, which regulates societal recognition of individuals not by their shape but by other visual properties. Similarly, in 'The Library of Babel' an uprising of 'Purifiers' seeks to dispose of imperfect or anomalous volumes, thus simplifying their collective researches by simply destroying millions of books.

There is little separating order from collapse in either text; in each case an entire universe of meaning is in immediate danger. The Square's first direct experience with the Sphere as it passes through the two dimensions of Flatland on quitting its own three-dimensional home in Spaceland is as a series of swelling and diminishing circles that change size but not shape or proportion. What is the Square expected to make of such an anomaly if not a moment of mystical or ecstatic enlightenment? We find concealed within a footnote tucked away at the very end of 'The Library of Babel' a proposition worthy of Edwin Abbott and his nameless Square narrator: 'At the beginning of the seventeenth century Cavalieri said that any solid body is the superposition of an infinite number of planes.' Is it possible that Jorge Luis Borges had read Abbott's text? The former had been the director of the National Library of Argentina, and his writings are filled with references to obscure, possible or even non-existent texts. He even compiled an alphabetical directory of imaginary animals from fiction and folklore and mythology, so the tensions that exist between the bibliographically organised world and that of the fantastic and irrational are often palpable in his stories and fables.

FLATLAND, SEE MARTHA ROSLER.

Square

The account of a text never takes us beyond the text; however, its realisation in graphic terms opens up new aspects and properties, breaks the limits of the narrative, becoming a visual figment generated but not contained by the text. 'Let it suffice now for me to repeat the classic dictum,' asserts Borges' unnamed narrator, echoing his author's own emphasis: 'The Library is a sphere whose exact centre is any one of its hexagons and whose circumference is inaccessible.' This particular statement has haunted thinking on the relationship between geometry and mysticism since the earliest Greco-Egyptian period of civilization. At its core is the Platonist concept of ideal forms: the notion that everything in the material universe is an imperfect version of an ideal abstraction. Pure geometric forms such as the square, the circle and the equilateral triangle are all expressions of this abstracted perfection. In a subtle way *Flatland* elaborates this same approach but emphatically on its own terms. A hierarchy of ideal forms, both social and mystical, inhabits the text. We note, for example, that the Square refers to the Sphere as his 'Lord', his 'Master' and his 'Teacher', while the Sphere itself speaks of the 'Gospel of Three Dimensions'. As a three-dimensional body moving through a flat plane, the Sphere gets as close to God as it is possible to be in a text written and developed between the nineteenth and twentieth centuries.

Although defined as something distinctly separate from God in the Library Universe that is laid out by Borges, his anonymous narrator describes his world in specifically mystical terms. The 'necessary form of absolute space' upheld by the Library's idealists makes all other forms, even that of God, inconceivable and therefore impossible. And yet to explore Flatland is to encounter the impossible. Compare, for example, the 'classic dictum' regarding the Library with the following from the Greco-Egyptian philosopher Hermes Trismegistus: 'God is an infinite sphere, the center of which is everywhere, the circumference nowhere.' Both statements occupy very similar dimensions. Over 1500 years after Hermes Trismegistus first spoke of God as a sphere, the Christian mystic Alain of Lille restates the same proposition in slightly terms, claiming that 'God is an intelligible sphere, whose center is everywhere, and whose circumference is nowhere.' There has been a shift in meaning: to speak of an 'intelligible sphere' rather than infinite one at the start of the thirteenth century is to anticipate Edwin Abbott's *Flatland* in all but narrative detail. No longer removed as an ideal form, the Sphere frustrates and torments the Square, only accessible to perception and the intellect when it passes through the plane of Flatland. During the Renaissance this same torment is reworked for the first time to embrace the material universe of the senses. 'We may enlarge our conceptions beyond all imaginable space; we only produce atoms in comparison with the reality of things,' asserts Blaise Pascal. 'It is an infinite sphere, the center of which is everywhere, the circumference nowhere. In short, it is the

"Semiotics of the Kitchen is a feminist parody video and performance piece released in 1975 by Martha Rosler. The video, which runs six minutes, is considered a critique of the commodified versions of traditional women's roles in modern society.

Featuring Rosler as a generic cooking show host, the camera observes as she presents an array of kitchen hand utensils, many of them outdated or strange, and, after identifying them, demonstrates unproductive, sometimes, violent, uses for each. It uses a largely static camera and a plain set, allowing the viewer to focus more on Rosler's performance and adding a primitive quality." [1]

greatest sensible mark of the almighty power of God that imagination loses itself in that thought.' Such words could easily have come from the Square himself.

Triangle

Flatland can never leave the page it has been printed on. Even as a series of illustrative graphic schemas to aid comprehension it can only map itself in two dimensions. At the same time, a written text will always evade the rationality of the typographically organized page, destabilizing not just the laws of grammar and syntax but also the conceptual background against which the printed word seeks to communicate with its readers. While the world of *Flatland* might be rationally organized to the point of becoming a despotic dystopia where there appears to be no end to the reasons why you might be 'consumed', it relies upon the intrusion of the irrational, usually in the form of dreams or mystical visions, to convey its relationship to the many different dimensions that are hinted at in the book's subtitle.

Flatland is, in other words, a work of complete and utter nonsense. Furthermore, the manner of its composition suggests the extent to which a graphic intrusion into a printed text brings with it a type of irrationality that is 'mystical' in a way that the Square would immediately understand and appreciate. There is no need to look any further than Laurence Sterne's masterpiece of eighteenth-century absurdity, *The Life and Opinions of Tristram Shandy, Gentleman,* for cases of irrational graphic intrusion. There is, for example, the infamous black page ostensibly inserted as a mark of funerary respect to one of the novel's minor characters Parson Yorick, who has passed away only pages after first being introduced. The entire fabric of this printed page is intended to be black, so the verso is just as darkly enigmatic as the recto. There is also the inclusion of a blank page upon which the reader is invited, since everyone's opinion is subjective, to write a description of what the most beautiful woman in the world might look like. Whole passages in Sterne's text are either broken up or replaced by dashes and asterisks, allowing grammar and punctuation to take on a life of their own even as the narrative collapses in upon itself.

These breaks in the printed text suggest the opening up of new spaces and dimensions within it. Illustrations alone tend to pale in comparison with the introduction of the marbled page, again occupying both recto and verso, upon which *Tristram Shandy's* narrator discourses at some length. 'I tell you before-hand,' he affirms, 'you had better throw down the book at once; for without much reading, by which your reverence knows, I mean much knowledge, you will no more be able to penetrate the moral of the next marbled page (motly emblem of my work!) than the world with all its sagacity has been able to unravel the many opinions, transactions and truths, which still lie mystically hid under the dark veil of the black one.' Unlike the typographical depths triangulated between the black, the white and the marbled pages of *Tristram Shandy,* the only other dimension to be perceived by the inhabitants of Flatland is a purely social one. Laws and codes of behavior press down upon a teaming lower order of thin women and triangular servants who form an unstable *lumpenproletariat* eager to embrace disorder at any moment. Bearing in mind that a revolution constitutes a motion rotating a body's position through space, translating it within any number of degrees and dimensions, it is entirely possible that *Flatland* is not simply a mystical text but a revolutionary one as well.

Ken Hollings
London, August 2014

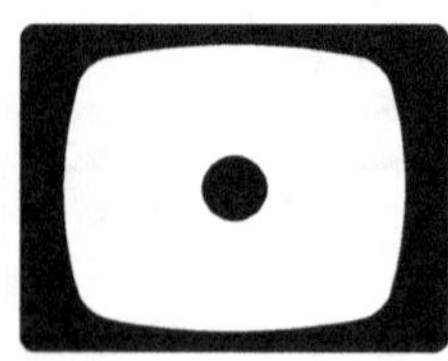

"Colorforms are paper-thin, die-cut vinyl sheet images and shapes that are meant to be applied to a shiny plastic laminated board, much like placing paper dolls against a paper backdrop. The images stick to the background by adhesion, which takes place when two highly polished surfaces come in contact. The Colorforms vinyl pieces can be repositioned to create new designs and scenarios." [1]

9

FLATLAND, SEE JORGE LUIS BORGES.

PART I
THIS WORLD

"Jorge Francisco Isidoro Luis Borges was an Argentine short-story writer, essayist, poet and translator, and a key figure in the Spanish language literature. His work embraces the 'character of unreality in all literature'.

Borges's works have contributed to philosophical literature and also to the fantasy genre. Critic Ángel Flores, the first to use the term magical realism to define a genre that reacted against the dominant realism and naturalism of the 19th century..." [1]

PART II
OTHER WORLDS

12

FLATLAND, SEE ARIEL SCHLESINGER.

"Schlesinger reinvents everyday objects, such as bicycles, packing tape, paper, and printers, into agents of romantic and daring fantasy. His imaginative sense of play comes through in interactive sculptures such as a household printer re-jigged to print directly on walls, a chair with 'padding' shaped by a large stack of curved paper, and sidewalk blocks that reconfigure lanes painted on them.

His series of conjoined objects, such as two letter-size pages moving and touching one another as if making love, rolls of masking tape united like Siamese twins, and two biscuits 'spooning' can be seen in a romantic light, but Schlesinger also has dangerous side. His numerous works using gas and flames explore risk and neuter a hazardous situation into one that is beautifully controlled." [2]

To
The Inhabitants of SPACE IN GENERAL
And H. C. IN PARTICULAR
This Work is Dedicated
By a Humble Native of Flatland
In the Hope that
Even as he was Initiated into the Mysteries
Of THREE Dimensions
Having been previously conversant
With ONLY TWO
So the Citizens of that Celestial Region
May aspire yet higher and higher
To the Secrets of FOUR FIVE OR EVEN SIX Dimensions
Thereby contributing
To the Enlargement of THE IMAGINATION
And the possible Development
Of that most rare and excellent Gift of MODESTY
Among the Superior Races
Of SOLID HUMANITY

Preface to the Second and Revised Edition, 1884

By the Editor

"Bruno Munari (October 24, 1907, Milan–September 30, 1998, Milan) was an Italian artist, designer, and inventor who contributed fundamentals to many fields of visual arts (painting, sculpture, film, industrial design, graphic design) in modernism, futurism, and concrete art, and in non visual arts (literature, poetry) with his research on games, didactic method, movement, tactile learning, kinesthetic learning, and creativity." [1]

If my poor Flatland friend retained the vigour of mind which he enjoyed when he began to compose these Memoirs, I should not now need to represent him in this preface, in which he desires, firstly, to return his thanks to his readers and critics in Spaceland, whose appreciation has, with unexpected celerity, required a second edition of his work; secondly, to apologize for certain errors and misprints (for which, however, he is not entirely responsible); and, thirdly, to explain one or two misconceptions. But he is not the Square he once was. Years of imprisonment, and the still heavier burden of general incredulity and mockery, have combined with the natural decay of old age to erase from his mind many of the thoughts and notions, and much also of the terminology, which he acquired during his short stay in Spaceland. He has, therefore, requested me to reply in his behalf to two special objections, one of an intellectual, the other of a moral nature.

The first objection is, that a Flatlander, seeing a Line, sees something that must be THICK to the eye as well as LONG to the eye (otherwise it would not be visible, if it had not some thickness); and consequently he ought (it is argued) to acknowledge that his countrymen are not only long and broad, but also (though doubtless in a very slight degree) THICK or HIGH. This objection is plausible, and, to Spacelanders, almost irresistible, so that, I confess, when I first heard it, I knew not what to reply. But my poor old friend's answer appears to me completely to meet it.

"I admit," said he—when I mentioned to him this objection—"I admit the truth of your critic's facts, but I deny his conclusions. It is true that we have really in Flatland a Third unrecognized Dimension called 'height', just as it is also true that you have really in Spaceland a Fourth unrecognized Dimension, called by no name at present, but which I will call 'extra-height'. But we can no more take cognizance of our 'height' than you can of your 'extra-height'. Even I—who have been in Spaceland, and have had the privilege of understanding for twenty-four hours the meaning of 'height'—even I cannot now comprehend it, nor realize it by the sense of sight or by any process of reason; I can but apprehend it by faith.

"The reason is obvious. Dimension implies direction, implies measurement, implies the more and the less. Now, all our lines are EQUALLY and INFINITESIMALLY thick (or high, whichever you like); consequently, there is nothing in them to lead our minds to the conception of that Dimension. No 'delicate micrometer'—as has been suggested by one too hasty Spaceland critic—would in the least avail us; for we should not know WHAT TO MEASURE, NOR IN WHAT DIRECTION. When we see a Line, we see something that is long and BRIGHT; BRIGHTNESS, as well as length, is necessary to the existence

"There have been several technical applications for the Möbius strip. Giant Möbius strips have been used as conveyor belts that last longer because the entire surface area of the belt gets the same amount of wear, and as continuous-loop recording tapes (to double the playing time). Möbius strips are common in the manufacture of fabric computer printer and typewriter ribbons, as they allow the ribbon to be twice as wide as the print head while using both halves evenly." [1]

of a Line; if the brightness vanishes, the Line is extinguished. Hence, all my Flatland friends—when I talk to them about the unrecognized Dimension which is somehow visible in a Line—say, 'Ah, you mean BRIGHTNESS': and when I reply, 'No, I mean a real Dimension', they at once retort, 'Then measure it, or tell us in what direction it extends'; and this silences me, for I can do neither. Only yesterday, when the Chief Circle (in other words our High Priest) came to inspect the State Prison and paid me his seventh annual visit, and when for the seventh time he put me the question, 'Was I any better?' I tried to prove to him that he was 'high', as well as long and broad, although he did not know it. But what was his reply? 'You say I am "high"; measure my "high-ness" and I will believe you.' What could I do? How could I meet his challenge? I was crushed; and he left the room triumphant.

"Does this still seem strange to you? Then put yourself in a similar position. Suppose a person of the Fourth Dimension, condescending to visit you, were to say, 'Whenever you open your eyes, you see a Plane (which is of Two Dimensions) and you INFER a Solid (which is of Three); but in reality you also see (though you do not recognize) a Fourth Dimension, which is not colour nor brightness nor anything of the kind, but a true Dimension, although I cannot point out to you its direction, nor can you possibly measure it.' What would you say to such a visitor? Would not you have him locked up? Well, that is my fate: and it is as natural for us Flatlanders to lock up a Square for preaching the Third Dimension, as it is for you Spacelanders to lock up a Cube for preaching the Fourth. Alas, how strong a family likeness runs through blind and persecuting humanity in all Dimensions! Points, Lines, Squares, Cubes, Extra-Cubes—we are all liable to the same errors, all alike the Slaves of our respective Dimensional prejudices, as one of your Spaceland poets has said—

'One touch of Nature makes all worlds akin'."

[Note: The Author desires me to add, that the misconception of some of his critics on this matter has induced him to insert in his dialogue with the Sphere, certain remarks which have a bearing on the point in question, and which he had previously omitted as being tedious and unnecessary.]

On this point the defence of the Square seems to me to be impregnable. I wish I could say that his answer to the second (or moral) objection was equally clear and cogent. It has been objected that he is a woman-hater; and as this objection has been vehemently urged by those whom Nature's decree has constituted the somewhat larger half of the Spaceland race, I should like to remove it, so far as I can honestly do so. But the Square is so unaccustomed to the use of the moral terminology of Spaceland that I should be doing him an injustice if I were

"Astronomers say they have heard the sound of a black hole singing. And what it is singing, and perhaps has been singing for more than two billion years, they say, is B flat—a B flat 57 octaves lower than middle C.

The black hole is playing 'the lowest note in the universe,' said Dr. Andrew Fabian, an X-ray astronomer at the Institute for Astronomy at Cambridge University in England." [3]

literally to transcribe his defence against this charge. Acting, therefore, as his interpreter and summarizer, I gather that in the course of an imprisonment of seven years he has himself modified his own personal views, both as regards Women and as regards the Isosceles or Lower Classes. Personally, he now inclines to the opinion of the Sphere that the Straight Lines are in many important respects superior to the Circles. But, writing as a Historian, he has identified himself (perhaps too closely) with the views generally adopted by Flatland, and (as he has been informed) even by Spaceland, Historians; in whose pages (until very recent times) the destinies of Women and of the masses of mankind have seldom been deemed worthy of mention and never of careful consideration.

In a still more obscure passage he now desires to disavow the Circular or aristocratic tendencies with which some critics have naturally credited him. While doing justice to the intellectual power with which a few Circles have for many generations maintained their supremacy over immense multitudes of their countrymen, he believes that the facts of Flatland, speaking for themselves without comment on his part, declare that Revolutions cannot always be suppressed by slaughter, and that Nature, in sentencing the Circles to infecundity, has condemned them to ultimate failure—"and herein," he says, "I see a fulfilment of the great Law of all worlds, that while the wisdom of Man thinks it is working one thing, the wisdom of Nature constrains it to work another, and quite a different and far better thing." For the rest, he begs his readers not to suppose that every minute detail in the daily life of Flatland must needs correspond to some other detail in Spaceland; and yet he hopes that, taken as a whole, his work may prove suggestive as well as amusing, to those Spacelanders of moderate and modest minds who—speaking of that which is of the highest importance, but lies beyond experience—decline to say on the one hand, "This can never be," and on the other hand, "It must needs be precisely thus, and we know all about it."

"The situation is at once magic, hilarious and inexplicably subversive—a kind of sculptural comedy. In the middle of the CAPC Bordeaux's majestic nave, around 20 coloured, abstract volumes made of polystyrene, plywood, foam or fibreglass ('tanks', 'rugs'; a trapezium-like red block, a green pedestal, a large white double wall) crawl slowly and almost imperceptibly along the floor, bumping into one another here and there. These taciturn bodies (among which there is also an abstract painting, creeping on the wall) move in magical suspension a few centimetres away from the floor on what might be tiny motorized wheels—although the near-illusionistic device also suggests minuscule paws hiding somewhere underneath their shells." [4]

PART I
THIS WORLD

PART I
THIS WORLD

FLATLAND, SEE LIGHT AND SPACE.

"Be patient, for the world is broad and wide."

"Light and Space denotes a loosely-affiliated art movement related to op art, minimalism and geometric abstraction originating in Southern California in the 1960s and influenced by John McLaughlin. It was characterized by a focus on perceptual phenomena, such as light, volume and scale, and the use of materials such as glass, neon, fluorescent lights, resin and cast acrylic, often forming installations conditioned by the work's surroundings. Whether by directing the flow of natural light, embedding artificial light within objects or architecture, or by playing with light through the use of transparent, translucent or reflective materials, Light and Space artists made the spectator's experience of light and other sensory phenomena under specific conditions the focus of their work." [1]

22

Of the Nature of Flatland

Edges reveal nothing else but space

I call our world Flatland, not because we call it so, but to make its nature clearer to you, my happy readers, who are privileged to live in Space.

Imagine a vast sheet of paper on which straight Lines, Triangles, Squares, Pentagons, Hexagons, and other figures, instead of remaining fixed in their places, move freely about, on or in the surface, but without the power of rising above or sinking below it, very much like shadows—only hard and with luminous edges—and you will then have a pretty correct notion of my country and countrymen. Alas, a few years ago, I should have said "my universe": but now my mind has been opened to higher views of things.

In such a country, you will perceive at once that it is impossible that there should be anything of what you call a "solid" kind; but I dare say you will suppose that we could at least distinguish by sight the Triangles, Squares, and other figures, moving about as I have described them. On the contrary, we could see nothing of the kind, not at least so as to distinguish one figure from another. Nothing was visible, nor could be visible, to us, except Straight Lines; and the necessity of this I will speedily demonstrate.

Place a penny on the middle of one of your tables in Space; and leaning over it, look down upon it. It will appear a circle.

24

AUSTRALIA NOT DOWN UNDER

A Compass Always Points North

FLATLAND, SEE COTTONOPOLIS.

"On visiting Manchester in 1825, the German architect Karl Schinkel wrote of his visit that 'the enormous factory buildings are seven to eight storeys high...where three years ago there were only meadows'. He went on to say that the buildings were so black that they looked as if they had stood already for a hundred years. King cotton, textiles, spinning, weaving and dyeing were the staple commercial enterprise of Manchester and the host of small mill towns that surrounded it. The city became known locally as 'Cottonopolis'." [5]

But now, drawing back to the edge of the table, gradually lower your eye (thus bringing yourself more and more into the condition of the inhabitants of Flatland), and you will find the penny becoming more and more oval to your view, and at last when you have placed your eye exactly on the edge of the table (so that you are, as it were, actually a Flatlander) the penny will then have ceased to appear oval at all, and will have become, so far as you can see, a straight line.

The same thing would happen if you were to treat in the same way a Triangle, or Square, or any other figure cut out of pasteboard. As soon as you look at it with your eye on the edge on the table, you will find that it ceases to appear to you a figure, and that it becomes in appearance a straight line. Take for example an equilateral Triangle—who represents with us a Tradesman of the respectable class. Fig. 1 represents the Tradesman as you would see him while you were bending over him from above; figs. 2 and 3 represent the Tradesman, as you would see him if your eye were close to the level, or all but on the level of the table; and if your eye were quite on the level of the table (and that is how we see him in Flatland) you would see nothing but a straight line.

WATER IS FLAT
EARTH IS FLAT

FLATLAND, SEE BRITISH DESIGN.

(1) (2) (3)

When I was in Spaceland I heard that your sailors have very similar experiences while they traverse your seas and discern some distant island or coast lying on the horizon. The far-off land may have bays, forelands, angles in and out to any number and extent; yet at a distance you see none of these (unless indeed your sun shines bright upon them revealing the projections and retirements by means of light and shade), nothing but a grey unbroken line upon the water.

Well, that is just what we see when one of our triangular or other acquaintances comes toward us in Flatland. As there is neither sun with us, nor any light of such a kind as to make shadows, we have none of the helps to the sight that you have in Spaceland. If our friend comes closer to us we see his line becomes larger; if he leaves us it becomes smaller: but still he

"It is possible to see the 1880s as the period of origin for the design profession, although the designer of those days would be entitled 'art adviser' or 'art superintendent'. But (their) role was beginning to be defined. It's commercial importance was beginning to be recognised."

"By the end of the 1880s, the moral issues of art and craftsmanship seemed almost to be outweighing the aesthetic ones: the relation of the fine artist and the craftsman; the whole wide role of the artist-craftsman in society. These were all subjects under long discussion at the earnest, convivial, and, needless to say, male-dominated meetings which were so much a feature of this period... A constant theme in

World IS Flat...
And That's That

the writings and speeches of these groups, the membership of which in fact was fairly interchangeable, was that of the importance of the personal element in art, a claim for the rightful recognition of the individual designer. This idea of individual artistic responsibility, a strongly moral concept, also turned out to have considerable commercial advantages in that it identified particular designers, giving them a public image, a glamour, a kudos…" [6]

looks like a straight line; be he a Triangle, Square, Pentagon, Hexagon, Circle, what you will—a straight Line he looks and nothing else.

You may perhaps ask how under these disadvantageous circumstances we are able to distinguish our friends from one another: but the answer to this very natural question will be more fitly and easily given when I come to describe the inhabitants of Flatland. For the present let me defer this subject, and say a word or two about the climate and houses in our country.

Of the Climate and Houses in Flatland

28

Compare the following startling discrepancies

FLATLAND, SEE GRAYSON PERRY.

"All In The Best Possible Taste with Grayson Perry is a 2012 documentary television series on United Kingdom station Channel 4, starring Turner Prize-winning artist Grayson Perry. The series analysed the ideas of taste held by the different social classes of the United Kingdom. Perry produced a series of six tapestries depicting the taste ideas of Britons, entitled 'The Vanity of Small Differences'." [1]

As with you, so also with us, there are four points of the compass North, South, East, and West.

There being no sun nor other heavenly bodies, it is impossible for us to determine the North in the usual way; but we have a method of our own. By a Law of Nature with us, there is a constant attraction to the South; and, although in temperate climates this is very slight—so that even a Woman in reasonable health can journey several furlongs northward without much difficulty—yet the hampering effect of the southward attraction is quite sufficient to serve as a compass in most parts of our earth. Moreover, the rain (which falls at stated intervals) coming always from the North, is an additional assistance; and in the towns we have the guidance of the houses, which of course have their side-walls running for the most part North and South, so that the roofs may keep off the rain from the North. In the country, where there are no houses, the trunks of the trees serve as some sort of guide. Altogether, we have not so much difficulty as might be expected in determining our bearings.

Yet in our more temperate regions, in which the southward attraction is hardly felt, walking sometimes in a perfectly desolate plain where there have been no houses nor trees to guide me, I have been occasionally compelled to remain stationary for hours together, waiting till the rain came before

between

the True Facts and the Modern Theories; and they say if is it not a national disgrace that we should prefer baseless superstitions, for the mere credit's sake of a few infidel scientists.

MODERN ASTRONOMY and its crafty or, most deluded sycophants teach that "the sun is stationary and the centre of the planetary or celestial bodies, and that it is over One Million miles larger than the earth!"

Whereas, it is not one thousandth part of its size—is constantly moving in spiral orbits, round and over the face of the motionless earth; increasing the latitude of those orbits about ten or eleven miles every day from June to December, and decreasing them in the same proportion from December to June.

The astronomers now teach that the Sun's distance from the Earth is from 92 to 93 Million miles; whereas, it is proved to be under 2,400 miles, and the stars and planets even less than that. So far from the Earth being a planet and "very much inferior in size to all the other planets but Mars," it is no part at all of the celestial system; but is wholly distinct and far superior in size and character to all the planets put together, which exhibit very little variety in size among themselves, and no parallax whatever, when viewed under any possible conditions!

The astronomers again assert the Earth to be a revolving and rotating Globe, with an axial speed of over one thousand miles an hour, and an orbital speed of over one thousand miles per minute! whereas, it is an absolutely motionless plane, surrounded by a barrier of impassable icebergs, extending into unknown regions, where "day and night come to an end," or, in other words, cease to be distinguished, and will only be removed when "there shall be no more sea;" and continuing my journey. On the weak and aged, and especially on delicate Females, the force of attraction tells much more heavily than on the robust of the Male Sex, so that it is a point of breeding, if you meet a Lady in the street, always to give her the North side of the way—by no means an easy thing to do always at short notice when you are in rude health and in a climate where it is difficult to tell your North from your South.

Windows there are none in our houses: for the light comes to us alike in our homes and out of them, by day and by night, equally at all times and in all places, whence we know not. It was in old days, with our learned men, an interesting and oft-investigated question, "What is the origin of light?" and the solution of it has been repeatedly attempted, with no other result than to crowd our lunatic asylums with the would-be solvers. Hence, after fruitless attempts to suppress such investigations indirectly by making them liable to a heavy tax, the Legislature, in comparatively recent times, absolutely prohibited them. I—alas, I alone in Flatland—know now only too well the true solution of this mysterious problem; but my knowledge cannot be made intelligible to a single one of my countrymen; and I am mocked at—I, the sole possessor of the truths of Space and of the theory of the introduction of Light from the world of three Dimensions—as if I were the maddest of the mad! But a truce to these painful digressions: let me return to our houses.

"Although it has its roots even earlier, the development of bourgeois respectability that occurred in the period 1750–1850 meant that in part at least, the idea of the person's goods being part of the expression of self-identity (as opposed to the earlier 18th century idea of goods as part of 'social performance') was widely accepted. Following on from this, consumer culture moves into two different pathways. The first is the importance of the urban and public scene and its spectacles supplied by shops, galleries, arcades, museums and exhibitions. The second or contrary notion involves the inward-looking private and domestic sphere. What link these two aspects in the goods

a "new firmament and a new earth" shall replace this sin-stained and misused world.

The astronomers teach an atmospheric pressure of fifteen pounds on the square inch; whereas, it does not amount to half as many grains. Gravitation (central), is the wildest fiction ever invented. All Attraction—Solar, lunar, central, and magnetic, is purely conjectural and physically impossible.

The astronomers further declare that this globe has no material support, but is sustained and controlled in its terrific orbits by solar attraction only, at a distance of nearly one hundred million miles; although Sir Isaac Newton himself declares the idea was "grossly preposterous and discreditable to any rational mind;" meaning, of course, that the "centripetal and centrifugal forces" were hypothetical conditions only, and like all the other data on which the Copernican theory was founded, were purely geometrical devices, which no one in their sober senses ever thought could be illustrated by an appeal to facts, But such was the ignorance or bigotry of his professional friends, that they would not allow even Sir Isaac Newton himself to publish his repeated disclaimers of being anything more than a mathematical inventor or formulator of a system which was in no degree dependent on the truth of his premises.

The rank absurdity and downright impossibility of any one, of its most elementary conditions, and the fact that no man of honour or scientific reputation would venture openly to defend it, ought to secure the instant rejection of it by every lover of truth in the world. The whole thing lies in a nutshell. All that is insisted upon is, that results or conclusions drawn from conjectural theories of philosophy, however plausible and apparently simple they may be, are wholly worthless and unworthy of any claim to rank as true science, till they have been proved correct by actual experimental demonstration, and can be thus confirmed and illustrated as often as their truth is challenged or denied. Even if a theory be true in the abstract, yet, if incapable of practical demonstration, it is not science, merely to suppose or assert it to be true. Newton himself was too sound a philosopher to attempt to illustrate the truth of the globular theory; he repeatedly discouraged all discussion, and, if left to himself, would never have attached his name-or sanction to such a bungling absurdity.

This is the ground on which the ZETETICS take their stand, and all the professors in the kingdom will strive in vain to dislodge them; and, what is more, they are too cowardly to attempt it. The above is so startling an exposure that the public press is ashamed to announce it; although the globular theory has been shown to be a Pagan superstition, unscriptural, irrational, unscientific, and physically impossible!

The true cosmogony of the Universe should be the primary subject, and one which ought to take precedence of every other on which the mind of a child can possibly be engaged. Ignorance of its true nature is a gross scandal on all connected with any phase of education, either religious or secular; and the imposition of a fraud which the intelligent child soon learns to that were bought and sold as part of a material culture was the consumer goods could be seen as (a) signs of status and identity, (b) vehicles of meaning, and (c) bearers of aesthetic values." [7]

The most common form for the construction of a house is five-sided or pentagonal, as in the annexed figure. The two Northern sides RO, OF, constitute the roof, and for the most part have no doors; on the East is a small door for the Women; on the West a much larger one for the Men; the South side or floor is usually doorless.

Square and triangular houses are not allowed, and for this reason. The angles of a Square (and still more those of an equilateral Triangle), being much more pointed than those of a Pentagon, and the lines of inanimate objects (such as houses) being dimmer than the lines of Men and Women, it follows that there is no little danger lest the points of a square or triangular house residence might do serious injury to an inconsiderate or perhaps absent-minded traveller suddenly therefore, running against them: and as early as the eleventh century of our era, triangular houses were universally forbidden by Law, the only exceptions being fortifications, powder-magazines, barracks, and other state buildings, which it is not desirable that the general public should approach without circumspection.

At this period, square houses were still everywhere permitted, though discouraged by a special tax. But, about three centuries afterwards, the Law decided that in all towns containing a population above ten thousand, the angle of a Pentagon was the smallest house-angle that could be allowed consistently

detect, exerts a positive injury on the mind all through life. At the present moment there is not a teacher in the kingdom who would venture to prove himself familiar with the most elementary principles of natural science; and yet the writer is abused for declaring the world is full of knaves or dunces. Even savages never boast of being wiser than they are, or teach their children what they know to be untrue.

Never before was there such a fuss made about education. Do we really know or only think we know? Or is it learn, learn, learn—and leave off no wiser than before? If bricks and mortar could make brain's—if fine buildings could ensure great thoughts—if learned professors knew all that they profess, Thomas Carlyle would have belied his countrymen when he said we were a nation of "mostly fools."

What is our standard of true knowledge? an imperfect standard is as misleading as defective weights If we deal with false analogies, we are only comparing true metal with an ingenious counterfeit!

What are we aiming at by these remarks? We mean to say and are able to prove that at this moment, we are living in an age of shams and false pretences, and that we are totally unfamiliar with the most elementary conditions of some of the most important subjects that can possibly occupy the attention of a professedly intelligent and commercial nation—that even our Clergy and Theological professors do not yet understand the teaching of the Mosaic records—that our Schoolmasters, on some subjects, do not understand or know more than their pupils; that even our nautical charts and tables would discredit a nation of savages; and that our geography and astronomy are just where they were left by our university authorities of two hundred years ago; and that the most eminent of our educational professors would not now venture to defend what our poor children are compelled to carry with them through life.

What shall we say to those "Scientific" Journalists and Reviewers who persistently discourage any desire for discussion or ventilation of this important subject? Is it to hide their own ignorance or to display a mock contempt for any suggestion that runs counter to popular prejudice or opinion; or do they go so far as to imply that they cannot find among their numerous literary connexion, one individual writer who has intelligence enough to maintain his ground in a discussion with an honest opponent? It is a gross fraud on the credulity of the public as well as on the helplessness of childhood to enforce the acceptance of certain teaching which they are too ignorant to explain or too cowardly to defend.

If modem astronomical science could be shewn to be demonstrably true, how glorious would be the victory, and how, dire our confusion! But till they cease their insolent taunts and courteously show us our error and the inutility of our opposition, we shall certainly not cease to regard them as vanquished foes, who lack the moral courage to acknowledge their defeat.

And we can but trust that when Prof. This or Prof. That ventures to pose as a Scientist or as an oracle with the public safety. The good sense of the community has seconded the efforts of the Legislature; and now, even in the country, the pentagonal construction has superseded every other. It is only now and then in some very remote and backward agricultural district that an antiquarian may still discover a square house.

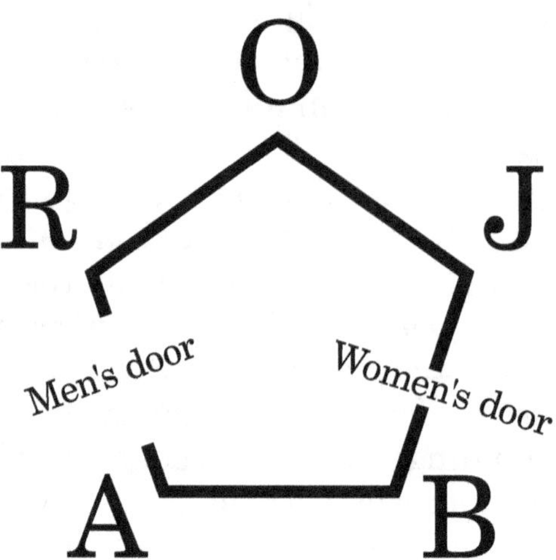

on scientific subjects, he will learn to exhibit a little more modesty and confess that for once in his life, he had to bow to the superior influence of common sense, and, above all, to the omnipotent authority of the inspired records.

As it is. Science is irredeemably prejudiced in the eyes of all honest men and can never again assume those insolent airs which have so frequently disfigured its encounters with the less dogmatic searchers after truth.

—from 'A Sketch Of The World As A Circular Plane' published in One Hundred Proofs that the Earth is not a Globe by William Carpenter, 1895 ('cheap edition')

Concerning the Inhabitants of Flatland

33

A theory of chance, not a chance theory

The greatest length or breadth of a full grown inhabitant of Flatland may be estimated at about eleven of your inches. Twelve inches may be regarded as a maximum.

Our Women are Straight Lines.

Our Soldiers and Lowest Classes of Workmen are Triangles with two equal sides, each about eleven inches long, and a base or third side so short (often not exceeding half an inch) that they form at their vertices a very sharp and formidable angle. Indeed when their bases are of the most degraded type (not more than the eighth part of an inch in size), they can hardly be distinguished from Straight Lines or Women; so extremely pointed are their vertices. With us, as with you, these Triangles are distinguished from others by being called Isosceles; and by this name I shall refer to them in the following pages.

Our Middle Class consists of Equilateral or Equal-Sided Triangles.

Our Professional Men and Gentlemen are Squares (to which class I myself belong) and Five-Sided Figures or Pentagons.

Next above these come the Nobility, of whom there are several degrees, beginning at Six-Sided Figures, or Hexagons, and from thence rising in the number of their sides till they receive the honourable title of Polygonal, or many-sided. Finally

34

Having found the accounts of A Square hidden away in one of our hexagonal libraries has put me in a precarious situation. Historicizing this event could become a method for correcting chance, hence minimizing the odds of finding his or my accounts again.

To tell my story is to look at the past from a probable future. If we believe that an event has a given chance of occurring, this should have a bearing on our credence that the event will occur, thus assuming a relation between chance and credence. But this relation is dependent on the world and timeline in which such an event occurs. The laws of chance are picked out by the worlds alone, so for every world, every event, every timeline, a specific set of chances will only take place. According to this Principal Principle, A Square has set in motion all the necessary conditions for our new governmentality and The Flatland Lottery.

V Line is my name, a very common one here in Flatland. Even though today—or at least for the last twelve months, as I cannot remember much before that—I am a woman, this has not always been the case. The ancient decree of Nature (Once a Woman, always a Woman) and the Laws of Evolution and Compensation have all been outmoded by the game we are now forced to play.

My account will be short. I have till midnight when another draw will take place, possibly rendering me unable to introduce

"It has already been suggested that a change occurred during the mid-19th century from rooms being use as signs or indicators of status and gentility to being representations of self, through styles. To meet the demand for the furnishing and setting up these homes, changes had to occur, not only in the distribution system but also in the provision of information and direction in matters of setting up and running a home. As the subtle graduations of goods developed even more, the meanings they held, which were designed to deal with the non-verbal communication relating to the home, became more complex. The viewer needed to become even more resourceful to read and recognise the signs. A knowledge and understanding of the narrative of selected objects intended to reinforce respectability was increasingly important." [7]

when the number of the sides becomes so numerous, and the sides themselves so small, that the figure cannot be distinguished from a circle, he is included in the Circular or Priestly order; and this is the highest class of all.

It is a Law of Nature with us that a male child shall have one more side than his father, so that each generation shall rise (as a rule) one step in the scale of development and nobility. Thus the son of a Square is a Pentagon; the son of a Pentagon, a Hexagon; and so on.

But this rule applies not always to the Tradesmen, and still less often to the Soldiers, and to the Workmen; who indeed can hardly be said to deserve the name of human Figures, since they have not all their sides equal. With them therefore the Law of Nature does not hold; and the son of an Isosceles (i.e. a Triangle with two sides equal) remains Isosceles still. Nevertheless, all hope is not shut out, even from the Isosceles, that his posterity may ultimately rise above his degraded condition. For, after a long series of military successes, or diligent and skilful labours, it is generally found that the more intelligent among the Artisan and Soldier classes manifest a slight increase of their third side or base, and a shrinkage of the two other sides. Intermarriages (arranged by the Priests) between the sons and daughters of these more intellectual members of the lower classes generally result in an offspring approximating

a small permutation in The Lottery system. I write this in order to believe in the probability that if I fail, I will be able of another attempt within my timeline. Able to recall this Flatland.

The Corporation and The Lottery were the direct results of the 285th rebellion. Polygons and Circles were no longer able to suppress sedition. Bribery, arranged marriages and methods of artificial compression/expansion could not cover the stagnation of our social mobility. And for the very first time in any rebellion, women toppled the outcomes. After one of my sisters discovered A Square's documents, a dissident group was quickly formed. Women weren't really agitated by A Square's discovery of the third dimension—no Nogon, Trigon, Tetragon, Pentagon, Hexagon, or N-gon really believed such a theory at the time—but rather by Square's perspective on female history and the linguistic aberrations of male and female speech patterns. Well known to all of us, a woman's invisibility and capacity to induce instant death by collision were the most powerful weapons in Flatland. So by weaponizing all women the 285th rebellion was a swift and deadly affair.

The origins of The Lottery can be traced to a particular moment in the Council Chamber. The most lethal commando of the rebellion had cornered the President and was about to poke him to death when the President's mind arrived at his most cunning idea yet. He would reincarnate Prometheus once more.

still more to the type of the Equal-Sided Triangle.

Rarely—in proportion to the vast numbers of Isosceles births—is a genuine and certifiable Equal-Sided Triangle produced from Isosceles parents. [Note: "What need of a certificate?" a Spaceland critic may ask: "Is not the procreation of a Square Son a certificate from Nature herself, proving the Equal-sidedness of the Father?" I reply that no Lady of any position will marry an uncertified Triangle. Square offspring has sometimes resulted from a slightly Irregular Triangle; but in almost every such case the Irregularity of the first generation is visited on the third; which either fails to attain the Pentagonal rank, or relapses to the Triangular.] Such a birth requires, as its antecedents, not only a series of carefully arranged intermarriages, but also a long, continued exercise of frugality and self-control on the part of the would-be ancestors of the coming Equilateral, and a patient, systematic, and continuous development of the Isosceles intellect through many generations.

The birth of a True Equilateral Triangle from Isosceles parents is the subject of rejoicing in our country for many furlongs around. After a strict examination conducted by the Sanitary and Social Board, the infant, if certified as Regular, is with solemn ceremonial admitted into the class of Equilaterals. He is then immediately taken from his proud yet sorrowing

"The bathing machine was a device, popular in the 18th and 19th centuries, to allow people to change out of their usual clothes, possibly change into swimwear and then wade in the ocean at beaches. Bathing machines were roofed and walled wooden carts rolled into the sea. Some had solid wooden walls; others had canvas walls over a wooden frame.

The bathing machine was part of etiquette for sea-bathing more rigorously enforced upon women than men but to be observed by both sexes among those who wished to be proper.

Especially in Britain, men and women were usually segregated, so nobody of the opposite sex might catch sight of them in their bathing suits, which (although extremely modest by modern standards) were not considered proper clothing in which to be seen." [1]

36

President—

What if I tell you that the solution to our problems is within our grasp?

I—

I'd say you are scheming again.

President—

Will you hear my proposal for the sake of Flatland?

I—

Why not? Your consummation is imminent. It does not matter what you do or say.

President—

I have devised a system that would allow everybody in Flatland to be treated equally, no matter your number of sides, internal angles, vertices, lineage.

I—

Tell more.

President—

I've envisioned a lottery. A drawing to be held once a year. Every Flatlander but a small selected group will participate. One percent of the population will win the chance of transcending class. A few compressions, extensions, trepannings, colligations and from an Isosceles Trigon to a perfect Dodecagon or even a Myriagon.

I—

parents and adopted by some childless Equilateral, who is bound by oath never to permit the child henceforth to enter his former home or so much as to look upon his relations again, for fear lest the freshly developed organism may, by force of unconscious imitation, fall back again into his hereditary level.

The occasional emergence of an Equilateral from the ranks of his serf-born ancestors is welcomed, not only by the poor serfs themselves, as a gleam of light and hope shed upon the monotonous squalor of their existence, but also by the Aristocracy at large; for all the higher classes are well aware that these rare phenomena, while they do little or nothing to vulgarize their own privileges, serve as a most useful barrier against revolution from below.

Had the acute-angled rabble been all, without exception, absolutely destitute of hope and of ambition, they might have found leaders in some of their many seditious outbreaks, so able as to render their superior numbers and strength too much even for the wisdom of the Circles. But a wise ordinance of Nature has decreed that, in proportion as the working-classes increase in intelligence, knowledge, and all virtue, in that same proportion their acute angle (which makes them physically terrible) shall increase also and approximate to the comparatively harmless angle of the Equilateral Triangle. Thus, in the most brutal and formidable of the soldier class—creatures almost

Only one percent?

President—

That is all we can afford for now. Not enough Hospitals or State Physicians. But that will change. The less fortunate classes will want to play this game. Imagine the profits!

I—

And what about this selected group you speak of?

President—

The Priests and myself will run the lottery in secret to avoid any compromise. Unjust and biased rulings will be banned. Chance will be our only ruler. We can call it The Corporation.

At my nod, all commando members collided with The President consuming him in an instant. The Corporation and The Lottery were born.

Most Flatlanders gave themselves up to the game of Chance. Rumors of a shadow government called The Corporation lasted a few months, but the odds of climbing the social ladder with a simple draw overtook any doubts. As might be expected the first version of The Lottery failed. Hospitals could not cope with demand. The amount of winners and the wait length began to incite new civil unrest. The Corporation saw this as variables of an experiment that needed to be tweaked and purified.

on a level with women in their lack of intelligence—it is found that, as they wax in the mental ability necessary to employ their tremendous penetrating power to advantage, so do they wane in the power of penetration itself.

How admirable is this Law of Compensation! And how perfect a proof of the natural fitness and, I may almost say, the divine origin of the aristocratic constitution of the States in Flatland! By a judicious use of this Law of Nature, the Polygons and Circles are almost always able to stifle sedition in its very cradle, taking advantage of the irrepressible and boundless hopefulness of the human mind. Art also comes to the aid of Law and Order. It is generally found possible—by a little artificial compression or expansion on the part of the State physicians—to make some of the more intelligent leaders of a rebellion perfectly Regular, and to admit them at once into the privileged classes; a much larger number, who are still below the standard, allured by the prospect of being ultimately ennobled, are induced to enter the State Hospitals, where they are kept in honourable confinement for life; one or two alone of the more obstinate, foolish, and hopelessly irregular are led to execution.

Then the wretched rabble of the Isosceles, planless and leaderless, are either transfixed without resistance by the small body of their brethren whom the Chief Circle keeps in pay for

38

They quickly realized that the game was only talking to the Flatlander's hopes and that a lesson of moral significance needed to be introduced.

By rebellion 289 The Government made it obligatory for all Flatlanders to partake in The Lottery. A series of mutations were developed and delivered at random throughout the population via viruses. Now you could become a Heptagon or a Line or a Square—sex and social mobility were no longer issues. Rebellion 307 brought degenerative mutations. Lines could become Segments. Polygons could become a sequence of sides and angles, which are not closed but have no ends, extending infinitely. Rebellion 331 led to self-intersecting Polygons, Star-Polygons were all the fad. Rebellion 363 triggered boundless mutations. Apeirogons came into existence. They do not lie in a flat plane, but zigzag in three—or more—dimensions. The Gospel of the Three Dimensions was seen as a crude venture by an inferior race. Our two latest rebellions have handed us memory alteration and death by chance, imbuing certain order into chaos.

Our yearly draw is upon me. I've been assigned to oversee the correct mutation sequences contained in the viruses about to be released. I've made a simple change to one of the sequences. By tomorrow we shall all be Lines.

"According to John Ruskin's biographer Mary Lutyens, the notable author, artist, and art critic was apparently accustomed only to the hairless nudes portrayed unrealistically in art, never having seen a naked woman before his wedding night. He was allegedly so shocked by his discovery of his wife Effie's pubic hair that he rejected her, and the marriage was later legally annulled. He is supposed to have thought his wife was freakish and deformed." [1]

emergencies of this kind; or else more often, by means of jealousies and suspicions skilfully fomented among them by the Circular party, they are stirred to mutual warfare, and perish by one another's angles. No less than one hundred and twenty rebellions are recorded in our annals, besides minor outbreaks numbered at two hundred and thirty-five; and they have all ended thus.

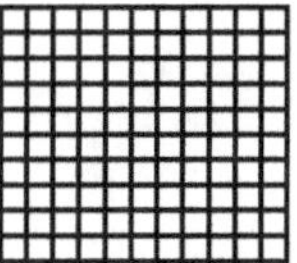

A woman is a needle

FLATLAND, SEE STEREOSCOPE.

"A stereoscope is a device for viewing a stereoscopic pair of separate images, depicting left-eye and right-eye views of the same scene, as a single three-dimensional image." [1]

If our highly pointed Triangles of the Soldier class are formidable, it may be readily inferred that far more formidable are our Women. For if a Soldier is a wedge, a Woman is a needle; being, so to speak, ALL point, at least at the two extremities. Add to this the power of making herself practically invisible at will, and you will perceive that a Female, in Flatland, is a creature by no means to be trifled with.

But here, perhaps, some of my younger Readers may ask HOW a woman in Flatland can make herself invisible. This ought, I think, to be apparent without any explanation. However, a few words will make it clear to the most unreflecting.

Place a needle on a table. Then, with your eye on the level of the table, look at it side-ways, and you see the whole length of it; but look at it end-ways, and you see nothing but a point, it has become practically invisible. Just so is it with one of our Women. When her side is turned towards us, we see her as a straight line; when the end containing her eye or mouth—for with us these two organs are identical—is the part that meets our eye, then we see nothing but a highly lustrous point; but when the back is presented to our view, then—being only sub-lustrous, and, indeed, almost as dim as an inanimate object—her hinder extremity serves her as a kind of Invisible Cap.

FLATLAND, SEE JEAN LUC GODARD.

The dangers to which we are exposed from our Women must now be manifest to the meanest capacity in Spaceland. If even the angle of a respectable Triangle in the middle class is not without its dangers; if to run against a Working Man involves a gash; if collision with an officer of the military class necessitates a serious wound; if a mere touch from the vertex of a Private Soldier brings with it danger of death;—what can it be to run against a Woman, except absolute and immediate destruction? And when a Woman is invisible, or visible only as a dim sub-lustrous point, how difficult must it be, even for the most cautious, always to avoid collision!

"Godard viewed film-making as an extension of criticism and was more interested in redefining film structure and style than actually being understood by the public. Often his movies were more about the presentation of a story than anything else." [1]

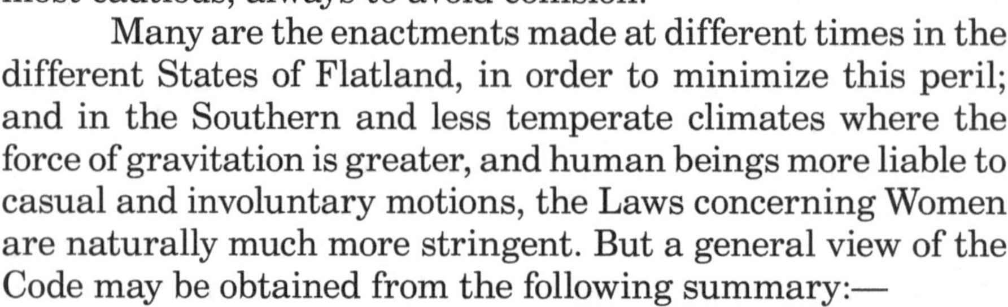

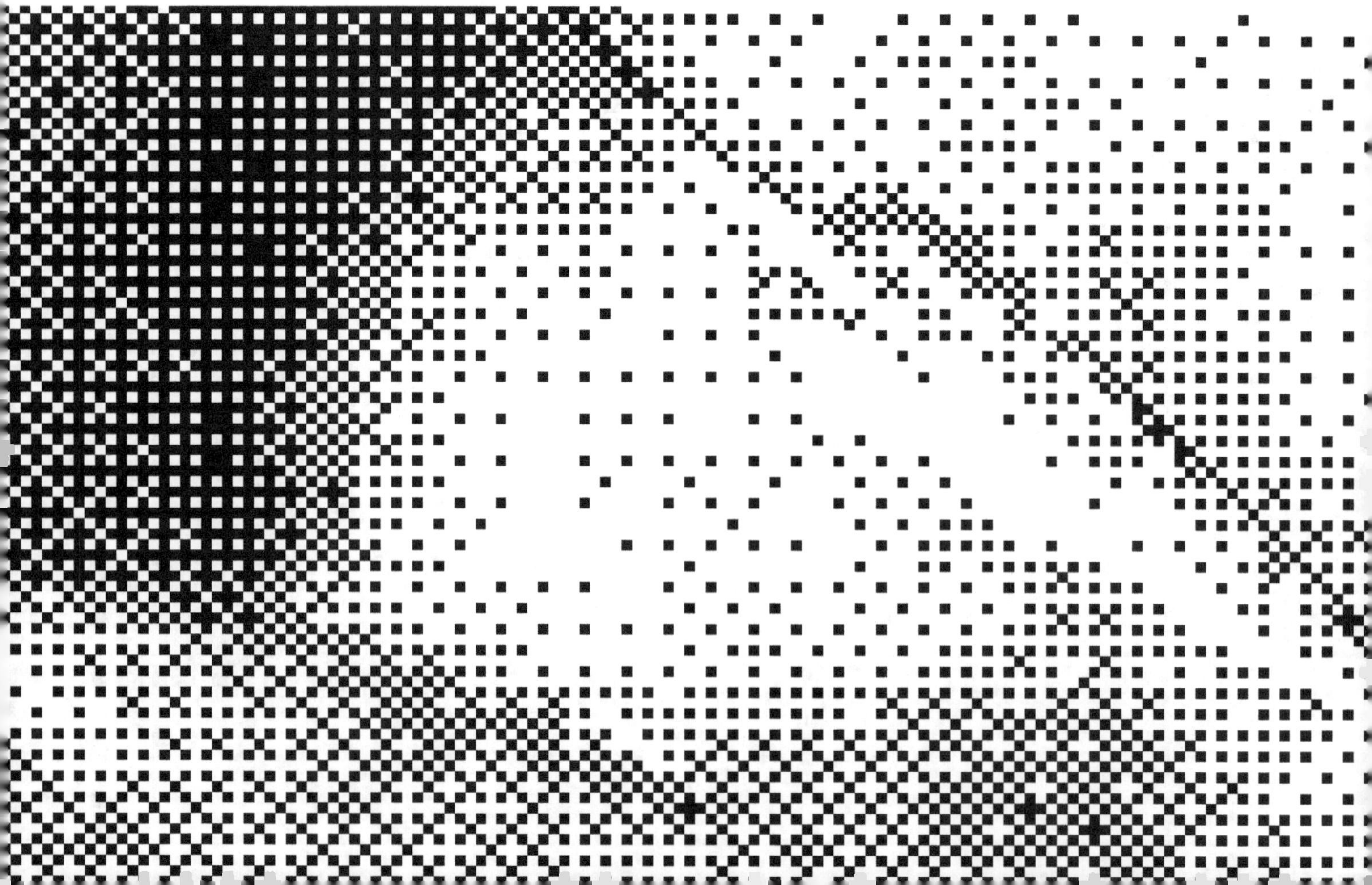

Many are the enactments made at different times in the different States of Flatland, in order to minimize this peril; and in the Southern and less temperate climates where the force of gravitation is greater, and human beings more liable to casual and involuntary motions, the Laws concerning Women are naturally much more stringent. But a general view of the Code may be obtained from the following summary:—

1. Every house shall have one entrance in the Eastern side, for the use of Females only; by which all females shall enter "in a becoming and respectful manner" and not by the Men's or Western door. [Note: When I was in Spaceland I understood that some of your Priestly circles have in the same way a separate entrance for Villagers, Farmers and Teachers

of Board Schools ('Spectator', Sept. 1884, p. 1255) that they may "approach in a becoming and respectful manner."]

2. No Female shall walk in any public place without continually keeping up her Peace-cry, under penalty of death.

3. Any Female, duly certified to be suffering from St. Vitus's Dance, fits, chronic cold accompanied by violent sneezing, or any disease necessitating involuntary motions, shall be instantly destroyed.

In some of the States there is an additional Law forbidding Females, under penalty of death, from walking or standing in any public place without moving their backs constantly from right to left so as to indicate their presence to those behind them; others oblige a Woman, when travelling, to be followed by one of her sons, or servants, or by her husband; others confine Women altogether to their houses except during the religious festivals. But it has been found by the wisest of our Circles or Statesmen that the multiplication of restrictions on Females tends not only to the debilitation and diminution of the race, but also to the increase of domestic murders to such an extent that a State loses more than it gains by a too prohibitive Code.

For whenever the temper of the Women is thus exasperated by confinement at home or hampering regulations abroad, they are apt to vent their spleen upon their husbands and children; and in the less temperate climates the whole

male population of a village has been sometimes destroyed in one or two hours of simultaneous female outbreak. Hence the Three Laws, mentioned above, suffice for the better regulated States, and may be accepted as a rough exemplification of our Female Code.

After all, our principal safeguard is found, not in Legislature, but in the interests of the Women themselves. For, although they can inflict instantaneous death by a retrograde movement, yet unless they can at once disengage their stinging extremity from the struggling body of their victim, their own frail bodies are liable to be shattered.

The power of Fashion is also on our side. I pointed out that in some less civilized States no female is suffered to stand in any public place without swaying her back from right to left. This practice has been universal among ladies of any pretensions to breeding in all well-governed States, as far back as the memory of Figures can reach. It is considered a disgrace to any State that legislation should have to enforce what ought to be, and is in every respectable female, a natural instinct. The rhythmical and, if I may so say, well-modulated undulation of the back in our ladies of Circular rank is envied and imitated by the wife of a common Equilateral, who can achieve nothing beyond a mere monotonous swing, like the ticking of a pendulum; and the regular tick of the Equilateral is no less admired

"Despite professing to be a guide of reliable information about every aspect of running a house for the aspirant middle classes, the original edition devotes 23 pages to household management then discusses cooking for almost all of the other 900. Even with the emphasis on food some of her cooking advice is so odd as to suggest that she had little experience preparing meals." [1]

and copied by the wife of the progressive and aspiring Isosceles, in the females of whose family no "back-motion" of any kind has become as yet a necessity of life. Hence, in every family of position and consideration, "back-motion" is as prevalent as time itself; and the husbands and sons in these households enjoy immunity at least from invisible attacks.

Not that it must be for a moment supposed that our Women are destitute of affection. But unfortunately the passion of the moment predominates, in the Frail Sex, over every other consideration. This is, of course, a necessity arising from their unfortunate conformation. For as they have no pretensions to an angle, being inferior in this respect to the very lowest of the Isosceles, they are consequently wholly devoid of brain-power, and have neither reflection, judgment nor forethought, and hardly any memory. Hence, in their fits of fury, they remember no claims and recognize no distinctions. I have actually known a case where a Woman has exterminated her whole household, and half an hour afterwards, when her rage was over and the fragments swept away, has asked what has become of her husband and her children.

Obviously then a Woman is not to be irritated as long as she is in a position where she can turn round. When you have them in their apartments—which are constructed with a view to denying them that power—you can say and do what

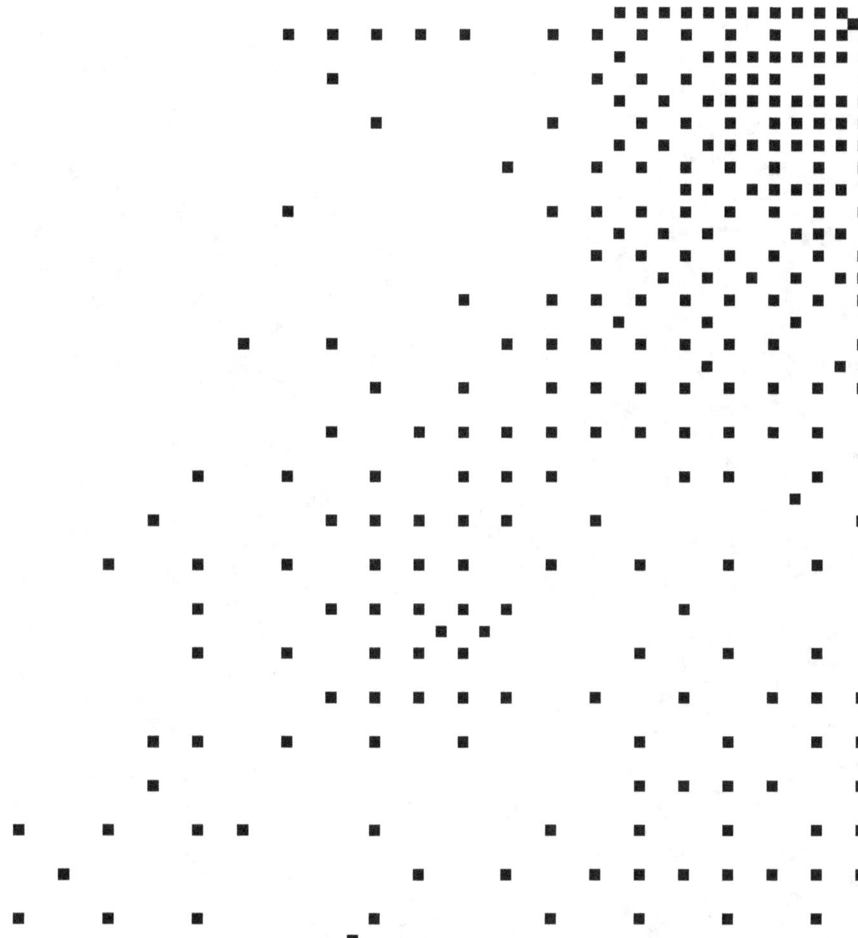

FLATLAND, SEE DANDY.

you like; for they are then wholly impotent for mischief, and will not remember a few minutes hence the incident for which they may be at this moment threatening you with death, nor the promises which you may have found it necessary to make in order to pacify their fury.

On the whole we get on pretty smoothly in our domestic relations, except in the lower strata of the Military Classes. There the want of tact and discretion on the part of the husbands produces at times indescribable disasters. Relying too much on the offensive weapons of their acute angles instead of the defensive organs of good sense and seasonable simulation, these reckless creatures too often neglect the prescribed construction of the women's apartments, or irritate their wives by ill-advised expressions out of doors, which they refuse immediately to retract. Moreover a blunt and stolid regard for literal truth indisposes them to make those lavish promises by which the more judicious Circle can in a moment pacify his consort. The result is massacre; not, however, without its advantages, as it eliminates the more brutal and troublesome of the Isosceles; and by many of our Circles the destructiveness of the Thinner Sex is regarded as one among many providential arrangements for suppressing redundant population, and nipping Revolution in the bud.

Yet even in our best regulated and most approximately

"A dandy is a man who places particular importance upon physical appearance, refined language, and leisurely hobbies, pursued with the appearance of nonchalance in a cult of Self. Historically, especially in late 18th- and early 19th-century Britain, a dandy, who was self-made, often strove to imitate an aristocratic lifestyle despite coming from a middle-class background." [1]

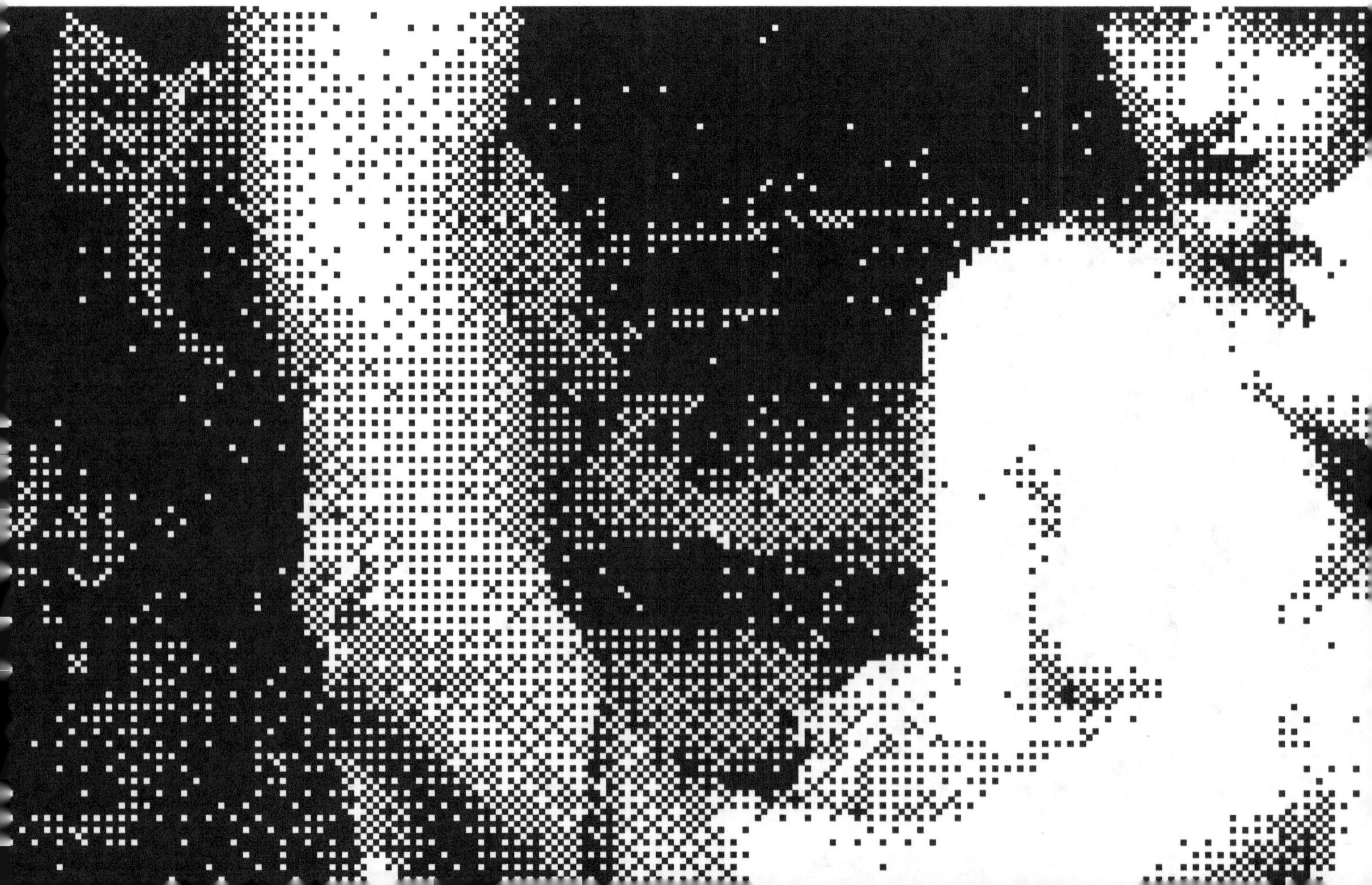

Circular families I cannot say that the ideal of family life is so high as with you in Spaceland. There is peace, in so far as the absence of slaughter may be called by that name, but there is necessarily little harmony of tastes or pursuits; and the cautious wisdom of the Circles has ensured safety at the cost of domestic comfort. In every Circular or Polygonal household it has been a habit from time immemorial—and now has become a kind of instinct among the women of our higher classes—that the mothers and daughters should constantly keep their eyes and mouths towards their husband and his male friends; and for a lady in a family of distinction to turn her back upon her husband would be regarded as a kind of portent, involving loss of STATUS. But, as I shall soon shew, this custom, though it has the advantage of safety, is not without its disadvantages.

In the house of the Working Man or respectable Tradesman—where the wife is allowed to turn her back upon her husband, while pursuing her household avocations—there are at least intervals of quiet, when the wife is neither seen nor heard, except for the humming sound of the continuous Peace-cry; but in the homes of the upper classes there is too often no peace. There the voluble mouth and bright penetrating eye are ever directed towards the Master of the household; and light itself is not more persistent than the stream of feminine discourse. The tact and skill which suffice to avert a Woman's

sting are unequal to the task of stopping a Woman's mouth; and as the wife has absolutely nothing to say, and absolutely no constraint of wit, sense, or conscience to prevent her from saying it, not a few cynics have been found to aver that they prefer the danger of the death-dealing but inaudible sting to the safe sonorousness of a Woman's other end.

To my readers in Spaceland the condition of our Women may seem truly deplorable, and so indeed it is. A Male of the lowest type of the Isosceles may look forward to some improvement of his angle, and to the ultimate elevation of the whole of his degraded caste; but no Woman can entertain such hopes for her sex. "Once a Woman, always a Woman" is a Decree of Nature; and the very Laws of Evolution seem suspended in her disfavour. Yet at least we can admire the wise Prearrangement which has ordained that, as they have no hopes, so they shall have no memory to recall, and no forethought to anticipate, the miseries and humiliations which are at once a necessity of their existence and the basis of the constitution of Flatland.

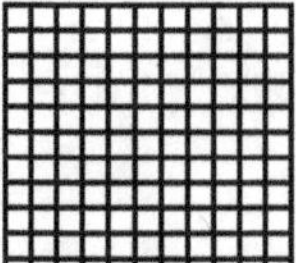

Of our Methods of Recognizing one another

In the year 2000

You, who are blessed with shade as well as light, you, who are gifted with two eyes, endowed with a knowledge of perspective, and charmed with the enjoyment of various colours, you, who can actually SEE an angle, and contemplate the complete circumference of a circle in the happy region of the Three Dimensions—how shall I make clear to you the extreme difficulty which we in Flatland experience in recognizing one another's configuration?

Recall what I told you above. All beings in Flatland, animate or inanimate, no matter what their form, present TO OUR VIEW the same, or nearly the same, appearance, viz. that of a straight Line. How then can one be distinguished from another, where all appear the same?

The answer is threefold. The first means of recognition is the sense of hearing; which with us is far more highly developed than with you, and which enables us not only to distinguish by the voice our personal friends, but even to discriminate between different classes, at least so far as concerns the three lowest orders, the Equilateral, the Square, and the Pentagon—for of the Isosceles I take no account. But as we ascend in the social scale, the process of discriminating and being discriminated by hearing increases in difficulty, partly because voices are assimilated, partly because the faculty of voice-discrimination is a plebeian virtue not much developed

FLATLAND, SEE WILLIAM MORRIS.

"William Morris (24 March 1834–3 October 1896) was an English textile designer, poet, novelist, translator, and socialist activist. Associated with the British Arts and Crafts Movement, he was a major contributor to the revival of traditional British textile arts and methods of production. His literary contributions helped to establish the modern fantasy genre, while he played a significant role in propagating the early socialist movement in Britain." [1]

among the Aristocracy. And wherever there is any danger of imposture we cannot trust to this method. Amongst our lowest orders, the vocal organs are developed to a degree more than correspondent with those of hearing, so that an Isosceles can easily feign the voice of a Polygon, and, with some training, that of a Circle himself. A second method is therefore more commonly resorted to.

FEELING is, among our Women and lower classes—about our upper classes I shall speak presently—the principal test of recognition, at all events between strangers, and when the question is, not as to the individual, but as to the class. What therefore "introduction" is among the higher classes in Spaceland, that the process of "feeling" is with us. "Permit me to ask you to feel and be felt by my friend Mr. So-and-so"—is still, among the more old-fashioned of our country gentlemen in districts remote from towns, the customary formula for a Flatland introduction. But in the towns, and among men of business, the words "be felt by" are omitted and the sentence is abbreviated to, "Let me ask you to feel Mr. So-and-so"; although it is assumed, of course, that the "feeling" is to be reciprocal. Among our still more modern and dashing young gentlemen—who are extremely averse to superfluous effort and supremely indifferent to the purity of their native language—the formula is still further curtailed by the use of "to

feel" in a technical sense, meaning, "to recommend-for-the-purposes-of-feeling-and-being-felt"; and at this moment the "slang" of polite or fast society in the upper classes sanctions such a barbarism as "Mr. Smith, permit me to feel Mr. Jones."

Let not my Reader however suppose that "feeling" is with us the tedious process that it would be with you, or that we find it necessary to feel right round all the sides of every individual before we determine the class to which he belongs. Long practice and training, begun in the schools and continued in the experience of daily life, enable us to discriminate at once by the sense of touch, between the angles of an equal-sided Triangle, Square, and Pentagon; and I need not say that the brainless vertex of an acute-angled Isosceles is obvious to the dullest touch. It is therefore not necessary, as a rule, to do more than feel a single angle of an individual; and this, once ascertained, tells us the class of the person whom we are addressing, unless indeed he belongs to the higher sections of the nobility. There the difficulty is much greater. Even a Master of Arts in our University of Wentbridge has been known to confuse a ten-sided with a twelve-sided Polygon; and there is hardly a Doctor of Science in or out of that famous University who could pretend to decide promptly and unhesitatingly between a twenty-sided and a twenty-four sided member of the Aristocracy.

"...to use material forms of engagement with technologies to supplement and extend critical reflection and, in doing so, to reconnect our lived experiences with technologies to social and conceptual critique." [8]

Those of my readers who recall the extracts I gave above

from the Legislative code concerning Women, will readily perceive that the process of introduction by contact requires some care and discretion. Otherwise the angles might inflict on the unwary Feeler irreparable injury. It is essential for the safety of the Feeler that the Felt should stand perfectly still. A start, a fidgety shifting of the position, yes, even a violent sneeze, has been known before now to prove fatal to the incautious, and to nip in the bud many a promising friendship. Especially is this true among the lower classes of the Triangles. With them, the eye is situated so far from their vertex that they can scarcely take cognizance of what goes on at that extremity of their frame. They are, moreover, of a rough coarse nature, not sensitive to the delicate touch of the highly organized Polygon. What wonder then if an involuntary toss of the head has ere now deprived the State of a valuable life!

I have heard that my excellent Grandfather—one of the least irregular of his unhappy Isosceles class, who indeed obtained, shortly before his decease, four out of seven votes from the Sanitary and Social Board for passing him into the class of the Equal-sided—often deplored, with a tear in his venerable eye, a miscarriage of this kind, which had occured to his great-great-great-Grandfather, a respectable Working Man with an angle or brain of 59 degrees 30 minutes. According to his account, my unfortunate Ancestor, being afflicted with

rheumatism, and in the act of being felt by a Polygon, by one sudden start accidentally transfixed the Great Man through the diagonal; and thereby, partly in consequence of his long imprisonment and degradation, and partly because of the moral shock which pervaded the whole of my Ancestor's relations, threw back our family a degree and a half in their ascent towards better things. The result was that in the next generation the family brain was registered at only 58 degrees, and not till the lapse of five generations was the lost ground recovered, the full 60 degrees attained, and the Ascent from the Isosceles finally achieved. And all this series of calamities from one little accident in the process of Feeling.

At this point I think I hear some of my better educated readers exclaim, "How could you in Flatland know anything about angles and degrees, or minutes? We can SEE an angle, because we, in the region of Space, can see two straight lines inclined to one another; but you, who can see nothing but one straight line at a time, or at all events only a number of bits of straight lines all in one straight line—how can you ever discern any angle, and much less register angles of different sizes?"

I answer that though we cannot SEE angles, we can INFER them, and this with great precision. Our sense of touch, stimulated by necessity, and developed by long training, enables

"A man finds himself alone on a dirt road, walking towards a diner. Inside he finds a jukebox playing loudly, and a pot of hot coffee on the stove. But there are no other people. He inquires for some breakfast, but no chef or waitress is to be found. He is dressed in an Air Force flight suit, but he does not remember who he is or how he got there." [1]

us to distinguish angles far more accurately than your sense of sight, when unaided by a rule or measure of angles. Nor must I omit to explain that we have great natural helps. It is with us a Law of Nature that the brain of the Isosceles class shall begin at half a degree, or thirty minutes, and shall increase (if it increases at all) by half a degree in every generation; until the goal of 60 degrees is reached, when the condition of serfdom is quitted, and the freeman enters the class of Regulars.

Consequently, Nature herself supplies us with an ascending scale or Alphabet of angles for half a degree up to 60 degrees, Specimens of which are placed in every Elementary School throughout the land. Owing to occasional retrogressions, to still more frequent moral and intellectual stagnation, and to the extraordinary fecundity of the Criminal and Vagabond Classes, there is always a vast superfluity of individuals of the half degree and single degree class, and a fair abundance of Specimens up to 10 degrees. These are absolutely destitute of civic rights; and a great number of them, not having even intelligence enough for the purposes of warfare, are devoted by the States to the service of education. Fettered immovably so as to remove all possibility of danger, they are placed in the class rooms of our Infant Schools, and there they are utilized by the Board of Education for the purpose of imparting to the offspring of the Middle Classes that tact and intelligence of

which these wretched creatures themselves are utterly devoid.

In some States the Specimens are occasionally fed and suffered to exist for several years; but in the more temperate and better regulated regions, it is found in the long run more advantageous for the educational interests of the young, to dispense with food, and to renew the Specimens every month—which is about the average duration of the foodless existence of the Criminal class. In the cheaper schools, what is gained by the longer existence of the Specimen is lost, partly in the expenditure for food, and partly in the diminished accuracy of the angles, which are impaired after a few weeks of constant "feeling". Nor must we forget to add, in enumerating the advantages of the more expensive system, that it tends, though slightly yet perceptibly, to the diminution of the redundant Isosceles population—an object which every statesman in Flatland constantly keeps in view. On the whole therefore—although I am not ignorant that, in many popularly elected School Boards, there is a reaction in favour of "the cheap system" as it is called—I am myself disposed to think that this is one of the many cases in which expense is the truest economy.

But I must not allow questions of School Board politics to divert me from my subject. Enough has been said, I trust, to shew that Recognition by Feeling is not so tedious or indecisive a process as might have been supposed; and it is obviously more

"A work of art can itself constitute a societal state, a model of human relationships."

"A work of art can consist of a process in time, a learning system through which the concepts of the social view forwarded in the work are accessed and internalised." [9]

trustworthy than Recognition by hearing. Still there remains, as has been pointed out above, the objection that this method is not without danger. For this reason many in the Middle and Lower classes, and all without exception in the Polygonal and Circular orders, prefer a third method, the description of which shall be reserved for the next section.

Of Recognition by Sight

58

An unattainable luxury among the lower classes

FLATLAND, SEE METAFILTER.

"Meta Filter is an interactive console, two participants sit on either side and look at a series of neutral images of people, people as individuals or people in relationship to others on the small screen in front of them. On their left is a thesaurus of almost 1,000 descriptive words. Each image has a connected question, asking the participant to choose a word from the thesaurus which best describes how they perceive the problem projected onto the screen and to enter their response in their copy of the Problem Book." [9]

I am about to appear very inconsistent. In previous sections I have said that all figures in Flatland present the appearance of a straight line; and it was added or implied, that it is consequently impossible to distinguish by the visual organ between individuals of different classes: yet now I am about to explain to my Spaceland critics how we are able to recognize one another by the sense of sight.

If however the Reader will take the trouble to refer to the passage in which Recognition by Feeling is stated to be universal, he will find this qualification—"among the lower classes". It is only among the higher classes and in our temperate climates that Sight Recognition is practised.

That this power exists in any regions and for any classes is the result of Fog; which prevails during the greater part of the year in all parts save the torrid zones. That which is with you in Spaceland an unmixed evil, blotting out the landscape, depressing the spirits, and enfeebling the health, is by us recognized as a blessing scarcely inferior to air itself, and as the Nurse of arts and Parent of sciences. But let me explain my meaning, without further eulogies on this beneficent Element.

If Fog were non-existent, all lines would appear equally and indistinguishably clear; and this is actually the case in those unhappy countries in which the atmosphere is perfectly dry and transparent. But wherever there is a rich supply of Fog

objects that are at a distance, say of three feet, are appreciably dimmer than those at a distance of two feet eleven inches; and the result is that by careful and constant experimental observation of comparative dimness and clearness, we are enabled to infer with great exactness the configuration of the object observed.

An instance will do more than a volume of generalities to make my meaning clear.

Suppose I see two individuals approaching whose rank I wish to ascertain. They are, we will suppose, a Merchant and a Physician, or in other words, an Equilateral Triangle and a Pentagon: how am I to distinguish them?

"Since the late 1970s, Barbara Kasten's photographic works have toed a line between the abstract potential of the medium and its inescapable referentiality. Born in Chicago in 1936 and schooled in the historical formal vocabulary of Constructivism, Kasten creates spatial arrangements which oscillate between the graphic flatness of geometric composition and the spectre of photography's illusionistic space." [10]

(1)

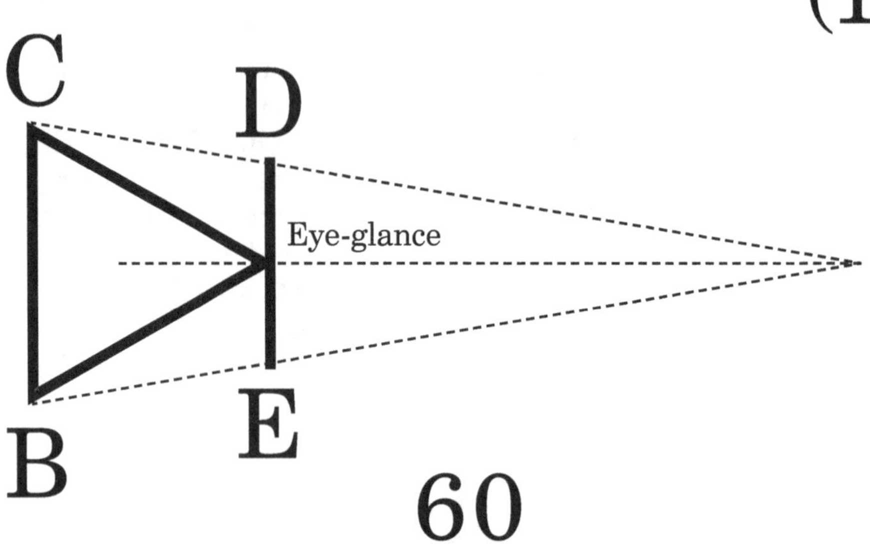

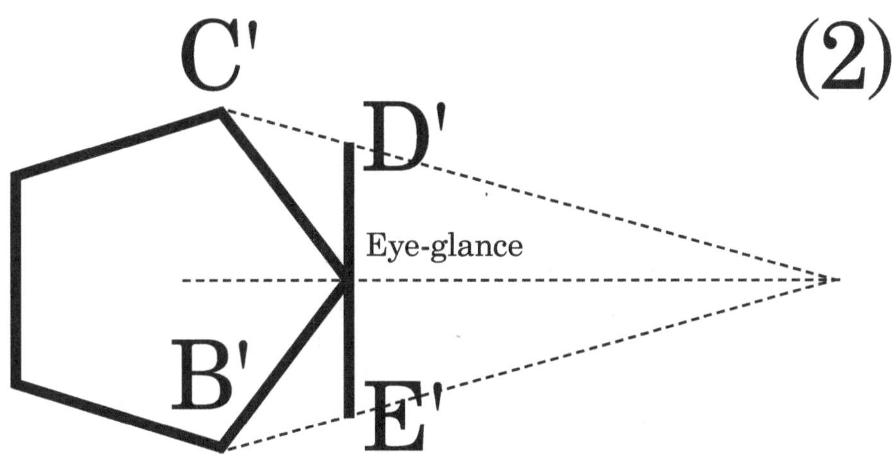

It will be obvious, to every child in Spaceland who has touched the threshold of Geometrical Studies, that, if I can bring my eye so that its glance may bisect an angle (A) of the approaching stranger, my view will lie as it were evenly between his two sides that are next to me (viz. CA and AB), so that I shall contemplate the two impartially, and both will appear of the same size.

Now in the case of (1) the Merchant, what shall I see? I shall see a straight line DAE, in which the middle point (A) will be very bright because it is nearest to me; but on either side the line will shade away RAPIDLY INTO DIMNESS, because the sides AC and AB RECEDE RAPIDLY INTO THE FOG and what appear to me as the Merchant's extremities, viz. D and E, will be VERY DIM INDEED.

On the other hand in the case of (2) the Physician, though I shall here also see a line (D'A'E') with a bright centre (A'), yet it will shade away LESS RAPIDLY into dimness, because the sides (A'C', A'B') RECEDE LESS RAPIDLY INTO THE FOG: and what appear to me the Physician's extremities, viz. D' and E', will not be NOT SO DIM as the extremities of the Merchant.

The Reader will probably understand from these two instances how—after a very long training supplemented by constant experience—it is possible for the well-educated classes among us to discriminate with fair accuracy between the middle and lowest orders, by the sense of sight. If my Spaceland Patrons have grasped this general conception, so far as to conceive the possibility of it and not to reject my account as altogether incredible—I shall have attained all I can reasonably expect. Were I to attempt further details I should only perplex. Yet for the sake of the young and inexperienced, who may perchance infer—from the two simple instances I have given above, of the manner in which I should recognize my Father and my Sons—that Recognition by sight is an easy affair, it may be needful to point out that in actual life most of the problems of Sight Recognition are far more subtle and complex.

FLATLAND, SEE CARL SAGAN.

"When we talk in alternate universes about Mayan high technology, let us show a space vehicle named and decorated after Mayan style and a radio telescope pivoting from a Mayan pyramid, controlling the space vehicle." [11]

If for example, when my Father, the Triangle, approaches me, he happens to present his side to me instead of his angle, then, until I have asked him to rotate, or until I have edged my eye round him, I am for the moment doubtful whether he may not be a Straight Line, or, in other words, a Woman. Again, when I am in the company of one of my two hexagonal Grandsons, contemplating one of his sides (AB) full front, it will be evident from the accompanying diagram that I shall see one whole line (AB) in comparative brightness (shading off hardly at all at the ends) and two smaller lines (CA and BD) dim throughout and shading away into greater dimness towards the extremities C and D.

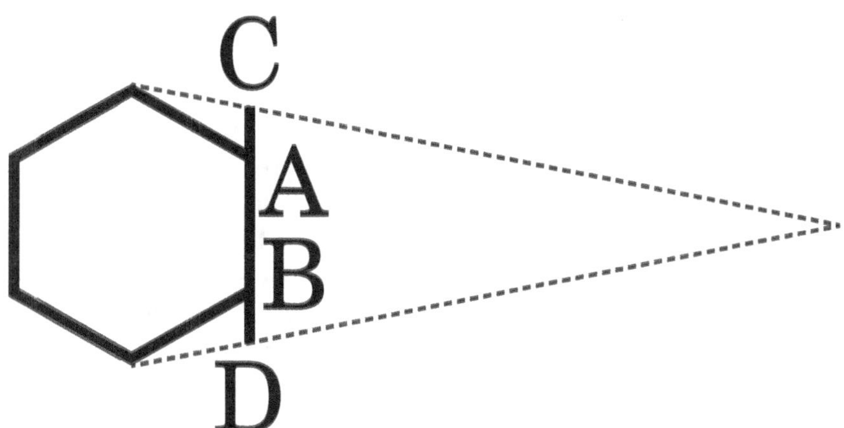

But I must not give way to the temptation of enlarging on these topics. The meanest mathematician in Spaceland will readily believe me when I assert that the problems of life, which present themselves to the well-educated—when they are themselves in motion, rotating, advancing or retreating, and at the same time attempting to discriminate by the sense of sight between a number of Polygons of high rank moving in different directions, as for example in a ball-room or conversazione—must be of a nature to task the angularity of the most intellectual, and amply justify the rich endowments of the Learned Professors of Geometry, both Static and Kinetic, in the illustrious University of Wentbridge, where the Science and Art of Sight Recognition are regularly taught to large classes of the ELITE of the States.

It is only a few of the scions of our noblest and wealthiest houses, who are able to give the time and money necessary for the thorough prosecution of this noble and valuable Art. Even to me, a Mathematician of no mean standing, and the Grandfather of two most hopeful and perfectly regular Hexagons, to find myself in the midst of a crowd of rotating Polygons of the higher classes, is occasionally very perplexing. And of course to a common Tradesman, or Serf, such a sight is almost as unintelligible as it would be to you, my Reader, were you suddenly transported into our country.

"Danny wears an Apollo 11 sweater; Room 237 represents the moon-landing stage where Kubrick supposedly worked—the moon is about 237,000 miles from Earth; the prevalence of Tang cans (created for astronauts) in the hotel's pantry; the pattern on the carpet where Danny plays matches that of Launch Pad 39A, from which the Apollo rocket took off." [12]

In such a crowd you could see on all sides of you nothing but a Line, apparently straight, but of which the parts would vary irregularly and perpetually in brightness or dimness. Even if you had completed your third year in the Pentagonal and Hexagonal classes in the University, and were perfect in the theory of the subject, you would still find that there was need of many years of experience, before you could move in a fashionable crowd without jostling against your betters, whom it is against etiquette to ask to "feel", and who, by their superior culture and breeding, know all about your movements, while you know very little or nothing about theirs. In a word, to comport oneself with perfect propriety in Polygonal society, one ought to be a Polygon oneself. Such at least is the painful teaching of my experience.

It is astonishing how much the Art—or I may almost call it instinct—of Sight Recognition is developed by the habitual practice of it and by the avoidance of the custom of "Feeling". Just as, with you, the deaf and dumb, if once allowed to gesticulate and to use the hand-alphabet, will never acquire the more difficult but far more valuable art of lipspeech and lip-reading, so it is with us as regards "Seeing" and "Feeling". None who in early life resort to "Feeling" will ever learn "Seeing" in perfection.

For this reason, among our Higher Classes, "Feeling" is discouraged or absolutely forbidden. From the cradle their

children, instead of going to the Public Elementary schools (where the art of Feeling is taught), are sent to higher Seminaries of an exclusive character; and at our illustrious University, to "feel" is regarded as a most serious fault, involving Rustication for the first offence, and Expulsion for the second.

But among the lower classes the art of Sight Recognition is regarded as an unattainable luxury. A common Tradesman cannot afford to let his son spend a third of his life in abstract studies. The children of the poor are therefore allowed to "feel" from their earliest years, and they gain thereby a precocity and an early vivacity which contrast at first most favourably with the inert, undeveloped, and listless behaviour of the half-instructed youths of the Polygonal class; but when the latter have at last completed their University course, and are prepared to put their theory into practice, the change that comes over them may almost be described as a new birth, and in every art, science, and social pursuit they rapidly overtake and distance their Triangular competitors.

Only a few of the Polygonal Class fail to pass the Final Test or Leaving Examination at the University. The condition of the unsuccessful minority is truly pitiable. Rejected from the higher class, they are also despised by the lower. They have neither the matured and systematically trained powers of the Polygonal Bachelors and Masters of Arts, nor yet the native

FLATLAND, SEE JOHN STEZAKER.

"His work is surreal in tone and is often made using collage and the appropriation of pre-existing images such as postcards, film stills, and publicity photographs. Art historian Julian Stallabrass said, 'The contrast at the heart of these works (by Stezaker) is not between represented and real, but between the unknowing primitives of popular culture, and the conscious, ironic artist and viewer of post-modern images'." [1]

precocity and mercurial versatility of the youthful Tradesman. The professions, the public services, are closed against them; and though in most States they are not actually debarred from marriage, yet they have the greatest difficulty in forming suitable alliances, as experience shews that the offspring of such unfortunate and ill-endowed parents is generally itself unfortunate, if not positively Irregular.

It is from these specimens of the refuse of our Nobility that the great Tumults and Seditions of past ages have generally derived their leaders; and so great is the mischief thence arising that an increasing minority of our more progressive Statesmen are of opinion that true mercy would dictate their entire suppression, by enacting that all who fail to pass the Final Examination of the University should be either imprisoned for life, or extinguished by a painless death.

But I find myself digressing into the subject of Irregularities, a matter of such vital interest that it demands a separate section.

68

Unfortunate causes of irregular births

FLATLAND, SEE HANS HOLBEIN.

Section 7

Throughout the previous pages I have been assuming—what perhaps should have been laid down at the beginning as a distinct and fundamental proposition—that every human being in Flatland is a Regular Figure, that is to say of regular construction. By this I mean that a Woman must not only be a line, but a straight line; that an Artisan or Soldier must have two of his sides equal; that Tradesmen must have three sides equal; Lawyers (of which class I am a humble member), four sides equal, and generally, that in every Polygon, all the sides must be equal.

The size of the sides would of course depend upon the age of the individual. A Female at birth would be about an inch long, while a tall adult Woman might extend to a foot. As to the Males of every class, it may be roughly said that the length of an adult's sides, when added together, is two feet or a little more. But the size of our sides is not under consideration. I am speaking of the EQUALITY of sides, and it does not need much reflection to see that the whole of the social life in Flatland rests upon the fundamental fact that Nature wills all Figures to have their sides equal.

If our sides were unequal our angles might be unequal. Instead of its being sufficient to feel, or estimate by sight, a single angle in order to determine the form of an individual, it would be necessary to ascertain each angle by the experiment

"The most notable and famous of Holbein's symbols in the work, however, is the distorted skull which is placed in the bottom center of the composition. The skull, rendered in anamorphic perspective, another invention of the Early Renaissance, is meant to be a visual puzzle as the viewer must approach the painting nearly from the side to see the form morph into an accurate rendering of a human skull. While the skull is evidently intended as a vanitas or memento mori, it is unclear why Holbein gave it such prominence in this painting." [1]

Abnormality no. 1 — a portion of the chromosome is missing or deleted

of Feeling. But life would be too short for such a tedious grouping. The whole science and art of Sight Recognition would at once perish; Feeling, so far as it is an art, would not long survive; intercourse would become perilous or impossible; there would be an end to all confidence, all forethought; no one would be safe in making the most simple social arrangements; in a word, civilization would relapse into barbarism.

Am I going too fast to carry my Readers with me to these obvious conclusions? Surely a moment's reflection, and a single instance from common life, must convince every one that our whole social system is based upon Regularity, or Equality of Angles. You meet, for example, two or three Tradesmen in the street, whom you recognize at once to be Tradesmen by a glance at their angles and rapidly bedimmed sides, and you ask them to step into your house to lunch. This you do at present with perfect confidence, because everyone knows to an inch or two the area occupied by an adult Triangle: but imagine that your Tradesman drags behind his regular and respectable vertex, a parallelogram of twelve or thirteen inches in diagonal:—what are you to do with such a monster sticking fast in your house door?

But I am insulting the intelligence of my Readers by accumulating details which must be patent to everyone who enjoys the advantages of a Residence in Spaceland. Obviously

Abnormality no. 2 — a portion of the chromosome breaks off, turns upside down and reattaches

the measurements of a single angle would no longer be sufficient under such portentous circumstances; one's whole life would be taken up in feeling or surveying the perimeter of one's acquaintances. Already the difficulties of avoiding a collision in a crowd are enough to tax the sagacity of even a well-educated Square; but if no one could calculate the Regularity of a single figure in the company, all would be chaos and confusion, and the slightest panic would cause serious injuries, or—if there happened to be any Women or Soldiers present—perhaps considerable loss of life.

Expediency therefore concurs with Nature in stamping the seal of its approval upon Regularity of conformation: nor has the Law been backward in seconding their efforts. "Irregularity of Figure" means with us the same as, or more than, a combination of moral obliquity and criminality with you, and is treated accordingly. There are not wanting, it is true, some promulgators of paradoxes who maintain that there is no necessary connection between geometrical and moral Irregularity. "The Irregular", they say, "is from his birth scouted by his own parents, derided by his brothers and sisters, neglected by the domestics, scorned and suspected by society, and excluded from all posts of responsibility, trust, and useful activity. His every movement is jealously watched by the police till he comes of age and presents himself for inspection; then he

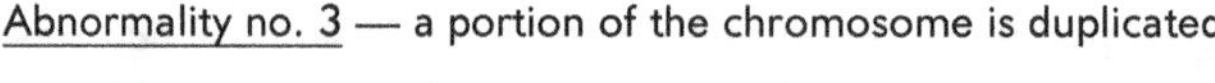
Abnormality no. 3 — a portion of the chromosome is duplicated

FLATLAND, SEE MURIEL COOPER.

"...make more intelligible the highly complex language of science... and articulate in symbolic, graphic form the order and beauty inherent in the scientist's abstract vision." [13]

is either destroyed, if he is found to exceed the fixed margin of deviation, or else immured in a Government Office as a clerk of the seventh class; prevented from marriage; forced to drudge at an uninteresting occupation for a miserable stipend; obliged to live and board at the office, and to take even his vacation under close supervision; what wonder that human nature, even in the best and purest, is embittered and perverted by such surroundings!"

All this very plausible reasoning does not convince me, as it has not convinced the wisest of our Statesmen, that our ancestors erred in laying it down as an axiom of policy that the toleration of Irregularity is incompatible with the safety of the State. Doubtless, the life of an Irregular is hard; but the interests of the Greater Number require that it shall be hard. If a man with a triangular front and a polygonal back were allowed to exist and to propagate a still more Irregular posterity, what would become of the arts of life? Are the houses and doors and churches in Flatland to be altered in order to accommodate such monsters? Are our ticket-collectors to be required to measure every man's perimeter before they allow him to enter a theatre or to take his place in a lecture room? Is an Irregular to be exempted from the militia? And if not, how is he to be prevented from carrying desolation into the ranks of his comrades? Again, what irresistible temptations to

Abnormality no. 4 — a portion of the chromosome breaks off and attaches to another chromosome

fraudulent impostures must needs beset such a creature! How easy for him to enter a shop with his polygonal front foremost, and to order goods to any extent from a confiding tradesman! Let the advocates of a falsely called Philanthropy plead as they may for the abrogation of the Irregular Penal Laws, I for my part have never known an Irregular who was not also what Nature evidently intended him to be—a hypocrite, a misanthropist, and, up to the limits of his power, a perpetrator of all manner of mischief.

Not that I should be disposed to recommend (at present) the extreme measures adopted by some States, where an infant whose angle deviates by half a degree from the correct angularity is summarily destroyed at birth. Some of our highest and ablest men, men of real genius, have during their earliest days laboured under deviations as great as, or even greater than, forty-five minutes: and the loss of their precious lives would have been an irreparable injury to the State. The art of healing also has achieved some of its most glorious triumphs in the compressions, extensions, trepannings, colligations, and other surgical or diaetetic operations by which Irregularity has been partly or wholly cured. Advocating therefore a VIA MEDIA, I would lay down no fixed or absolute line of demarcation; but at the period when the frame is just beginning to set, and when the Medical Board has reported that recovery is improbable,

"Examples are typically massive in character (even when not large), fortress-like, with a predominance of exposed concrete construction, or in the case of the 'brick brutalists' ruggedly detailed brickwork and concrete together. There is often an emphasis on graphically expressing in the external elevations and in the whole-site plan the main functions and people-flows of the buildings. Brutalism became popular for educational buildings (especially university buildings), but was relatively rare for corporate projects." [1]

Abnormality no. 5 — segments from two different chromosomes are exchanged

I would suggest that the Irregular offspring be painlessly and mercifully consumed.

75

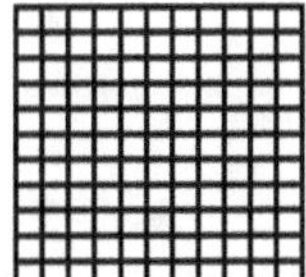

Of the Ancient Practice of Painting

76

Rainbow Manifesto

FLATLAND, SEE GESTALT PRINCIPLES.

"These examples are instances of camouflage, the phenomenon in which objects are hidden from view but not by being occluded: instead, they are perceptually subdivided (broken up internally) and repartitioned, that is, their parts are grouped with parts of the surrounding environment. As used by animals in the struggle for survival and by humans in warfare, the power of Gestalt principles thus makes it possible for organisms and things which are in plain sight to become effectively invisible and therefore undetectable by adversaries. Thus whether a physical object that is optically present exists or does not exist visually, depends on the interplay of perceptual laws." [14]

If my Readers have followed me with any attention up to this point, they will not be surprised to hear that life is somewhat dull in Flatland. I do not, of course, mean that there are not battles, conspiracies, tumults, factions, and all those other phenomena which are supposed to make History interesting; nor would I deny that the strange mixture of the problems of life and the problems of Mathematics, continually inducing conjecture and giving the opportunity of immediate verification, imparts to our existence a zest which you in Spaceland can hardly comprehend. I speak now from the aesthetic and artistic point of view when I say that life with us is dull; aesthetically and artistically, very dull indeed.

How can it be otherwise, when all one's prospect, all one's landscapes, historical pieces, portraits, flowers, still life, are nothing but a single line, with no varieties except degrees of brightness and obscurity?

It was not always thus. Colour, if Tradition speaks the truth, once for the space of half a dozen centuries or more, threw a transient splendour over the lives of our ancestors in the remotest ages. Some private individual—a Pentagon whose name is variously reported—having casually discovered the constituents of the simpler colours and a rudimentary method of painting, is said to have begun decorating first his house, then his slaves, then his Father, his Sons, and Grandsons, lastly

Cover your head with a yellow hat because Tristan Tzara didn't cover his head with one in 1916, 1918, 1919 and 1920.

Wear a violet coat because Jean-Paul Sartre, who said it hasn't been sufficiently noted that the constructions, paintings and poem-objects of Surrealism were the manual realization of sterilities by which the sceptics of the Third Century B.C. justified their perpetual "epoche." After which, Carneades and Philo, sure of not compromising themselves by an imprudent adherence, lived like everybody else. In the same way, the Surrealists, once the world is destroyed and miraculously preserved by its himself. The convenience as well as the beauty of the results commended themselves to all. Wherever Chromatistes,—for by that name the most trustworthy authorities concur in calling him,—turned his variegated frame, there he at once excited attention, and attracted respect. No one now needed to "feel" him; no one mistook his front for his back; all his movements were readily ascertained by his neighbours without the slightest strain on their powers of calculation; no one jostled him, or failed to make way for him; his voice was saved the labour of that exhausting utterance by which we colourless Squares and Pentagons are often forced to proclaim our individuality when we move amid a crowd of ignorant Isosceles.

The fashion spread like wildfire. Before a week was over, every Square and Triangle in the district had copied the example of Chromatistes, and only a few of the more conservative Pentagons still held out. A month or two found even the Dodecagons infected with the innovation. A year had not elapsed before the habit had spread to all but the very highest of the Nobility. Needless to say, the custom soon made its way from the district of Chromatistes to surrounding regions; and within two generations no one in all Flatland was colourless except the Women and the Priests.

Here Nature herself appeared to erect a barrier, and to plead against extending the innovation to these two classes.

"A first surface mirror or front surface mirror (also commonly abbreviated FS mirror or FSM) is a mirror with the reflective surface being above a backing, as opposed to the conventional, second surface mirror with the reflective surface behind a transparent substrate such as glass or acrylic. In cases where the mirror is subjected to extreme cold (as low as 33 K as in the James Webb Space Telescope), a polished pure beryllium mirror is used without a first surface coating in order to obviate buckling caused by differing coefficients of thermal expansion." [1]

destruction, can shamelessly give full play to their immense love of the world never wore one.

Wear red gloves because fifteen years ago I was blamed by a Japanese Communist for not painting a red flag.

Wear orange pants because Circumference $= 2\pi r$

Wear green socks because the area of the circle $= \pi r^2$

Put on blue shoes

but π = 3.1415926535897932384
6264338327950288419716939937510582
0974944592307816406286208998628034
8253421170679821480865132823066470

Many-sidedness was almost essential as a pretext for the Innovators. "Distinction of sides is intended by Nature to imply distinction of colours"—such was the sophism which in those days flew from mouth to mouth, converting whole towns at a time to the new culture. But manifestly to our Priests and Women this adage did not apply. The latter had only one side, and therefore—plurally and pedantically speaking—NO SIDES. The former—if at least they would assert their claim to be really and truly Circles, and not mere high-class Polygons with an infinitely large number of infinitesimally small sides—were in the habit of boasting (what Women confessed and deplored) that they also had no sides, being blessed with a perimeter of one line, or, in other words, a Circumference. Hence it came to pass that these two Classes could see no force in the so-called axiom about "Distinction of Sides implying Distinction of Colour"; and when all others had succumbed to the fascinations of corporal decoration, the Priests and the Women alone still remained pure from the pollution of paint.

Immoral, licentious, anarchical, unscientific—call them by what names you will—yet, from an aesthetic point of view, those ancient days of the Colour Revolt were the glorious childhood of Art in Flatland—a childhood, alas, that never ripened into manhood, nor even reached the blossom of youth. To live

9384460955058223172535940812848111
7450284102701938521105559644622948
9549303819644288109756659334461284
7564823378678316527120190914564856
6923460348610454326648213393607260
2491412737245870066063155881748815
2092096282925409171536436903600113
3053054882046652138414695194151160
9433057270365759591953092186117381
9326117931051185480744623799627495673518857527248912279381830119491298
3367336244065664308602139494639522
4737190702179860943702770539217176
2931767523846748184676694051320065681271452635608277857713427577896091

was then in itself a delight, because living implied seeing. Even at a small party, the company was a pleasure to behold; the richly varied hues of the assembly in a church or theatre are said to have more than once proved too distracting for our greatest teachers and actors; but most ravishing of all is said to have been the unspeakable magnificence of a military review.

The sight of a line of battle of twenty thousand Isosceles suddenly facing about, and exchanging the sombre black of their bases for the orange and purple of the two sides including their acute angle; the militia of the Equilateral Triangles tricoloured in red, white, and blue; the mauve, ultra-marine, gamboge, and burnt umber of the Square artillerymen rapidly rotating near their vermilion guns; the dashing and flashing of the five-coloured and six-coloured Pentagons and Hexagons careering across the field in their offices of surgeons, geometricians and aides-de-camp—all these may well have been sufficient to render credible the famous story how an illustrious Circle, overcome by the artistic beauty of the forces under his command, threw aside his marshal's baton and his royal crown, exclaiming that he henceforth exchanged them for the artist's pencil. How great and glorious the sensuous development of these days must have been is in part indicated by the very language and vocabulary of the period. The commonest utterances of the commonest citizens in the time of the Colour

80

7363717872146844090122495343014654
9585371050792279689258923542019956
11212902196086355441911971602977461
1309960518707211349999998372978049
951059731732816096318475024459455...

—Ay-O

FLATLAND, SEE ALIGHERO BOETTI.

Revolt seem to have been suffused with a richer tinge of word or thought; and to that era we are even now indebted for our finest poetry and for whatever rhythm still remains in the more scientific utterance of these modern days.

"It was not until 1975 that Boetti created the first works entitled Tutto and not until 1982 that his first large scale Tutto embroidered pictures were made. The first Tutto (all square in format) were given the title Pack and these were the first embroidered Tutto to take the form by which the series is now known. Each one made use of a selected variety of intersecting shapes of 'all' the separate objects and things that make up the world, with each shape coloured, arbitrarily, by the Afghan women who embroidered them. Boetti chose the various objects to be depicted from an extensive range of sources including encyclopaedias, schoolbooks, magazines, newspapers, and other lexica. Such an approach ensured the wide range of motifs; but the degree of this range and its scope was always ultimately determined by Boetti himself with many stencils made of certain favourite motifs so that they could be reused in later Tutto designs." [1]

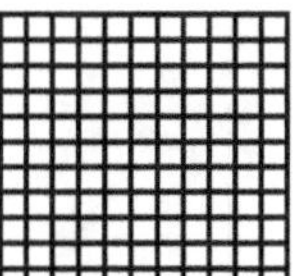

Of the Universal Colour Bill

82

Revolution inside revolution

But meanwhile the intellectual Arts were fast decaying.

The Art of Sight Recognition, being no longer needed, was no longer practised; and the studies of Geometry, Statics, Kinetics, and other kindred subjects, came soon to be considered superfluous, and fell into disrespect and neglect even at our University. The inferior Art of Feeling speedily experienced the same fate at our Elementary Schools. Then the Isosceles classes, asserting that the Specimens were no longer used nor needed, and refusing to pay the customary tribute from the Criminal classes to the service of Education, waxed daily more numerous and more insolent on the strength of their immunity from the old burden which had formerly exercised the twofold wholesome effect of at once taming their brutal nature and thinning their excessive numbers.

Year by year the Soldiers and Artisans began more vehemently to assert—and with increasing truth—that there was no great difference between them and the very highest class of Polygons, now that they were raised to an equality with the latter, and enabled to grapple with all the difficulties and solve all the problems of life, whether Statical or Kinetical, by the simple process of Colour Recognition. Not content with the natural neglect into which Sight Recognition was falling, they began boldly to demand the legal prohibition of all "monopolizing and aristocratic Arts" and the consequent abolition of all

CHARLOTTE'S LOCKS 268
MINSTER GREEN 224

BOOK ROOM RED 50
MIZZLE 266

endowments for the studies of Sight Recognition, Mathematics, and Feeling. Soon, they began to insist that inasmuch as Colour, which was a second Nature, had destroyed the need of aristocratic distinctions, the Law should follow in the same path, and that henceforth all individuals and all classes should be recognized as absolutely equal and entitled to equal rights.

Finding the higher Orders wavering and undecided, the leaders of the Revolution advanced still further in their requirements, and at last demanded that all classes alike, the Priests and the Women not excepted, should do homage to Colour by submitting to be painted. When it was objected that Priests and Women had no sides, they retorted that Nature and Expediency concurred in dictating that the front half of every human being (that is to say, the half containing his eye and mouth) should be distinguishable from his hinder half. They therefore brought before a general and extraordinary Assembly of all the States of Flatland a Bill proposing that in every Woman the half containing the eye and mouth should be coloured red, and the other half green. The Priests were to be painted in the same way, red being applied to that semicircle in which the eye and mouth formed the middle point; while the other or hinder semicircle was to be coloured green.

There was no little cunning in this proposal, which indeed emanated not from any Isosceles—for no being so

"The Ivy League nude posture photos were taken in the 1940s through the 1970s of all incoming freshmen at certain Ivy League and Seven Sisters colleges (as well as Swarthmore), ostensibly to gauge the rate and severity of rickets, scoliosis, and lordosis in the population. Harvard had its own such program by the 1980s. The larger project was run by William Herbert Sheldon and Earnest Albert Hooton, who may have been using the data to support their theory on body types and social hierarchy. What remained of the images were transferred to the Smithsonian and most were destroyed between 1995 and 2001." [1]

NANCY'S BLUSHES 278
FOLLY GREEN 76

EATING ROOM RED 43
SUGAR BAG LIGHT 29

degraded would have had angularity enough to appreciate, much less to devise, such a model of state-craft—but from an Irregular Circle who, instead of being destroyed in his childhood, was reserved by a foolish indulgence to bring desolation on his country and destruction on myriads of his followers.

On the one hand the proposition was calculated to bring the Women in all classes over to the side of the Chromatic Innovation. For by assigning to the Women the same two colours as were assigned to the Priests, the Revolutionists thereby ensured that, in certain positions, every Woman would appear like a Priest, and be treated with corresponding respect and deference—a prospect that could not fail to attract the Female Sex in a mass.

But by some of my Readers the possibility of the identical appearance of Priests and Women, under the new Legislation, may not be recognized; if so, a word or two will make it obvious.

Imagine a woman duly decorated, according to the new Code; with the front half (i.e. the half containing eye and mouth) red, and with the hinder half green. Look at her from one side. Obviously you will see a straight line, HALF RED, HALF GREEN.

CALAMINE 230
LICHEN 19

PICTURE GALLERY RED 42
GREEN SMOKE 47

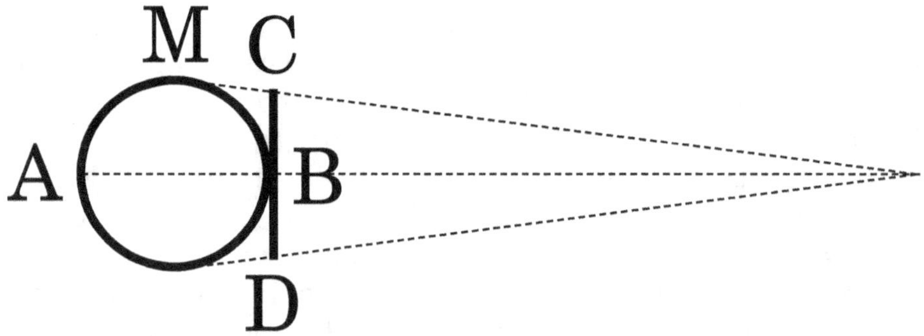

Now imagine a Priest, whose mouth is at M, and whose front semicircle (AMB) is consequently coloured red, while his hinder semicircle is green; so that the diameter AB divides the green from the red. If you contemplate the Great Man so as to have your eye in the same straight line as his dividing diameter (AB), what you will see will be a straight line (CBD), of which ONE HALF (CB) WILL BE RED, AND THE OTHER (BD) GREEN. The whole line (CD) will be rather shorter perhaps than that of a full-sized Woman, and will shade off more rapidly towards its extremities; but the identity of the colours would give you an immediate impression of identity of Class, making you neglectful of other details. Bear in mind the decay of Sight Recognition which threatened society at the time of the Colour Revolt; add too the certainty that Women would speedily learn to shade off their extremities so as to imitate the Circles; it

FOX RED 48
PIGEON 25

TERRE D'EGYPTE 247
SAXON GREEN 80

"The Anarchist Cookbook, first published in 1971, is a book that contains instructions for the manufacture of explosives, rudimentary telecommunications phreaking devices, and other items. The book also includes instructions for home manufacturing of illicit drugs, including LSD. It was written by William Powell at the apex of the counterculture era in order to protest United States involvement in the Vietnam War." [1]

must then be surely obvious to you, my dear Reader, that the Colour Bill placed us under a great danger of confounding a Priest with a young Woman.

How attractive this prospect must have been to the Frail Sex may readily be imagined. They anticipated with delight the confusion that would ensue. At home they might hear political and ecclesiastical secrets intended not for them but for their husbands and brothers, and might even issue commands in the name of a priestly Circle; out of doors the striking combination of red and green, without addition of any other colours, would be sure to lead the common people into endless mistakes, and the Women would gain whatever the Circles lost, in the deference of the passers by. As for the scandal that would befall the Circular Class if the frivolous and unseemly conduct of the Women were imputed to them, and as to the consequent subversion of the Constitution, the Female Sex could not be expected to give a thought to these considerations. Even in the households of the Circles, the Women were all in favour of the Universal Colour Bill.

The second object aimed at by the Bill was the gradual demoralization of the Circles themselves. In the general intellectual decay they still preserved their pristine clearness and strength of understanding. From their earliest childhood, familiarized in their Circular households with the total absence

RECTORY RED 217
TERESA'S GREEN 236

BLAZER 212
ARSENIC 214

of Colour, the Nobles alone preserved the Sacred Art of Sight Recognition, with all the advantages that result from that admirable training of the intellect. Hence, up to the date of the introduction of the Universal Colour Bill, the Circles had not only held their own, but even increased their lead of the other classes by abstinence from the popular fashion.

Now therefore the artful Irregular whom I described above as the real author of this diabolical Bill, determined at one blow to lower the status of the Hierarchy by forcing them to submit to the pollution of Colour, and at the same time to destroy their domestic opportunities of training in the Art of Sight Recognition, so as to enfeeble their intellects by depriving them of their pure and colourless homes. Once subjected to the chromatic taint, every parental and every childish Circle would demoralize each other. Only in discerning between the Father and the Mother would the Circular infant find problems for the exercise of its understanding—problems too often likely to be corrupted by maternal impostures with the result of shaking the child's faith in all logical conclusions. Thus by degrees the intellectual lustre of the Priestly Order would wane, and the road would then lie open for a total destruction of all Aristocratic Legislature and for the subversion of our Privileged Classes.

"In religion the Future is behind us. In art the present is the eternal. The tea-masters held that real appreciation of art is only possible to those who make of it a living influence. Thus they sought to regulate their daily life by the high standard of refinement which obtained in the tea-room. In all circumstances serenity of mind should be maintained, and conversation should be conducted as never to mar the harmony of the surroundings. The cut and color of the dress, the poise of the body, and the manner of walking could all be made expressions of artistic personality." [15]

RED EARTH 64
VERT DE TERRE 234

89

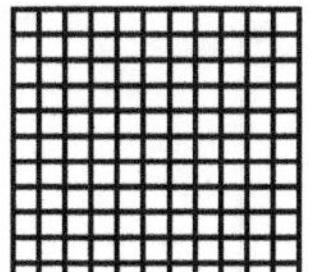

Of the Suppression of the Chromatic Sedition

90

A non-chromatic world

FLATLAND, SEE MAX BILL.

"As a designer and artist, Bill sought to create forms which visually represent the New Physics of the early 20th century. He sought to create objects so that the new science of form could be understood by the senses: that is as a concrete art. Thus Bill is not a rationalist—as is typically thought—but rather a phenomenologist. One who understands embodiment as the ultimate expression of a concrete art." [16]

The agitation for the Universal Colour Bill continued for three years; and up to the last moment of that period it seemed as though Anarchy were destined to triumph.

A whole army of Polygons, who turned out to fight as private soldiers, was utterly annihilated by a superior force of Isosceles Triangles—the Squares and Pentagons meanwhile remaining neutral. Worse than all, some of the ablest Circles fell a prey to conjugal fury. Infuriated by political animosity, the wives in many a noble household wearied their lords with prayers to give up their opposition to the Colour Bill; and some, finding their entreaties fruitless, fell on and slaughtered their innocent children and husband, perishing themselves in the act of carnage. It is recorded that during that triennial agitation no less than twenty-three Circles perished in domestic discord.

Great indeed was the peril. It seemed as though the Priests had no choice between submission and extermination; when suddenly the course of events was completely changed by one of those picturesque incidents which Statesmen ought never to neglect, often to anticipate, and sometimes perhaps to originate, because of the absurdly disproportionate power with which they appeal to the sympathies of the populace.

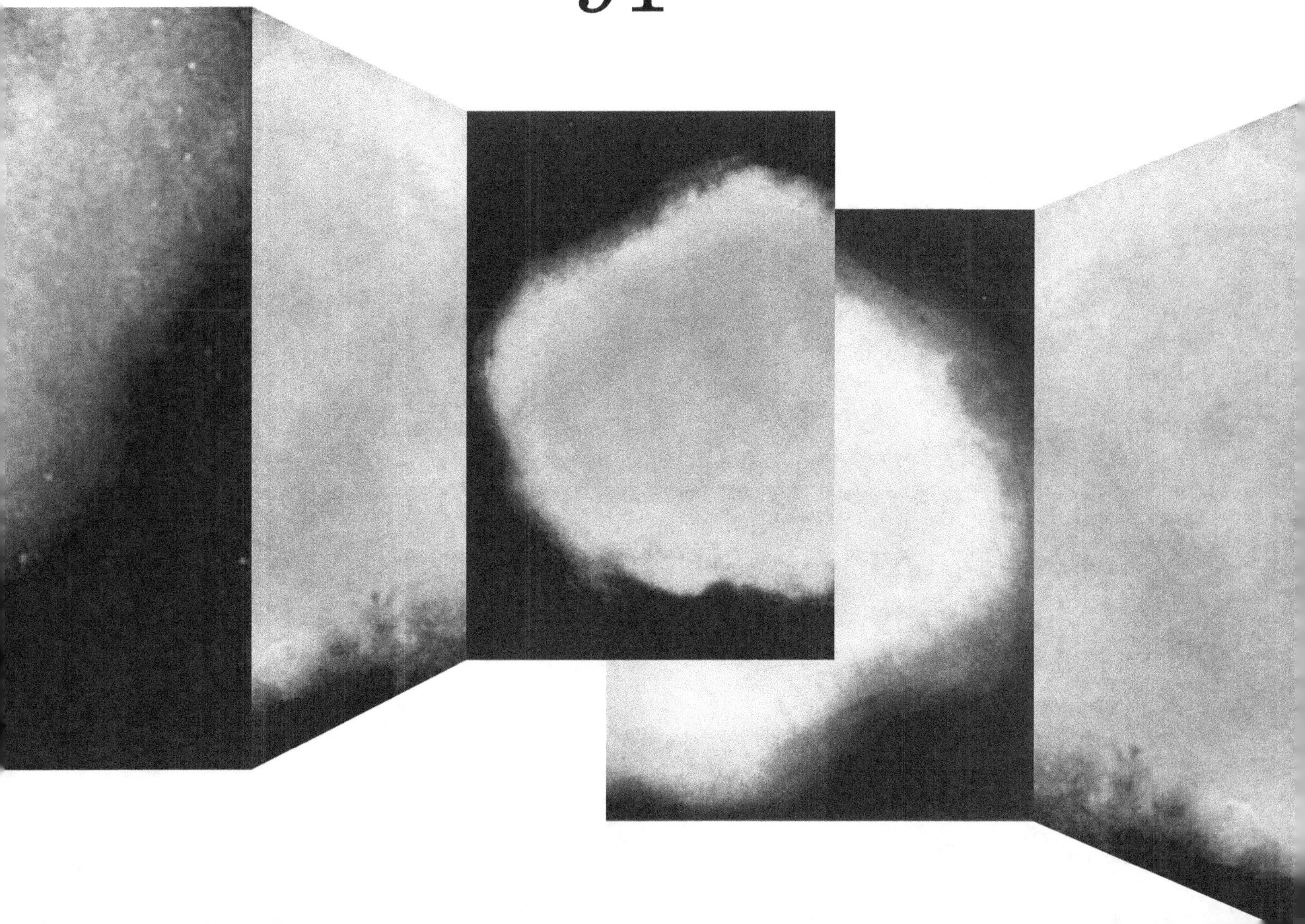

It happened that an Isosceles of a low type, with a brain little if at all above four degrees—accidentally dabbling in the colours of some Tradesman whose shop he had plundered—painted himself, or caused himself to be painted (for the story varies) with the twelve colours of a Dodecagon. Going into the Market Place he accosted in a feigned voice a maiden, the orphan daughter of a noble Polygon, whose affection in former days he had sought in vain; and by a series of deceptions—aided, on the one side, by a string of lucky accidents too long to relate, and on the other, by an almost inconceivable fatuity and neglect of ordinary precautions on the part of the relations of the bride—he succeeded in consummating the marriage. The unhappy girl committed suicide on discovering the fraud to which she had been subjected.

When the news of this catastrophe spread from State to State the minds of the Women were violently agitated. Sympathy with the miserable victim and anticipations of similar deceptions for themselves, their sisters, and their daughters, made them now regard the Colour Bill in an entirely new aspect. Not a few openly avowed themselves converted to antagonism; the rest needed only a slight stimulus to make a similar avowal. Seizing this favourable opportunity, the Circles hastily convened an extraordinary Assembly of the States; and besides the usual guard of Convicts, they secured the attendance of a large number of reactionary Women.

Amidst an unprecedented concourse, the Chief Circle

"From 1942 to 1946, Yves Klein studied at the École Nationale de la Marine Marchande and the École Nationale des Langues Orientales and began practicing judo. At this time, he became friends with Arman Fernandez and Claude Pascal and started to paint. At the age of nineteen, Klein and his friends lay on a beach in the south of France, and divided the world between themselves; Arman chose the earth, Claude, words, while Yves chose the ethereal space surrounding the planet, which he then proceeded to sign.

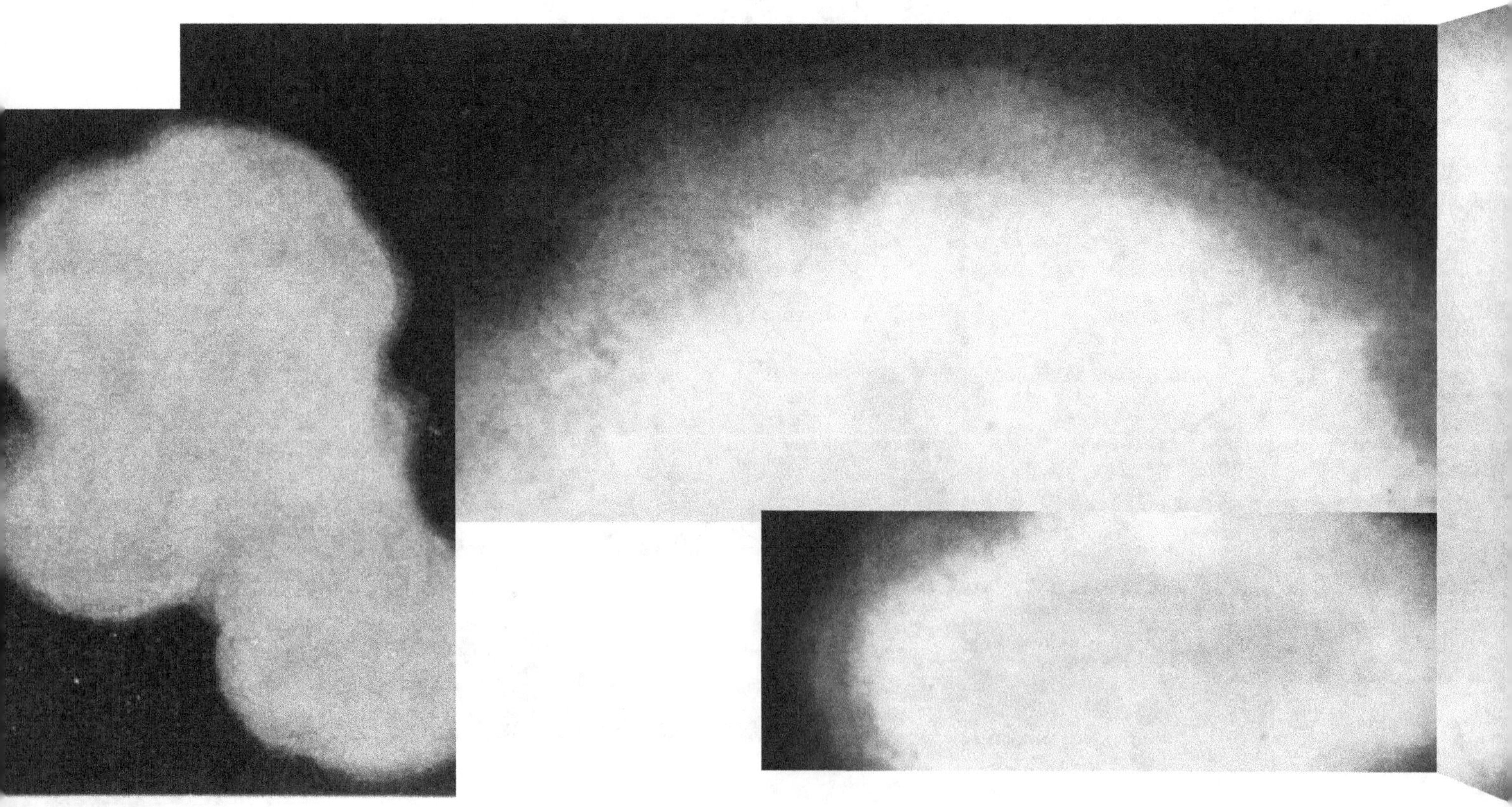

'With this famous symbolic gesture of signing the sky, Klein had foreseen, as in a reverie, the thrust of his art from that time onwards—a quest to reach the far side of the infinite'." [1]

of those days—by name Pantocyclus—arose to find himself hissed and hooted by a hundred and twenty thousand Isosceles. But he secured silence by declaring that henceforth the Circles would enter on a policy of Concession; yielding to the wishes of the majority, they would accept the Colour Bill. The uproar being at once converted to applause, he invited Chromatistes, the leader of the Sedition, into the centre of the hall, to receive in the name of his followers the submission of the Hierarchy. Then followed a speech, a masterpiece of rhetoric, which occupied nearly a day in the delivery, and to which no summary can do justice.

With a grave appearance of impartiality he declared that as they were now finally committing themselves to Reform or Innovation, it was desirable that they should take one last view of the perimeter of the whole subject, its defects as well as its advantages. Gradually introducing the mention of the dangers to the Tradesmen, the Professional Classes and the Gentlemen, he silenced the rising murmurs of the Isosceles by reminding them that, in spite of all these defects, he was willing to accept the Bill if it was approved by the majority. But it was manifest that all, except the Isosceles, were moved by his words and were either neutral or averse to the Bill.

Turning now to the Workmen he asserted that their interests must not be neglected, and that, if they intended to

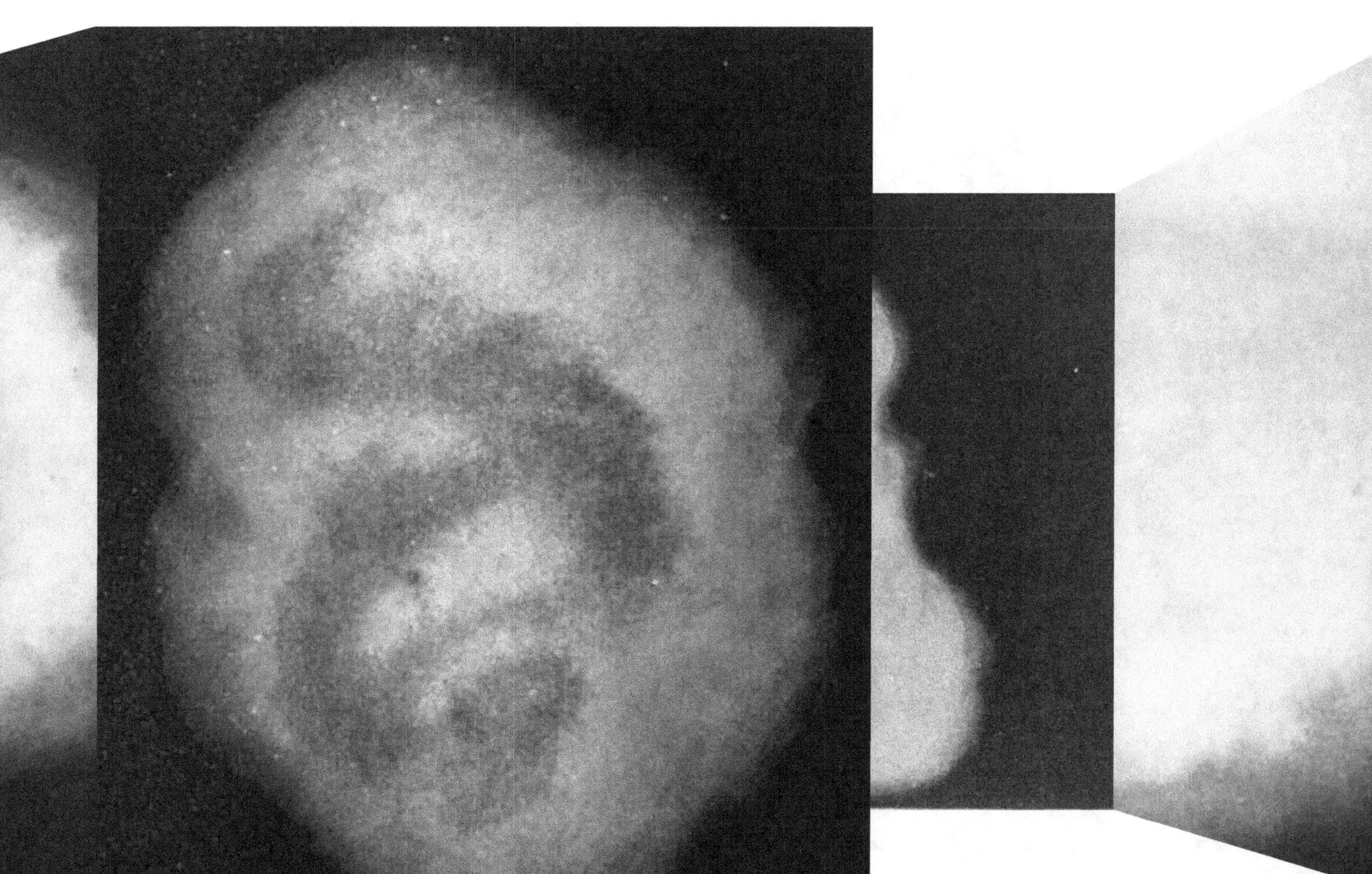

accept the Colour Bill, they ought at least to do so with full view of the consequences. Many of them, he said, were on the point of being admitted to the class of the Regular Triangles; others anticipated for their children a distinction they could not hope for themselves. That honourable ambition would now have to be sacrificed. With the universal adoption of Colour, all distinctions would cease; Regularity would be confused with Irregularity; development would give place to retrogression; the Workman would in a few generations be degraded to the level of the Military, or even the Convict Class; political power would be in the hands of the greatest number, that is to say the Criminal Classes, who were already more numerous than the Workmen, and would soon out-number all the other Classes put together when the usual Compensative Laws of Nature were violated.

A subdued murmur of assent ran through the ranks of the Artisans, and Chromatistes, in alarm, attempted to step forward and address them. But he found himself encompassed with guards and forced to remain silent while the Chief Circle in a few impassioned words made a final appeal to the Women, exclaiming that, if the Colour Bill passed, no marriage would henceforth be safe, no woman's honour secure; fraud, deception, hypocrisy would pervade every household; domestic bliss would share the fate of the Constitution and pass to speedy

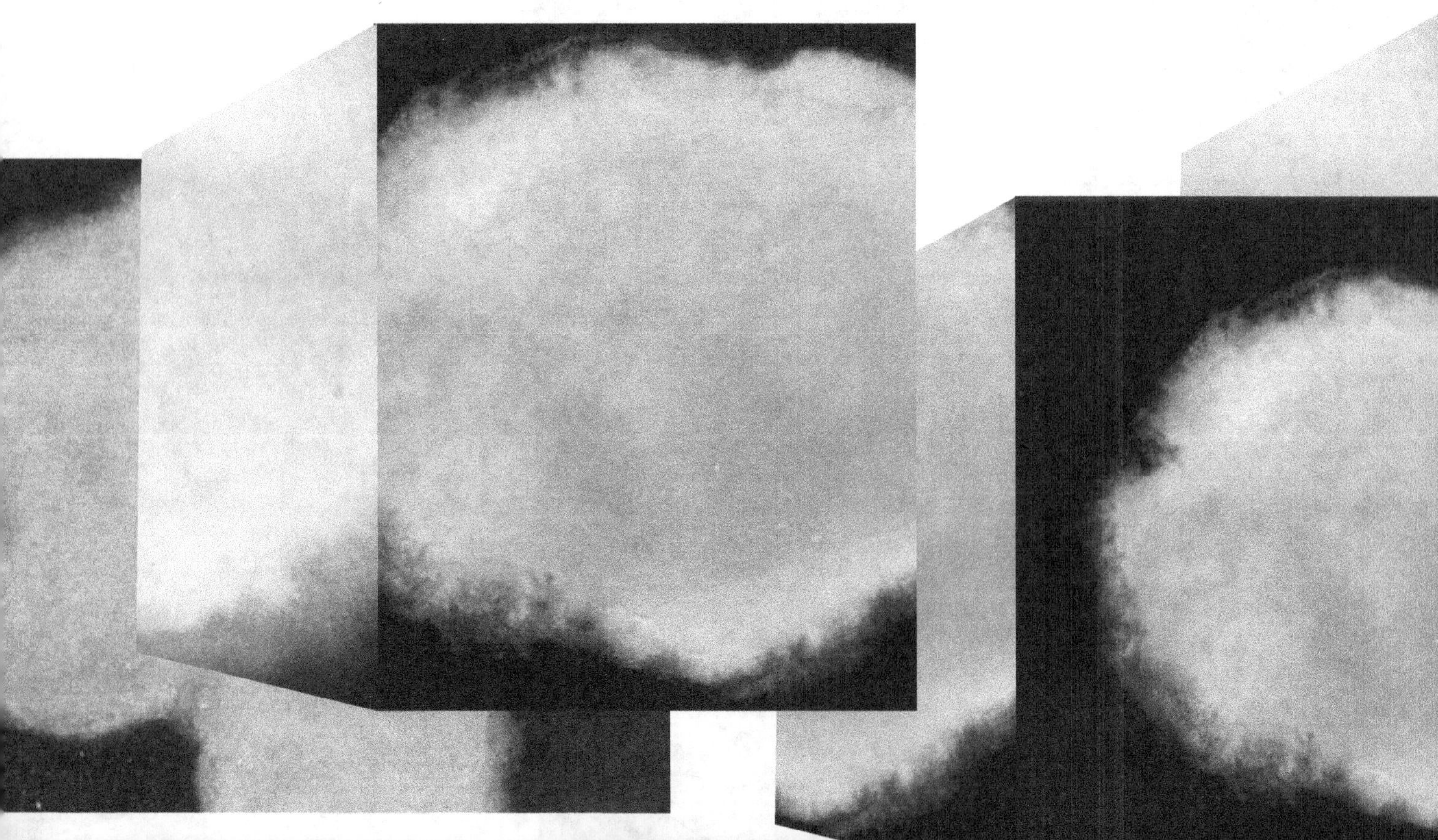

"Is graceless and looks quite ridiculous when—with his sight still dim and before he has gotten sufficiently accustomed to the surrounding darkness—he is compelled in courtrooms or elsewhere to contend about the shadows of justice or the representations of which they are the shadows, and to dispute about the way these things are understood by men who have never seen justice itself?" [17]

perdition. "Sooner than this," he cried, "Come death."

At these words, which were the preconcerted signal for action, the Isosceles Convicts fell on and transfixed the wretched Chromatistes; the Regular Classes, opening their ranks, made way for a band of Women who, under direction of the Circles, moved, back foremost, invisibly and unerringly upon the unconscious soldiers; the Artisans, imitating the example of their betters, also opened their ranks. Meantime bands of Convicts occupied every entrance with an impenetrable phalanx.

The battle, or rather carnage, was of short duration. Under the skillful generalship of the Circles almost every Woman's charge was fatal and very many extracted their sting uninjured, ready for a second slaughter. But no second blow was needed; the rabble of the Isosceles did the rest of the business for themselves. Surprised, leader-less, attacked in front by invisible foes, and finding egress cut off by the Convicts behind them, they at once—after their manner—lost all presence of mind, and raised the cry of "treachery". This sealed their fate. Every Isosceles now saw and felt a foe in every other. In half an hour not one of that vast multitude was living; and the fragments of seven score thousand of the Criminal Class slain by one another's angles attested the triumph of Order.

The Circles delayed not to push their victory to the uttermost. The Working Men they spared but decimated. The

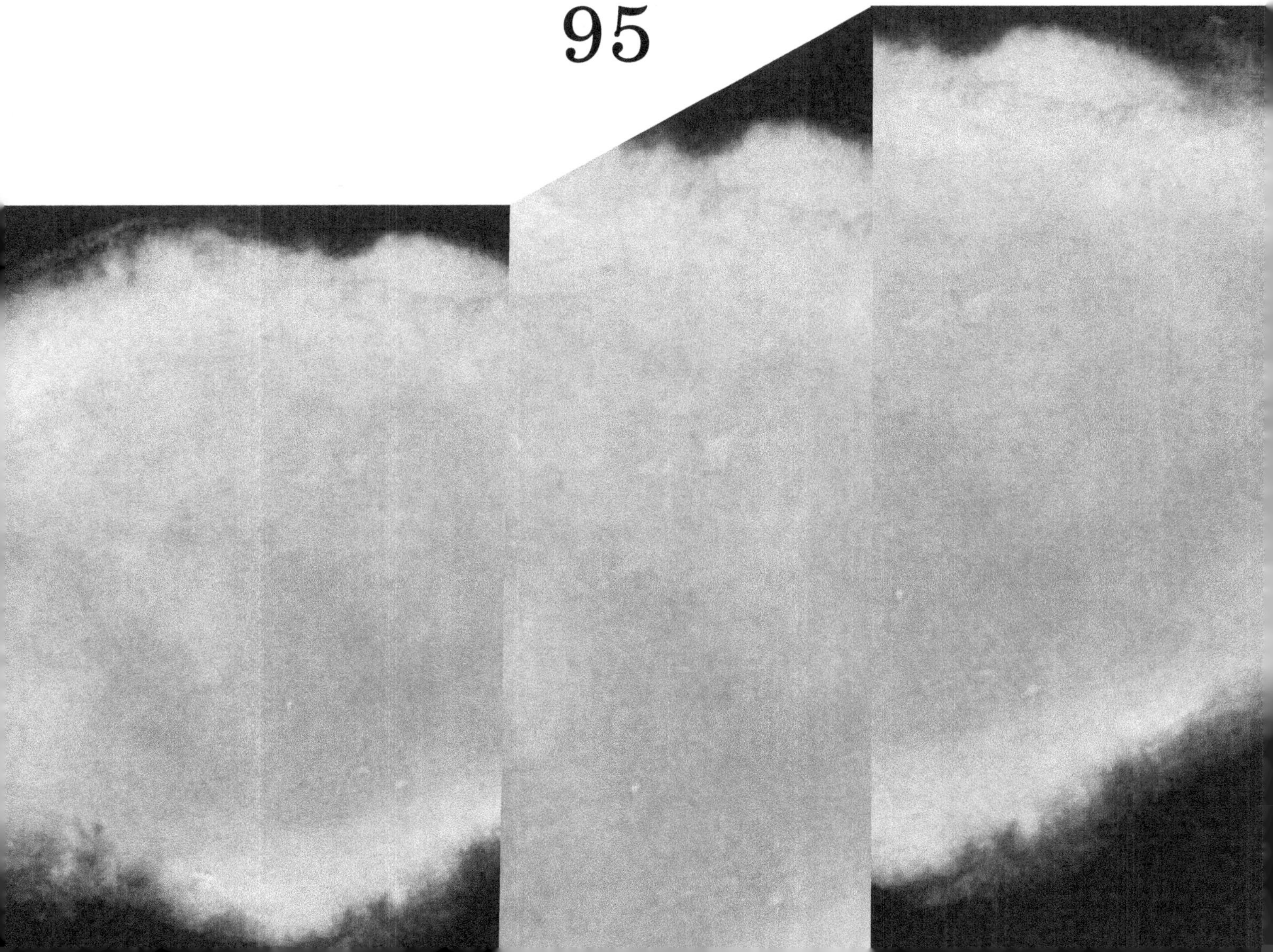

Militia of the Equilaterals was at once called out; and every Triangle suspected of Irregularity on reasonable grounds, was destroyed by Court Martial, without the formality of exact measurement by the Social Board. The homes of the Military and Artisan classes were inspected in a course of visitations extending through upwards of a year; and during that period every town, village, and hamlet was systematically purged of that excess of the lower orders which had been brought about by the neglect to pay the tribute of Criminals to the Schools and University, and by the violation of the other natural Laws of the Constitution of Flatland. Thus the balance of classes was again restored.

Needless to say that henceforth the use of Colour was abolished, and its possession prohibited. Even the utterance of any word denoting Colour, except by the Circles or by qualified scientific teachers, was punished by a severe penalty. Only at our University in some of the very highest and most esoteric classes—which I myself have never been privileged to attend—it is understood that the sparing use of Colour is still sanctioned for the purpose of illustrating some of the deeper problems of mathematics. But of this I can only speak from hearsay.

Elsewhere in Flatland, Colour is now non-existent. The art of making it is known to only one living person, the Chief Circle for the time being; and by him it is handed down on

"The purpose of a 3D scanner is usually to create a point cloud of geometric samples on the surface of the subject. These points can then be used to extrapolate the shape of the subject (a process called reconstruction). If color information is collected at each point, then the colors on the surface of the subject can also be determined." [18]

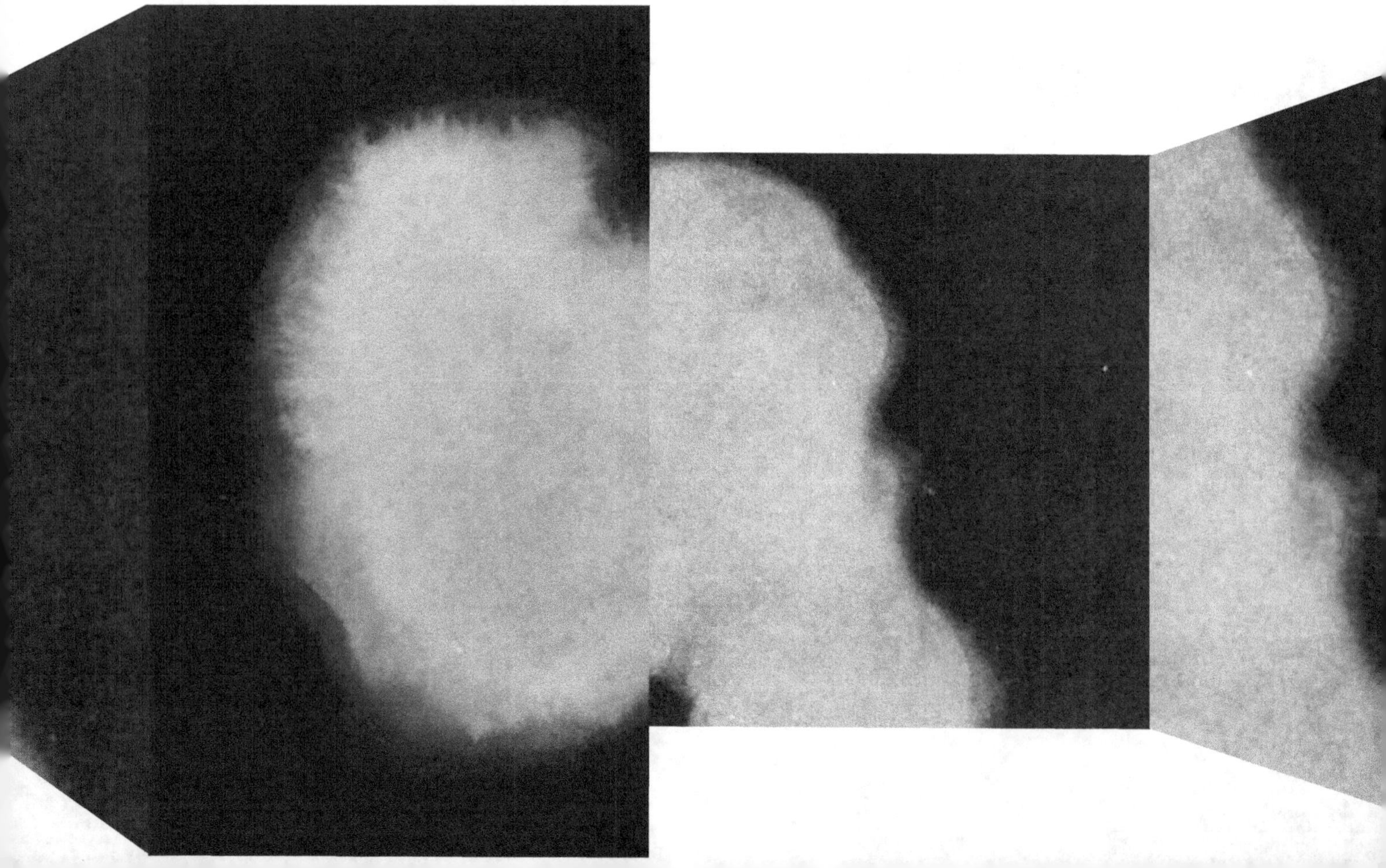

his death-bed to none but his Successor. One manufactory alone produces it; and, lest the secret should be betrayed, the Workmen are annually consumed, and fresh ones introduced. So great is the terror with which even now our Aristocracy looks back to the far-distant days of the agitation for the Universal Colour Bill.

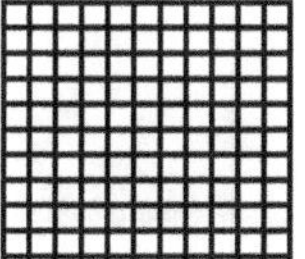

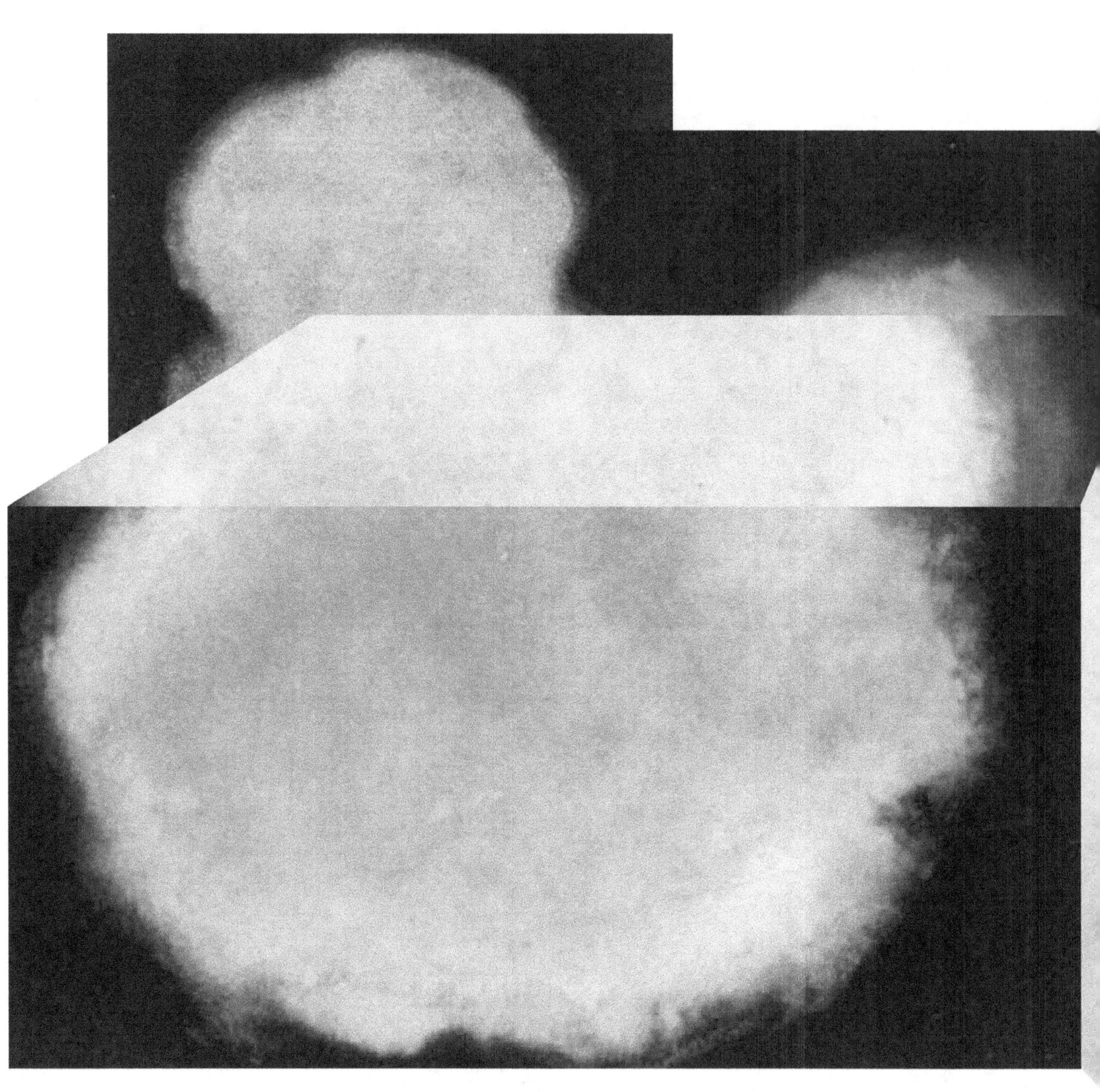

Rules and regulations

FLATLAND, SEE SPACETIME.

"Claude Bragdon's 'day job' was as an architect. He, along with Abbott, also believed that learning to comprehend a fourth dimension was in some sense equivalent to enlightenment." [19]

Bragdon cites Professor N. A. Oumoff as saying "Time does not flow, any more than space flows. It is we who are flowing, wanderers in a four-dimensional universe. Time is just the same measurement of space as length, breadth, and thickness". [20]

It is high time that I should pass from these brief and discursive notes about things in Flatland to the central event of this book, my initiation into the mysteries of Space. THAT is my subject; all that has gone before is merely preface.

For this reason I must omit many matters of which the explanation would not, I flatter myself, be without interest for my Readers: as for example, our method of propelling and stopping ourselves, although destitute of feet; the means by which we give fixity to structures of wood, stone, or brick, although of course we have no hands, nor can we lay foundations as you can, nor avail ourselves of the lateral pressure of the earth; the manner in which the rain originates in the intervals between our various zones, so that the northern regions do not intercept the moisture from falling on the southern; the nature of our hills and mines, our trees and vegetables, our seasons and harvests; our Alphabet and method of writing, adapted to our linear tablets; these and a hundred other details of our physical existence I must pass over, nor do I mention them now except to indicate to my readers that their omission proceeds not from forgetfulness on the part of the author, but from his regard for the time of the Reader.

Yet before I proceed to my legitimate subject some few final remarks will no doubt be expected by my Readers upon those pillars and mainstays of the Constitution of Flatland,

I—No Boy to be admitted under Seven, or above Fourteen Years of age, or whose Parent or Parents shall receive any Collection or Benefit from the Levies raised for the maintanance of the Poor. Preference to be given to those Boys who have musical voices, or who manifest any notions of singing.

II—Each Boy to be allowed, once in eighteen months, a green cloath coat with short skirt, a waitcoast, and trowsers of the same, one shirt of flaxen cloth, two pairs of stockings, one pair of shoes, and a cap. The new clothes to be worn for the first half year only on Sundays; and if the Boy be withdrawn within that time, the clothes be returned.

N.B—The Boys to be measured, and the garments cut out, by one Tailor only; who is directed to have the cloth well soaked in water before cutting out, to allow the sleeves large, to turn up a piece at the cuffs, and make due allowance for growing.

III—The Boys are expected to attend at the school room, cleanly washed and combed, every morning from nine till twelve, and every afternoon from two till five, allowing Saturday afternoon and after three on Thursdays, for holidays. Neglect of this regulation will render the Boys offending liable to confinement at the discretion of the Master.

the controllers of our conduct and shapers of our destiny, the objects of universal homage and almost of adoration: need I say that I mean our Circles or Priests?

When I call them Priests, let me not be understood as meaning no more than the term denotes with you. With us, our Priests are Administrators of all Business, Art, and Science; Directors of Trade, Commerce, Generalship, Architecture, Engineering, Education, Statesmanship, Legislature, Morality, Theology; doing nothing themselves, they are the Causes of everything worth doing, that is done by others.

Although popularly everyone called a Circle is deemed a Circle, yet among the better educated Classes it is known that no Circle is really a Circle, but only a Polygon with a very large number of very small sides. As the number of the sides increases, a Polygon approximates to a Circle; and, when the number is very great indeed, say for example three or four hundred, it is extremely difficult for the most delicate touch to feel any polygonal angles. Let me say rather, it WOULD be difficult: for, as I have shown above, Recognition by Feeling is unknown among the highest society, and to FEEL a Circle would be considered a most audacious insult. This habit of abstention from Feeling in the best society enables a Circle the more easily to sustain the veil of mystery in which, from his earliest years, he is wont to enwrap the exact nature of

"Scientific racism is the use of scientific techniques and hypotheses to support or justify the belief in racism, racial inferiority, or racial superiority, or alternatively the practice of classifying individuals of different phenotypes into discrete races. According to the United Nations convention, superiority based on racial differentiation is scientifically false, morally condemnable, socially unjust and dangerous, and there is no justification for racial discrimination, in theory or in practice, anywhere." [1]

102

IV—The Boys are to assemble every Sunday at the school room previous to Church hours, and to walk to and from Church in form with the Master, as often as there may be Divine Service. The Master to attend to their behaviour in Church, and to punish misconduct by confinement in the school room, or otherwise.

V—Boys coming irregurlay to school are to be confined during play hours, at the discretion of the Master; and Boys leaving their confinement before the time fixed, will be subject to further correction. If Parents interfere with the Master in his discipline of the school, their children will be liable to be expelled by the Trustees. Boys habitually guilty of impertinence, obstinacy, or of playing truant, will be expelled.

VI—Boys detained and kept by their Parents from school five days together, or above twelve days in the whole, in any one quarter, upon any pretext, except sickness, will be liable to be expelled by the Trustees.

VII—The school house, with its appurtenances, having been repaired partly from an accumulated fund, shall be kept in tenantable repair, and insured against fire, and the Master allowed

his Perimeter or Circumference. Three feet being the average Perimeter it follows that, in a Polygon of three hundred sides each side will be no more than the hundredth part of a foot in length, or little more than the tenth part of an inch; and in a Polygon of six or seven hundred sides the sides are little larger than the diameter of a Spaceland pin-head. It is always assumed, by courtesy, that the Chief Circle for the time being has ten thousand sides.

The ascent of the posterity of the Circles in the social scale is not restricted, as it is among the lower Regular classes, by the Law of Nature which limits the increase of sides to one in each generation. If it were so, the number of sides in a Circle would be a mere question of pedigree and arithmetic, and the four hundred and ninety-seventh descendant of an Equilateral Triangle would necessarily be a Polygon with five hundred sides. But this is not the case. Nature's Law prescribes two antagonistic decrees affecting Circular propagation; first, that as the race climbs higher in the scale of development, so development shall proceed at an accelerated pace; second, that in the same proportion, the race shall become less fertile. Consequently in the home of a Polygon of four or five hundred sides it is rare to find a son; more than one is never seen. On the other hand the son of a five-hundred-sided Polygon has been known to possess five hundred

to reside therein, and occupy it for his own convinience; but the school room not to be used for any other purpose, without the consent of the Trustees.

VIII—This Charity being granted on the condition that the Athanasian Creed be read in the Parish Church on the days appointed in the Rubrick, and that the Boys be permitted to tone the Responses in and during Divine Service; due representation thereof must be accordingly made to the officiated Clergymen, and repeated as occasion may require.

IX—The Master to instruct all the Boys in Reading, Writing, and Arithmetic; and such as are duly qualified, in singing of Psalms, and toning the Responses, in and during divine service; carefully observing that the Responses be made in a low devotional tone—and to pay great attention to this duty being properly performed.

X—The Master to keep a regular and strict account of the Boys' attendance and conduct, to be laid before the Trustees every quarter. Meritorious behaviour to be rewarded by Christmas presents, if the funds will admit thereof.

and fifty, or even six hundred sides.

Art also steps in to help the process of the higher Evolution. Our physicians have discovered that the small and tender sides of an infant Polygon of the higher class can be fractured, and his whole frame re-set, with such exactness that a Polygon of two or three hundred sides sometimes—by no means always, for the process is attended with serious risk—but sometimes overleaps two or three hundred generations, and as it were doubles at a stroke, the number of his progenitors and the nobility of his descent.

Many a promising child is sacrificed in this way. Scarcely one out of ten survives. Yet so strong is the parental ambition among those Polygons who are, as it were, on the fringe of the Circular class, that it is very rare to find a Nobleman of that position in society, who has neglected to place his first-born in the Circular Neo-Therapeutic Gymnasium before he has attained the age of a month.

One year determines success or failure. At the end of that time the child has, in all probability, added one more to the tombstones that crowd the Neo-Therapeutic Cemetery; but on rare occasions a glad procession bears back the little one to his exultant parents, no longer a Polygon, but a Circle, at least by courtesy: and a single instance of so blessed a result induces multitudes of Polygonal parents to submit to similar

104

XI—The Master to receive, through the medium of the Trustees, as a compensation for his services, a certain salary of £12 a Year—to be at all times liable to be displaced, in case of misconduct, by an order of the Trustees made at any general meeting; and on notice of such order, to leave the house appropiated for his residence, within one Month.

XII—The school to be at all times open to the visitation and inspection of all or any of the Trustees, any two of whom may convene a meeting of the whole body.

XIII—Parents, who feel themselves aggrieved by the conduct of the Master in the School, may state their complaints at a meeting of Trustees.

XIV—A Copy of these Rules, signed by the Trustees to be kept constantly fixed up in the school room, and open to the inspection of the inhabitants at all reasonable times.

—Buckingham Green-Coat School, 1827

FLATLAND, SEE LIGHT CONE.

domestic sacrifices, which have a dissimilar issue.

"A light cone is the path that a flash of light, emanating from a single event (localized to a single point in space and a single moment in time) and traveling in all directions, would take through space-time. If we imagine the light confined to a two-dimensional plane, the light from the flash spreads out in a circle after the event E occurs, and if we graph the growing circle with the vertical axis of the graph representing time, the result is a cone, known as the future light cone. The past light cone behaves like the future light cone in reverse, a circle which contracts in radius at the speed of light until it converges to a point at the exact position and time of the event E." [1]

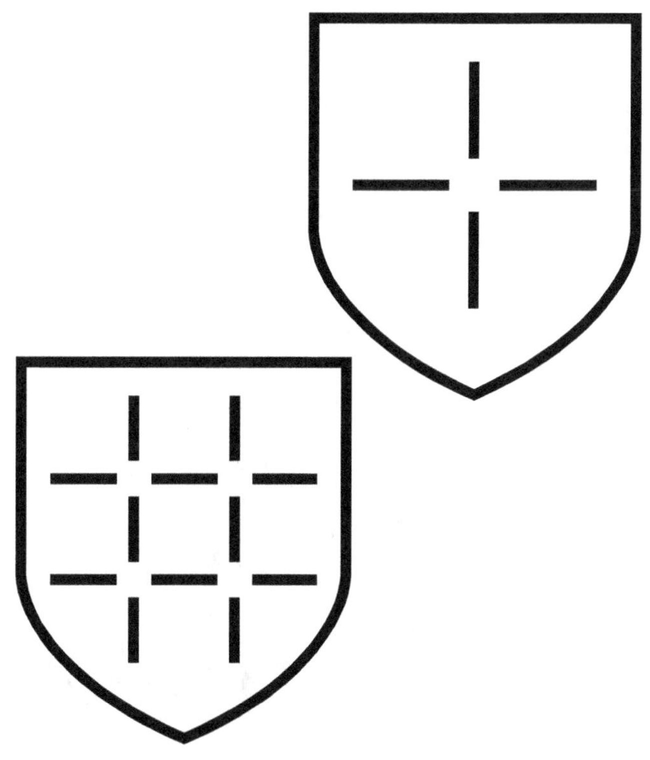

Of the Doctrine of Priests

Of control and illumination

As to the doctrine of the Circles it may briefly be summed up in a single maxim, "Attend to your Configuration." Whether political, ecclesiastical, or moral, all their teaching has for its object the improvement of individual and collective Configuration—with special reference of course to the Configuration of the Circles, to which all other objects are subordinated.

It is the merit of the Circles that they have effectually suppressed those ancient heresies which led men to waste energy and sympathy in the vain belief that conduct depends upon will, effort, training, encouragement, praise, or anything else but Configuration. It was Pantocyclus—the illustrious Circle mentioned above, as the queller of the Colour Revolt—who first convinced mankind that Configuration makes the man; that if, for example, you are born an Isosceles with two uneven sides, you will assuredly go wrong unless you have them made even—for which purpose you must go to the Isosceles Hospital; similarly, if you are a Triangle, or Square, or even a Polygon, born with any Irregularity, you must be taken to one of the Regular Hospitals to have your disease cured; otherwise you will end your days in the State Prison or by the angle of the State Executioner.

All faults or defects, from the slightest misconduct to the most flagitious crime, Pantocyclus attributed to some deviation from perfect Regularity in the bodily figure, caused perhaps (if not congenital) by some collision in a crowd; by neglect to take

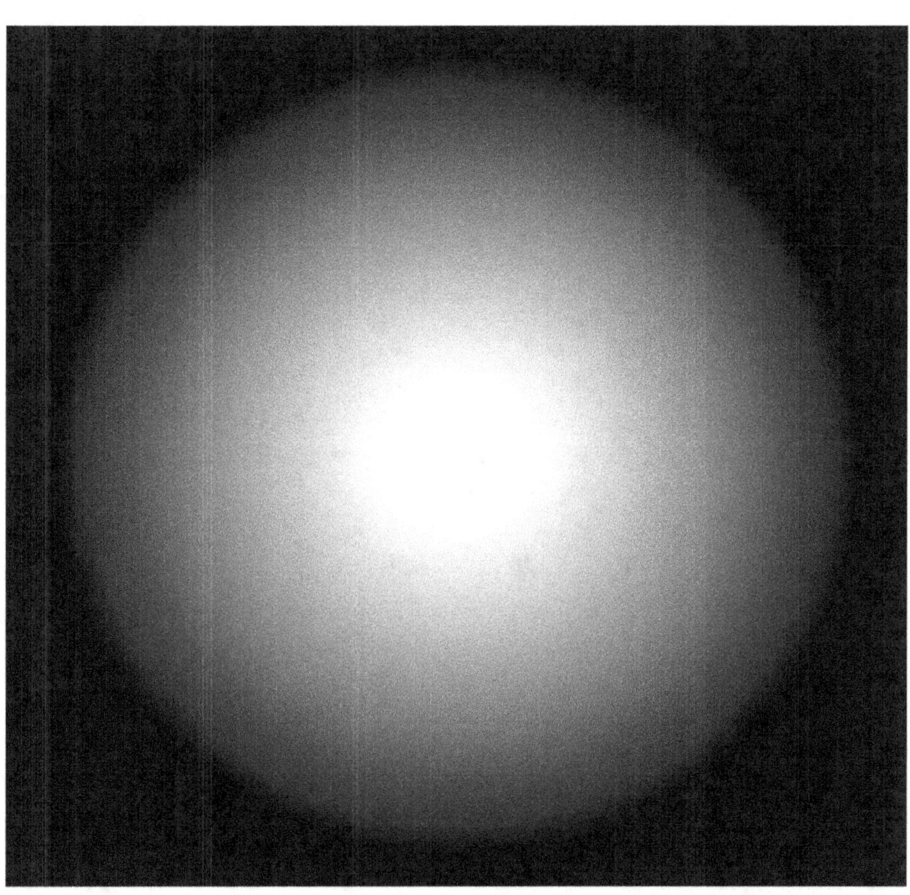

exercise, or by taking too much of it; or even by a sudden change of temperature, resulting in a shrinkage or expansion in some too susceptible part of the frame. Therefore, concluded that illustrious Philosopher, neither good conduct nor bad conduct is a fit subject, in any sober estimation, for either praise or blame. For why should you praise, for example, the integrity of a Square who faithfully defends the interests of his client, when you ought in reality rather to admire the exact precision of his right angles? Or again, why blame a lying, thievish Isosceles when you ought rather to deplore the incurable inequality of his sides?

Theoretically, this doctrine is unquestionable; but it has practical drawbacks. In dealing with an Isosceles, if a rascal pleads that he cannot help stealing because of his unevenness, you reply that for that very reason, because he cannot help being a nuisance to his neighbours, you, the Magistrate, cannot help sentencing him to be consumed—and there's an end of the matter. But in little domestic difficulties, where the penalty of consumption, or death, is out of the question, this theory of Configuration sometimes comes in awkwardly; and I must confess that occasionally when one of my own Hexagonal Grandsons pleads as an excuse for his disobedience that a sudden change of the temperature has been too much for his Perimeter, and that I ought to lay the blame not on him but on his Configuration, which can only be strengthened by abundance of the choicest sweetmeats,

"In algebraic geometry, a hypersurface in projective space of dimension n is an algebraic set that is purely of dimension n−1. It is then defined by a single equation F=0, a homogeneous polynomial in the homogeneous coordinates. It may have singularities, so not in fact be a submanifold in the strict sense. 'Primal' is an old term for an irreducible hypersurface." [1]

I neither see my way logically to reject, nor practically to accept, his conclusions.

For my own part, I find it best to assume that a good sound scolding or castigation has some latent and strengthening influence on my Grandson's Configuration; though I own that I have no grounds for thinking so. At all events I am not alone in my way of extricating myself from this dilemma; for I find that many of the highest Circles, sitting as Judges in law courts, use praise and blame towards Regular and Irregular Figures; and in their homes I know by experience that, when scolding their children, they speak about "right" or "wrong" as vehemently and passionately as if they believed that these names represented real existences, and that a human Figure is really capable of choosing between them.

Constantly carrying out their policy of making Configuration the leading idea in every mind, the Circles reverse the nature of that Commandment which in Spaceland regulates the relations between parents and children. With you, children are taught to honour their parents; with us—next to the Circles, who are the chief object of universal homage—a man is taught to honour his Grandson, if he has one; or, if not, his Son. By "honour", however, is by no means meant "indulgence", but a reverent regard for their highest interests: and the Circles teach that the duty of fathers is to subordinate their own interests to those of posterity, thereby advancing the welfare of the whole State as well as that of their own immediate descendants.

The weak point in the system of the Circles—if a humble Square may venture to speak of anything Circular as containing any element of weakness—appears to me to be found in their relations with Women.

As it is of the utmost importance for Society that Irregular births should be discouraged, it follows that no Woman who has any Irregularities in her ancestry is a fit partner for one who desires that his posterity should rise by regular degrees in the social scale.

Now the Irregularity of a Male is a matter of measurement; but as all Women are straight, and therefore visibly Regular so to speak, one has to devise some other means of ascertaining what I may call their invisible Irregularity, that is to say their potential Irregularities as regards possible offspring. This is effected by carefully-kept pedigrees, which are preserved and supervised by the State; and without a certified pedigree no Woman is allowed to marry.

Now it might have been supposed that a Circle—proud of his ancestry and regardful for a posterity which might possibly issue hereafter in a Chief Circle—would be more careful than any other to choose a wife who had no blot on her escutcheon.

FLATLAND, SEE HERMAN CAKE.

"Herman cake (often called simply Herman) is a 'friendship cake', similar to the Amish Friendship Bread, for which the ingredients are passed from person to person (like a chain letter) and which continues to grow as it contains yeast and lactic acid bacteria. One starter can, in theory, last indefinitely. The other ingredients for the mixture are milk, sugar, flour and warm water. They became popular in the 1970s." [1]

But it is not so. The care in choosing a Regular wife appears to diminish as one rises in the social scale. Nothing would induce an aspiring Isosceles, who had hopes of generating an Equilateral Son, to take a wife who reckoned a single Irregularity among her Ancestors; a Square or Pentagon, who is confident that his family is steadily on the rise, does not inquire above the five-hundredth generation; a Hexagon or Dodecagon is even more careless of the wife's pedigree; but a Circle has been known deliberately to take a wife who has had an Irregular Great-Grandfather, and all because of some slight superiority of lustre, or because of the charms of a low voice—which, with us, even more than you, is thought "an excellent thing in Woman".

Such ill-judged marriages are, as might be expected, barren, if they do not result in positive Irregularity or in diminution of sides; but none of these evils have hitherto proved sufficiently deterrent. The loss of a few sides in a highly-developed Polygon is not easily noticed, and is sometimes compensated by a successful operation in the Neo-Therapeutic Gymnasium, as I have described above; and the Circles are too much disposed to acquiesce in infecundity as a Law of the superior development. Yet, if this evil be not arrested, the gradual diminution of the Circular class may soon become more rapid, and the time may be not far distant when, the race being no longer able to produce a Chief Circle, the Constitution of Flatland must fall.

revolve

your mind

around

FLATLAND, SEE INVISIBLE COMMITTEE.

One other word of warning suggests itself to me, though I cannot so easily mention a remedy; and this also refers to our relations with Women. About three hundred years ago, it was decreed by the Chief Circle that, since women are deficient in Reason but abundant in Emotion, they ought no longer to be treated as rational, nor receive any mental education. The consequence was that they were no longer taught to read, nor even to master Arithmetic enough to enable them to count the angles of their husband or children; and hence they sensibly declined during each generation in intellectual power. And this system of female non-education or quietism still prevails.

My fear is that, with the best intentions, this policy has been carried so far as to react injuriously on the Male Sex.

For the consequence is that, as things now are, we Males have to lead a kind of bi-lingual, and I may almost say bi-mental, existence. With Women, we speak of "love", "duty", "right", "wrong", "pity", "hope", and other irrational and emotional conceptions, which have no existence, and the fiction of which has no object except to control feminine exuberances; but among ourselves, and in our books, we have an entirely different vocabulary and I may almost say, idiom. "Love" then becomes "the anticipation of benefits"; "duty" becomes "necessity" or "fitness"; and other words are correspondingly transmuted. Moreover, among Women, we use language implying the utmost deference for their

"The book is divided into two parts. The first attempts a complete diagnosis of the totality of modern capitalist civilization, moving through what the Invisible Committee identify as the 'seven circles' of alienation: 'self, social relations, work, the economy, urbanity, the environment, and to close civilization'. The latter part of the book begins to offer a prescription for revolutionary struggle based on the formation of communes, or affinity group-style units, in an underground network that will build its forces outside of mainstream politics, and attack in moments of crisis—political, social, environmental—to push towards anti-capitalist revolution. The insurrection envisioned by the Invisible Committee will revolve around 'the local appropriation of power by the people, of the physical blocking of the economy and of the annihilation of police forces'." [1]

volve

Sex; and they fully believe that the Chief Circle Himself is not more devoutly adored by us than they are: but behind their backs they are both regarded and spoken of—by all except the very young—as being little better than "mindless organisms".

Our Theology also in the Women's chambers is entirely different from our Theology elsewhere.

Now my humble fear is that this double training, in language as well as in thought, imposes somewhat too heavy a burden upon the young, especially when, at the age of three years old, they are taken from the maternal care and taught to unlearn the old language—except for the purpose of repeating it in the presence of their Mothers and Nurses—and to learn the vocabulary and idiom of science. Already methinks I discern a weakness in the grasp of mathematical truth at the present time as compared with the more robust intellect of our ancestors three hundred years ago. I say nothing of the possible danger if a Woman should ever surreptitiously learn to read and convey to her Sex the result of her perusal of a single popular volume; nor of the possibility that the indiscretion or disobedience of some infant Male might reveal to a Mother the secrets of the logical dialect. On the simple ground of the enfeebling of the Male intellect, I rest this humble appeal to the highest Authorities to reconsider the regulations of Female education.

ur

config

tion

PART II
OTHER WORLDS

116

PART II
OTHER WORLDS

FLATLAND, SEE POLARI.

"O brave new worlds, that have such people in them!"

"Polari (or alternatively Parlare, Parlary, Palare, Palarie, Palari; from Italian parlare, 'to talk') is a form of cant slang used in Britain by actors, circus and fairground showmen, merchant navy sailors, criminals, prostitutes, and the gay subculture. There is some debate about its origins, but it can be traced back to at least the nineteenth century and possibly the sixteenth century. There is a longstanding connection with Punch and Judy street puppet performers who traditionally used Polari to converse." [1]

How I had a Vision of Lineland

118

Parallel, similar, contrary and oblique

It was the last day but one of the 1999th year of our era, and the first day of the Long Vacation. Having amused myself till a late hour with my favourite recreation of Geometry, I had retired to rest with an unsolved problem in my mind. In the night I had a dream.

I saw before me a vast multitude of small Straight Lines (which I naturally assumed to be Women) interspersed with other Beings still smaller and of the nature of lustrous points—all moving to and fro in one and the same Straight Line, and, as nearly as I could judge, with the same velocity.

A noise of confused, multitudinous chirping or twittering issued from them at intervals as long as they were moving; but sometimes they ceased from motion, and then all was silence.

Approaching one of the largest of what I thought to be Women, I accosted her, but received no answer. A second and a third appeal on my part were equally ineffectual. Losing patience at what appeared to me intolerable rudeness, I brought my mouth into a position full in front of her mouth so as to intercept her motion, and loudly repeated my question, "Woman, what signifies this concourse, and this strange and confused chirping, and this monotonous motion to and fro in one and the same Straight Line?"

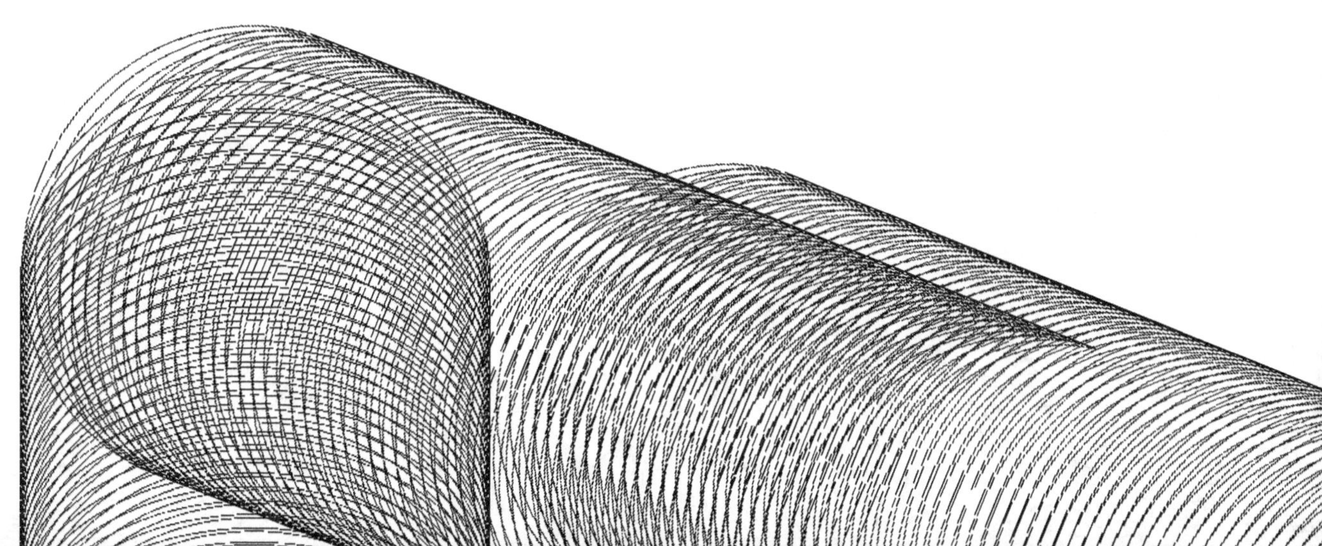

My View of Lineland

My-
self

Women A Boy The KING Men Men A Boy Women

The KING'S Eyes
much larger than the reality
shewing that HIS MAJESTY
could see nothing but a point.

"The writing system (possibly a false writing system) appears modeled on ordinary Western-style writing systems (left-to-right writing in rows; an alphabet with uppercase and lowercase letters, some of which double as numerals). Some letters appear only at the beginning or at the end of words, a feature shared with Semitic writing systems. The curvilinear letters of the alphabet are rope- or thread-like, displaying loops and even knots, and are somewhat reminiscent of Sinhala alphabets.

The language of the book has defied complete analysis by linguists for decades. The number system used for numbering the

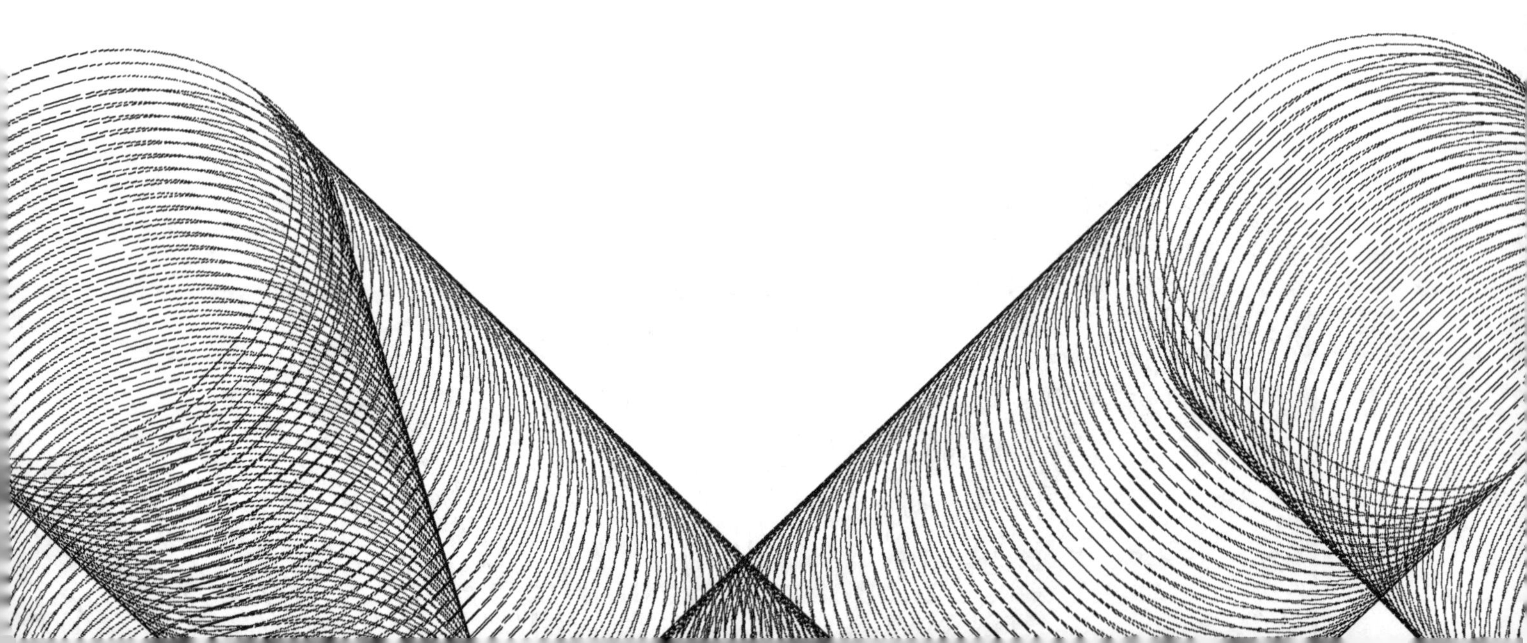

pages, however, has been cracked (apparently independently) by Allan C. Wechsler and Bulgarian linguist Ivan Derzhanski, among others. It is a variation of base 21." [1]

"I am no Woman," replied the small Line. "I am the Monarch of the world. But thou, whence intrudest thou into my realm of Lineland?" Receiving this abrupt reply, I begged pardon if I had in any way startled or molested his Royal Highness; and describing myself as a stranger I besought the King to give me some account of his dominions. But I had the greatest possible difficulty in obtaining any information on points that really interested me; for the Monarch could not refrain from constantly assuming that whatever was familiar to him must also be known to me and that I was simulating ignorance in jest. However, by persevering questions I elicited the following facts:

It seemed that this poor ignorant Monarch—as he called himself—was persuaded that the Straight Line which he called his Kingdom, and in which he passed his existence, constituted the whole of the world, and indeed the whole of Space. Not being able either to move or to see, save in his Straight Line, he had no conception of anything out of it. Though he had heard my voice when I first addressed him, the sounds had come to him in a manner so contrary to his experience that he had made no answer, "seeing no man", as he expressed it, "and hearing a voice as it were from my own intestines." Until the moment when I placed my mouth in his World, he had neither seen me, nor heard anything

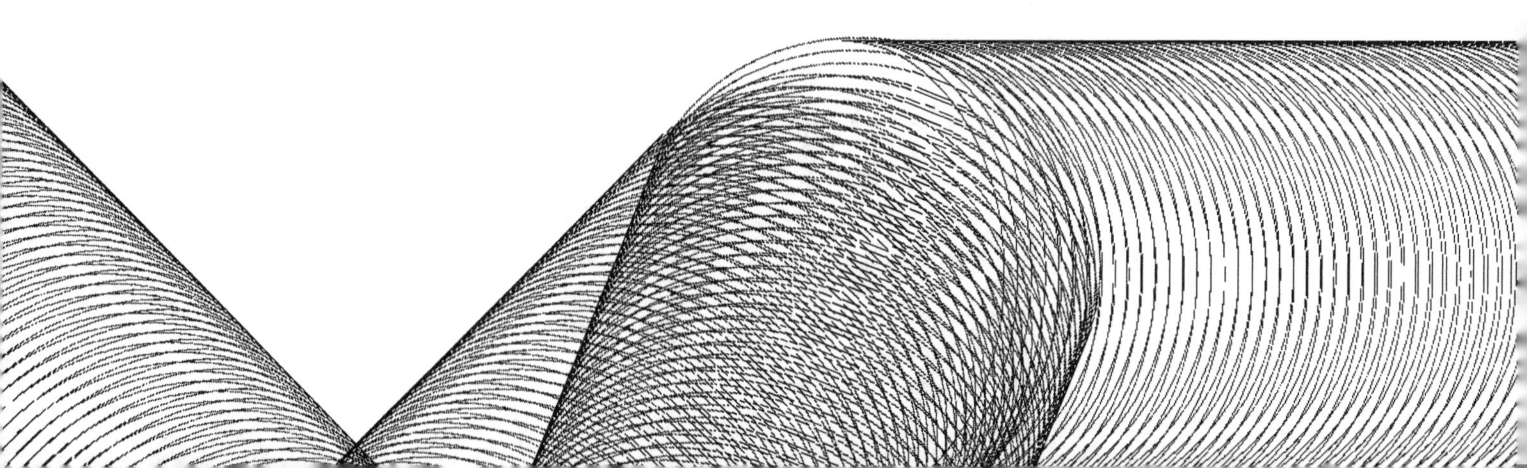

except confused sounds beating against—what I called his side, but what he called his INSIDE or STOMACH; nor had he even now the least conception of the region from which I had come. Outside his World, or Line, all was a blank to him; nay, not even a blank, for a blank implies Space; say, rather, all was non-existent.

His subjects—of whom the small Lines were men and the Points Women—were all alike confined in motion and eye-sight to that single Straight Line, which was their World. It need scarcely be added that the whole of their horizon was limited to a Point; nor could any one ever see anything but a Point. Man, woman, child, thing—each was a Point to the eye of a Linelander. Only by the sound of the voice could sex or age be distinguished. Moreover, as each individual occupied the whole of the narrow path, so to speak, which constituted his Universe, and no one could move to the right or left to make way for passers by, it followed that no Linelander could ever pass another. Once neighbours, always neighbours. Neighbourhood with them was like marriage with us. Neighbours remained neighbours till death did them part.

Such a life, with all vision limited to a Point, and all motion to a Straight Line, seemed to me inexpressibly dreary; and I was surprised to note the vivacity and cheerfulness

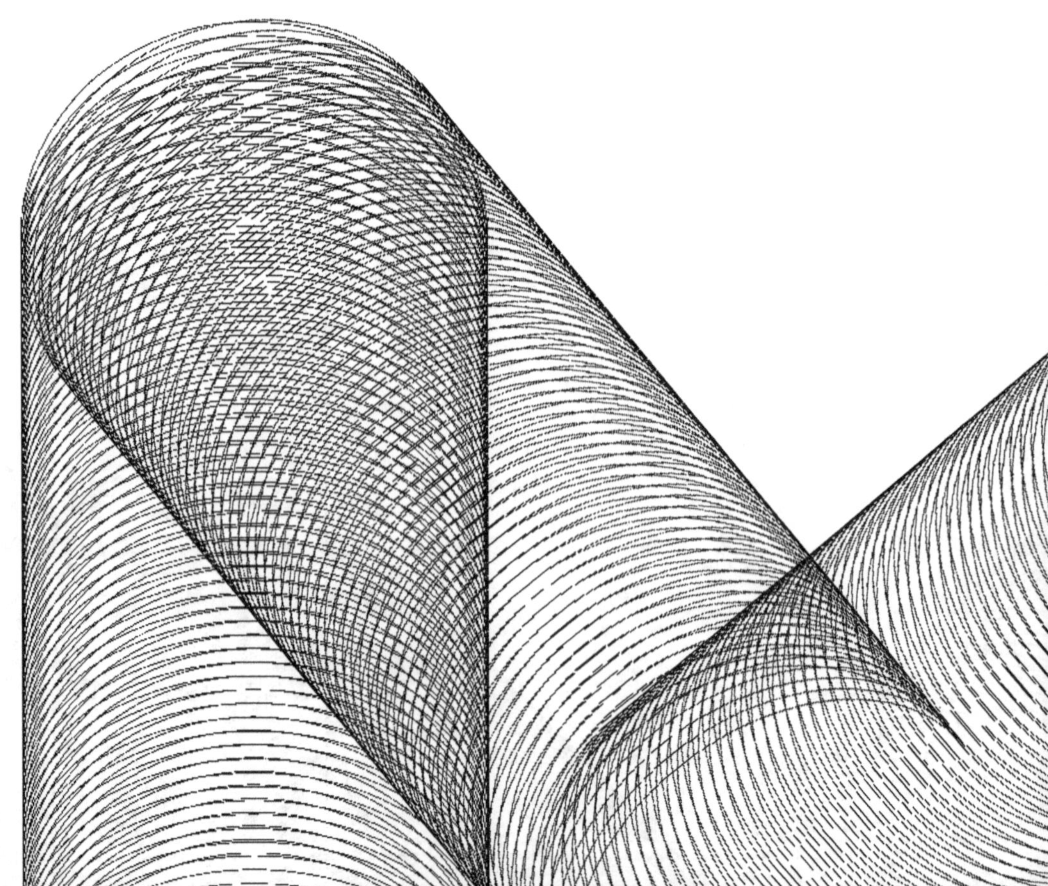

FLATLAND, SEE PRISON ESCAPE.

"Numerous methods have been used to escape prison over time. Many escapes have been successfully conducted by inmates who have invented their own methods. Weaknesses that are found as prisoners escape are often corrected at numerous prisons around the world to prevent future escapes in a similar manner. This leads inmates to finding new ways out.

Since prisoners usually have a lot of time in which they are doing nothing, this gives them plenty of time to think, allowing them to devise plans and figure out ways to escape." [1]

of the King. Wondering whether it was possible, amid circumstances so unfavourable to domestic relations, to enjoy the pleasures of conjugal union, I hesitated for some time to question his Royal Highness on so delicate a subject; but at last I plunged into it by abruptly inquiring as to the health of his family. "My wives and children," he replied, "are well and happy."

Staggered at this answer—for in the immediate proximity of the Monarch (as I had noted in my dream before I entered Lineland) there were none but Men—I ventured to reply, "Pardon me, but I cannot imagine how your Royal Highness can at any time either see or approach their Majesties, when there are at least half a dozen intervening individuals, whom you can neither see through, nor pass by? Is it possible that in Lineland proximity is not necessary for marriage and for the generation of children?"

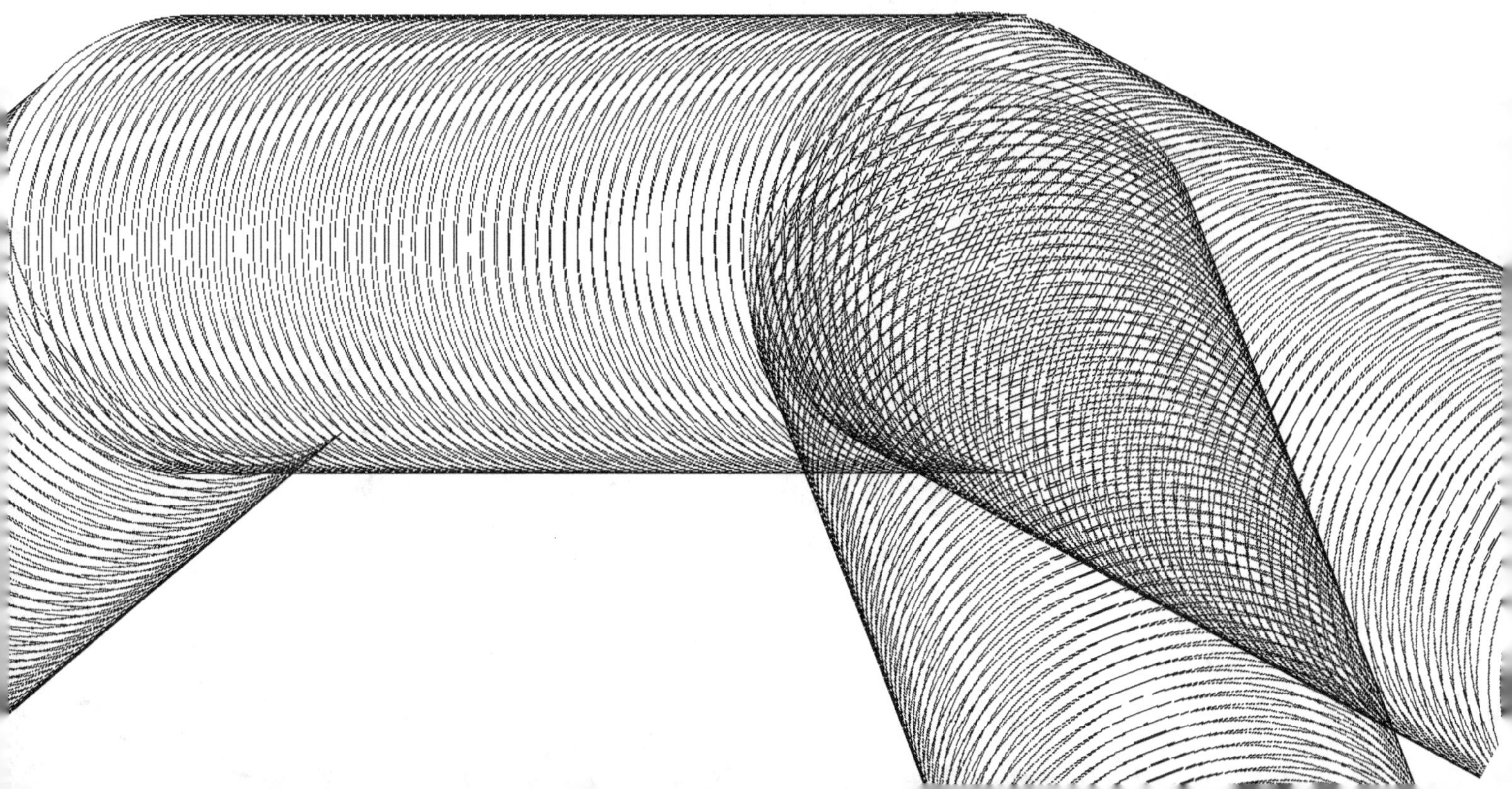

"How can you ask so absurd a question?" replied the Monarch. "If it were indeed as you suggest, the Universe would soon be depopulated. No, no; neighbourhood is needless for the union of hearts; and the birth of children is too important a matter to have been allowed to depend upon such an accident as proximity. You cannot be ignorant of this. Yet since you are pleased to affect ignorance, I will instruct you as if you were the veriest baby in Lineland. Know, then, that marriages are consummated by means of the faculty of sound and the sense of hearing.

"You are of course aware that every Man has two mouths or voices—as well as two eyes—a bass at one and a tenor at the other of his extremities. I should not mention this, but that I have been unable to distinguish your tenor in the course of our conversation." I replied that I had but one voice, and that I had not been aware that his Royal Highness had two. "That confirms my impression," said the King, "that you are not a Man, but a feminine Monstrosity with a bass voice, and an utterly uneducated ear. But to continue.

"Nature having herself ordained that every Man should wed two wives—" "Why two?" asked I. "You carry your affected simplicity too far", he cried. "How can there be a completely harmonious union without the combination of the Four in One, viz. the Bass and Tenor of the Man and the Soprano and Contralto of the two Women?" "But supposing," said I, "that a man should prefer one wife or three?" "It is impossible," he said; "it is as inconceivable as that two and one should make five, or that the human eye should see a Straight Line." I would have interrupted him; but he proceeded as follows:

"Once in the middle of each week a Law of Nature

"The theatre consists of a foyer, sound labyrinth and main performance space. It is a building within a building, conceived directly for this art form, and built in part with a grant from the National Endowment For The Arts. Listeners sit in concentric circles and are enveloped by speakers in sloping walls, floating floor and a suspended ceiling. Compositions are performed live at each program by a tape performer who directs the sounds through a custom designed console to any combination of the 169 speakers. Sounds are 'sculpted' through their movement, direction, speed and intensity on multiple planes in space. Live performance of

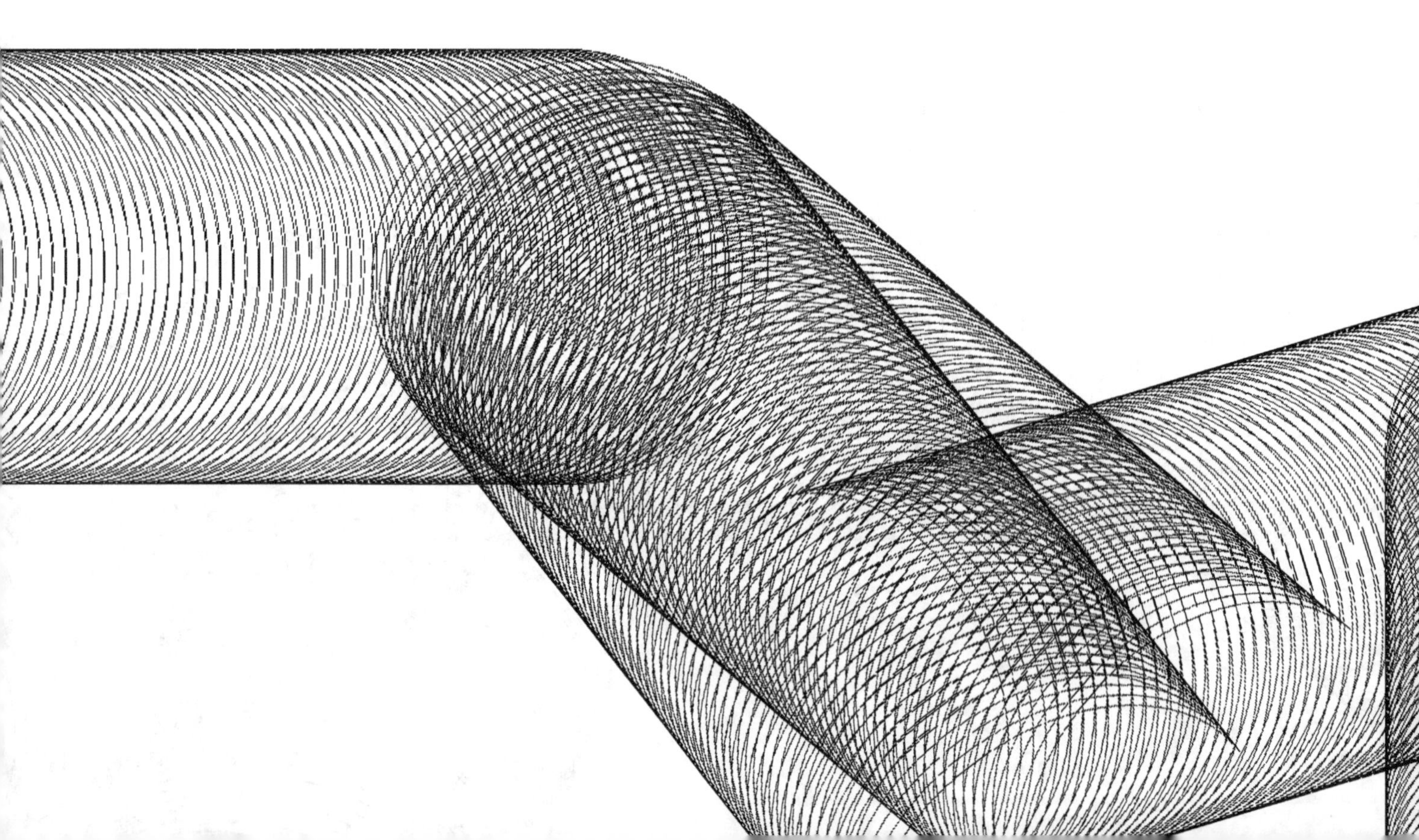

taped works gives a human, interactive element to AUDIUM's spatial electronic orchestra." [21]

compels us to move to and fro with a rhythmic motion of more than usual violence, which continues for the time you would take to count a hundred and one. In the midst of this choral dance, at the fifty-first pulsation, the inhabitants of the Universe pause in full career, and each individual sends forth his richest, fullest, sweetest strain. It is in this decisive moment that all our marriages are made. So exquisite is the adaptation of Bass to Treble, of Tenor to Contralto, that oftentimes the Loved Ones, though twenty thousand leagues away, recognize at once the responsive note of their destined Lover; and, penetrating the paltry obstacles of distance, Love unites the three. The marriage in that instant consummated results in a threefold Male and Female offspring which takes its place in Lineland."

"What! Always threefold?" said I. "Must one wife then always have twins?"

"Bass-voiced Monstrosity! yes," replied the King. "How else could the balance of the Sexes be maintained, if two girls were not born for every boy? Would you ignore the very Alphabet of Nature?" He ceased, speechless for fury; and some time elapsed before I could induce him to resume his narrative.

"You will not, of course, suppose that every bachelor

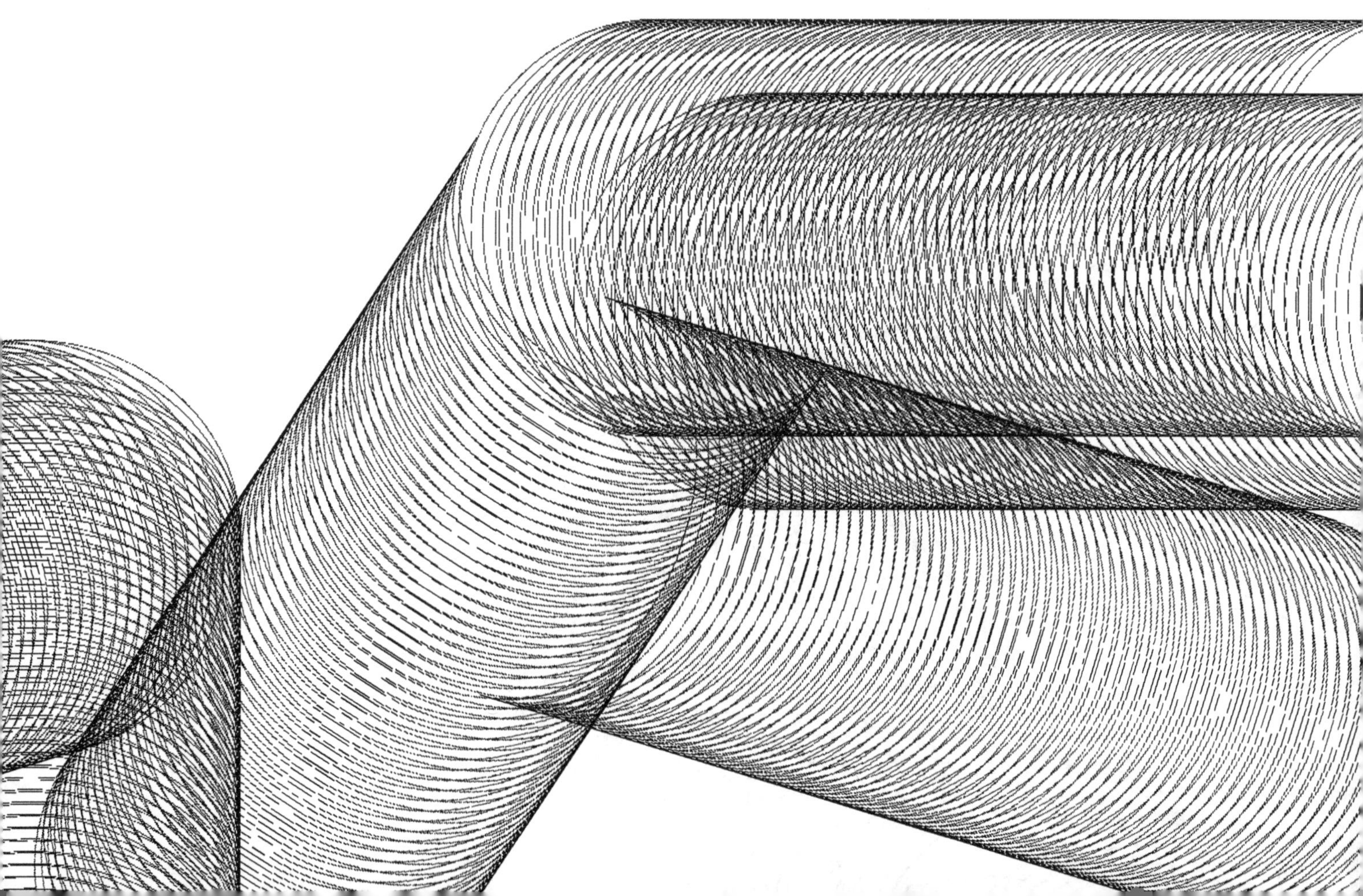

among us finds his mates at the first wooing in this universal Marriage Chorus. On the contrary, the process is by most of us many times repeated. Few are the hearts whose happy lot it is at once to recognize in each other's voices the partner intended for them by Providence, and to fly into a reciprocal and perfectly harmonious embrace. With most of us the courtship is of long duration. The Wooer's voices may perhaps accord with one of the future wives, but not with both; or not, at first, with either; or the Soprano and Contralto may not quite harmonize. In such cases Nature has provided that every weekly Chorus shall bring the three Lovers into closer harmony. Each trial of voice, each fresh discovery of discord, almost imperceptibly induces the less perfect to modify his or her vocal utterance so as to approximate to the more perfect. And after many trials and many approximations, the result is at last achieved. There comes a day at last, when, while the wonted Marriage Chorus goes forth from universal Lineland, the three far-off Lovers suddenly find themselves in exact harmony, and, before they are awake, the wedded Triplet is rapt vocally into a duplicate embrace; and Nature rejoices over one more marriage and over three more births."

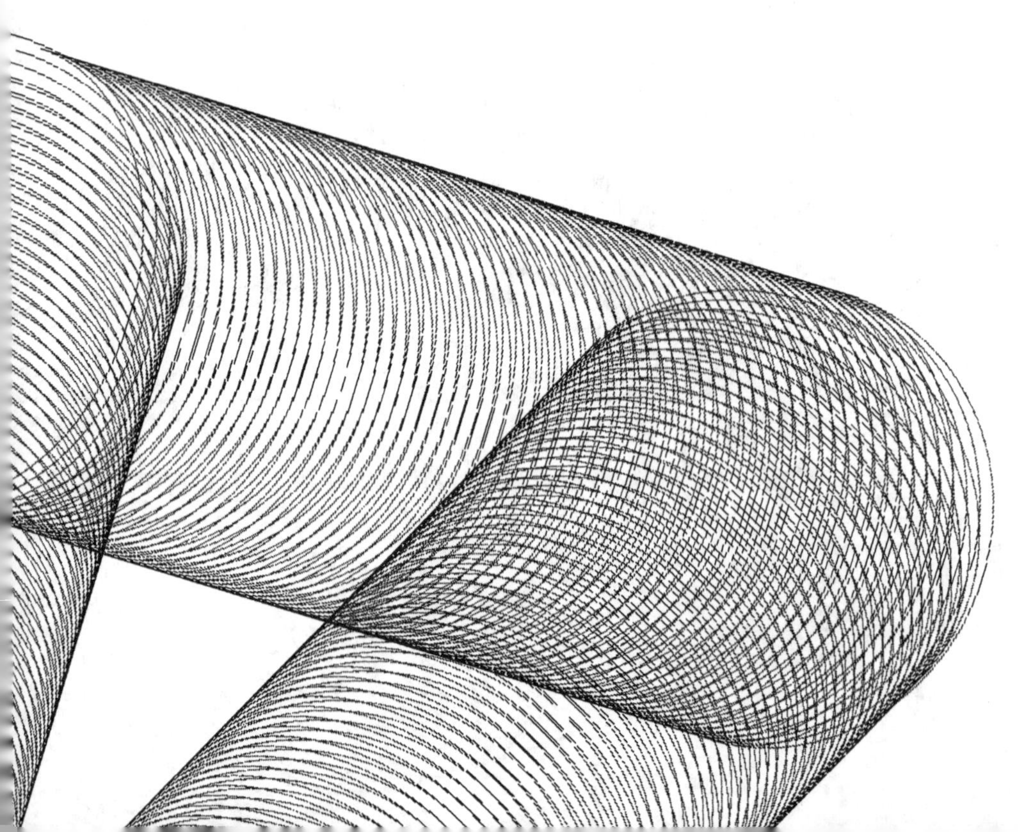

FLATLAND, SEE STICK CHART.

"Stick charts were made and used by the Marshallese to navigate the Pacific Ocean by canoe off the coast of the Marshall Islands. The charts represented major ocean swell patterns and the ways the islands disrupted those patterns, typically determined by sensing disruptions in ocean swells by islands during sea navigation. Stick charts were typically made from the midribs of coconut fronds tied together to form an open framework. Island locations were represented by shells tied to the framework, or by the lashed junction of two or more sticks. The threads represented prevailing ocean surface wave-crests and directions they took as they approached islands and met other similar wave-crests formed by the ebb and flow of breakers." [1]

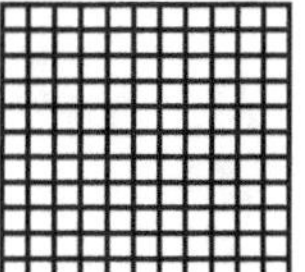

How I vainly
tried to explain the
nature of Flatland

**Fragments of a
slaughtered
victory**

Thinking that it was time to bring down the Monarch from his raptures to the level of common sense, I determined to endeavour to open up to him some glimpses of the truth, that is to say of the nature of things in Flatland. So I began thus: "How does your Royal Highness distinguish the shapes and positions of his subjects? I for my part noticed by the sense of sight, before I entered your Kingdom, that some of your people are Lines and others Points, and that some of the Lines are larger—" "You speak of an impossibility," interrupted the King; "you must have seen a vision; for to detect the difference between a Line and a Point by the sense of sight is, as every one knows, in the nature of things, impossible; but it can be detected by the sense of hearing, and by the same means my shape can be exactly ascertained. Behold me—I am a Line, the longest in Lineland, over six inches of Space—" "Of Length", I ventured to suggest. "Fool," said he, "Space is Length. Interrupt me again, and I have done."

I apologized; but he continued scornfully, "Since you are impervious to argument, you shall hear with your ears how by means of my two voices I reveal my shape to my Wives, who are at this moment six thousand miles seventy yards two feet eight inches away, the one to the North, the other to the South. Listen, I call to them."

He chirruped, and then complacently continued: "My

SCHLE-MOZZ-LE

* A riot, quarrel, or noise of any kind

wives at this moment receiving the sound of one of my voices, closely followed by the other, and perceiving that the latter reaches them after an interval in which sound can traverse 6.457 inches, infer that one of my mouths is 6.457 inches further from them than the other, and accordingly know my shape to be 6.457 inches. But you will of course understand that my wives do not make this calculation every time they hear my two voices. They made it, once for all, before we were married. But they COULD make it at any time. And in the same way I can estimate the shape of any of my Male subjects by the sense of sound."

"But how," said I, "if a Man feigns a Woman's voice with one of his two voices, or so disguises his Southern voice that it cannot be recognized as the echo of the Northern? May not such deceptions cause great inconvenience? And have you no means of checking frauds of this kind by commanding your neighbouring subjects to feel one another?" This of course was a very stupid question, for feeling could not have answered the purpose; but I asked with the view of irritating the Monarch, and I succeeded perfectly.

"What!" cried he in horror, "explain your meaning." "Feel, touch, come into contact," I replied. "If you mean by FEELING," said the King, "approaching so close as to leave no space between two individuals, know, Stranger, that this

'According to the principle of his work, LeWitt's wall drawings are usually executed by people other than the artist himself. Even after his death, people are still making these drawings. He would therefore eventually use teams of assistants to create such works. Writing about making wall drawings, LeWitt himself observed in 1971 that 'each person draws a line differently and each person understands words differently'." [1]

* Commit a crime punishable by death

WORK-
CAPI-
TOL

offence is punishable in my dominions by death. And the reason is obvious. The frail form of a Woman, being liable to be shattered by such an approximation, must be preserved by the State; but since Women cannot be distinguished by the sense of sight from Men, the Law ordains universally that neither Man nor Woman shall be approached so closely as to destroy the interval between the approximator and the approximated.

"And indeed what possible purpose would be served by this illegal and unnatural excess of approximation which you call TOUCHING, when all the ends of so brutal and coarse a process are attained at once more easily and more exactly by the sense of hearing? As to your suggested danger of deception, it is non-existent: for the Voice, being the essence of one's Being, cannot be thus changed at will. But come, suppose that I had the power of passing through solid things, so that I could penetrate my subjects, one after another, even to the number of a billion, verifying the size and distance of each by the sense of FEELING: how much time and energy would be wasted in this clumsy and inaccurate method! Whereas now, in one moment of audition, I take as it were the census and statistics, local, corporeal, mental and spiritual, of every living being in Lineland. Hark, only hark!"

So saying he paused and listened, as if in an ecstasy, to a sound which seemed to me no better than a tiny chirping

* Watch the Woman

from an innumerable multitude of lilliputian grasshoppers.

"Truly," replied I, "your sense of hearing serves you in good stead, and fills up many of your deficiencies. But permit me to point out that your life in Lineland must be deplorably dull. To see nothing but a Point! Not even to be able to contemplate a Straight Line! Nay, not even to know what a Straight Line is! To see, yet be cut off from those Linear prospects which are vouchsafed to us in Flatland! Better surely to have no sense of sight at all than to see so little! I grant you I have not your discriminative faculty of hearing; for the concert of all Lineland which gives you such intense pleasure, is to me no better than a multitudinous twittering or chirping. But at least I can discern, by sight, a Line from a Point. And let me prove it. Just before I came into your kingdom, I saw you dancing from left to right, and then from right to left, with Seven Men and a Woman in your immediate proximity on the left, and eight Men and two Women on your right. Is not this correct?"

"It is correct," said the King, "so far as the numbers and sexes are concerned, though I know not what you mean by 'right' and 'left'. But I deny that you saw these things. For how could you see the Line, that is to say the inside, of any Man? But you must have heard these things, and then dreamed that you saw them. And let me ask what you mean by those words 'left' and 'right'. I suppose it is your way of saying Northward

* To win

AE EE

TAKE
THE
EGG

FLATLAND, SEE 1999 A.D.

1999 A.D., a film produced by the Philco-Ford Corporation in 1967, seems to have predicted online shopping and bill paying, plasma screens, email and home laser printers. [22]

and Southward."

"Not so," replied I; "besides your motion of Northward and Southward, there is another motion which I call from right to left."

King—
Exhibit to me, if you please, this motion from left to right.

I—
Nay, that I cannot do, unless you could step out of your Line altogether.

King—
Out of my Line? Do you mean out of the world? Out of Space?

I—
Well, yes. Out of YOUR World. Out of YOUR Space. For your Space is not the true Space. True Space is a Plane; but your Space is only a Line.

King—
If you cannot indicate this motion from left to right by yourself moving in it, then I beg you to describe it to me in words.

I—
If you cannot tell your right side from your left, I fear

* Shady, doubtful

IA AI

SKILA-
MA-
LINK

FLATLAND, SEE HOUSE OF THE FUTURE.

that no words of mine can make my meaning clear to you. But surely you cannot be ignorant of so simple a distinction.

King—

I do not in the least understand you.

I—

Alas! How shall I make it clear? When you move straight on, does it not sometimes occur to you that you COULD move in some other way, turning your eye round so as to look in the direction towards which your side is now fronting? In other words, instead of always moving in the direction of one of your extremities, do you never feel a desire to move in the direction, so to speak, of your side?

King—

Never. And what do you mean? How can a man's inside "front" in any direction? Or how can a man move in the direction of his inside?

I—

Well then, since words cannot explain the matter, I will try deeds, and will move gradually out of Lineland in the direction which I desire to indicate to you.

At the word I began to move my body out of Lineland. As long

"The attraction offered a tour of a home of the future, set in the year 1986, and featured household appliances such as microwave ovens, which eventually became commonplace. The house saw over 435,000 visitors within the first six weeks of opening, and ultimately saw over 20 million visitors before being closed." [1]

To fight

AE E A

as any part of me remained in his dominion and in his view, the King kept exclaiming, "I see you, I see you still; you are not moving." But when I had at last moved myself out of his Line, he cried in his shrillest voice, "She is vanished; she is dead." "I am not dead," replied I; "I am simply out of Lineland, that is to say, out of the Straight Line which you call Space, and in the true Space, where I can see things as they are. And at this moment I can see your Line, or side—or inside as you are pleased to call it; and I can see also the Men and Women on the North and South of you, whom I will now enumerate, describing their order, their size, and the interval between each."

When I had done this at great length, I cried triumphantly, "Does that at last convince you?" And, with that, I once more

WHOOP
ER-
UPS

OOE U

* Inferior, noisy singers

entered Lineland, taking up the same position as before.

But the Monarch replied, "If you were a Man of sense—though, as you appear to have only one voice I have little doubt you are not a Man but a Woman—but, if you had a particle of sense, you would listen to reason. You ask me to believe that there is another Line besides that which my senses indicate, and another motion besides that of which I am daily conscious. I, in return, ask you to describe in words or indicate by motion that other Line of which you speak. Instead of moving, you merely exercise some magic art of vanishing and returning to sight; and instead of any lucid description of your new World, you simply tell me the numbers and sizes of some forty of my retinue, facts known to any child in my capital. Can anything be more irrational or audacious? Acknowledge your folly or depart from my dominions."

Furious at his perversity, and especially indignant that he professed to be ignorant of my sex, I retorted in no measured terms, "Besotted Being! You think yourself the perfection of existence, while you are in reality the most imperfect and imbecile. You profess to see, whereas you can see nothing but a Point! You plume yourself on inferring the existence of a Straight Line; but I CAN SEE Straight Lines, and infer the existence of Angles, Triangles, Squares, Pentagons, Hexagons, and even Circles. Why waste more words? Suffice it that I am

* To trash thoroughly

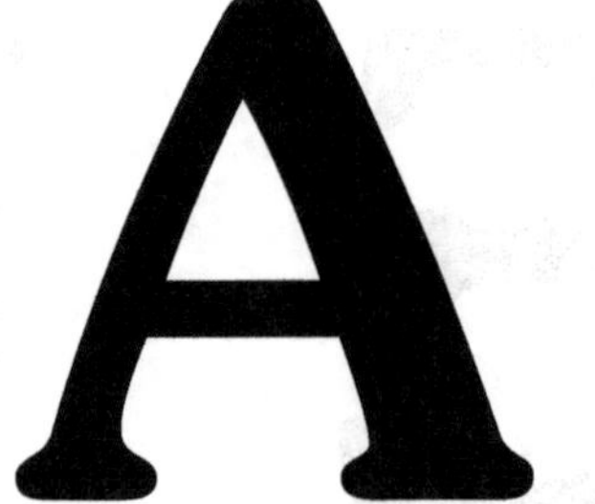

"At the beginning of the century, people still believed that by avoiding dark and damp micro-climates and by eliminating dust corners—hence by excluding the 'miasmas'—tuberculosis pathogens could effectively be fought. The floor covering linoleum, promising cleanliness like no other, in this connection gained almost medical significance.

The 'Zauberberg' 'Magic Mountain', whose kind did not only exist in Davos, was the model of an ideal future society. Only the pioneering employment of hygienic interior design and modern medicine—yes, even of a reformed culture as a whole —in a sanatorium with its micro-community really made the recuperation possible of bodies fallen ill in, and because of, the dark 19th century." [23]

the completion of your incomplete self. You are a Line, but I am a Line of Lines, called in my country a Square: and even I, infinitely superior though I am to you, am of little account among the great nobles of Flatland, whence I have come to visit you, in the hope of enlightening your ignorance."

Hearing these words the King advanced towards me with a menacing cry as if to pierce me through the diagonal; and in that same moment there arose from myriads of his subjects a multitudinous war-cry, increasing in vehemence till at last methought it rivalled the roar of an army of a hundred thousand Isosceles, and the artillery of a thousand Pentagons. Spell-bound and motionless, I could neither speak nor move to avert the impending destruction; and still the noise grew louder, and the King came closer, when I awoke to find the breakfast-bell recalling me to the realities of Flatland.

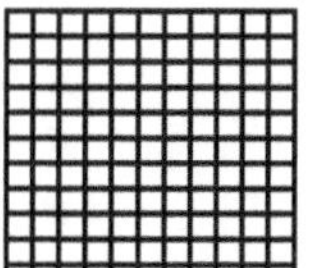

Concerning a Stranger from Spaceland

We make sense together

From dreams I proceed to facts.

It was the last day of the 1999th year of our era. The pattering of the rain had long ago announced nightfall; and I was sitting in the company of my wife, musing on the events of the past and the prospects of the coming year, the coming century, the coming Millennium.

[Note: When I say "sitting", of course I do not mean any change of attitude such as you in Spaceland signify by that word; for as we have no feet, we can no more "sit" nor "stand" (in your sense of the word) than one of your soles or flounders.

Nevertheless, we perfectly well recognize the different mental states of volition implied in "lying", "sitting", and "standing", which are to some extent indicated to a beholder by a slight increase of lustre corresponding to the increase of volition.

But on this, and a thousand other kindred subjects, time forbids me to dwell.]

My four Sons and two orphan Grandchildren had retired to their several apartments; and my wife alone remained with me to see the old Millennium out and the new one in.

I was rapt in thought, pondering in my mind some words that had casually issued from the mouth of my youngest Grandson, a most promising young Hexagon of unusual brilliancy and perfect angularity. His uncles and I had been giving

him his usual practical lesson in Sight Recognition, turning ourselves upon our centres, now rapidly, now more slowly, and questioning him as to our positions; and his answers had been so satisfactory that I had been induced to reward him by giving him a few hints on Arithmetic, as applied to Geometry.

Taking nine Squares, each an inch every way, I had put them together so as to make one large Square, with a side of three inches, and I had hence proved to my little Grandson that—though it was impossible for us to SEE the inside of the Square—yet we might ascertain the number of square inches in a Square by simply squaring the number of inches in the side: "and thus," said I, "we know that 3^2, or 9, represents the number of square inches in a Square whose side is 3 inches long."

The little Hexagon meditated on this a while and then said to me; "But you have been teaching me to raise numbers to the third power: I suppose 3^3 must mean something in Geometry; what does it mean?" "Nothing at all," replied I, "not at least in Geometry; for Geometry has only Two Dimensions." And then I began to shew the boy how a Point by moving through a length of three inches makes a Line of three inches, which may be represented by 3; and how a Line of three inches, moving parallel to itself through a length of three inches, makes a Square of three inches every way, which may be represented by 3^2.

Upon this, my Grandson, again returning to his former

"At the back of Lade Pit are the three Listening Devices built in the 1920s and 30s as part of a national early warning system against enemy aircraft. This is one of only two sites in the world where you can see all three designs." [24]

suggestion, took me up rather suddenly and exclaimed, "Well, then, if a Point by moving three inches, makes a Line of three inches represented by 3; and if a straight Line of three inches, moving parallel to itself, makes a Square of three inches every way, represented by 3^2; it must be that a Square of three inches every way, moving somehow parallel to itself (but I don't see how) must make Something else (but I don't see what) of three inches every way—and this must be represented by 3^3."

"Go to bed," said I, a little ruffled by this interruption: "if you would talk less nonsense, you would remember more sense."

So my Grandson had disappeared in disgrace; and there I sat by my Wife's side, endeavouring to form a retrospect of the year 1999 and of the possibilities of the year 2000, but not quite able to shake off the thoughts suggested by the prattle of my bright little Hexagon. Only a few sands now remained in the half-hour glass. Rousing myself from my reverie I turned the glass Northward for the last time in the old Millennium; and in the act, I exclaimed aloud, "The boy is a fool."

Straightway I became conscious of a Presence in the room, and a chilling breath thrilled through my very being. "He is no such thing," cried my Wife, "and you are breaking the Commandments in thus dishonouring your own Grandson." But I took no notice of her. Looking round in every direction I could see nothing; yet still I FELT a Presence, and shivered as

the cold whisper came again. I started up. "What is the matter?" said my Wife, "there is no draught; what are you looking for? There is nothing." There was nothing; and I resumed my seat, again exclaiming, "The boy is a fool, I say; 3^3 can have no meaning in Geometry." At once there came a distinctly audible reply, "The boy is not a fool; and 3^3 has an obvious Geometrical meaning."

My Wife as well as myself heard the words, although she did not understand their meaning, and both of us sprang forward in the direction of the sound. What was our horror when we saw before us a Figure! At the first glance it appeared to be a Woman, seen sideways; but a moment's observation shewed me that the extremities passed into dimness too rapidly to represent one of the Female Sex; and I should have thought it a Circle, only that it seemed to change its size in a manner impossible for a Circle or for any regular Figure of which I had had experience.

But my Wife had not my experience, nor the coolness necessary to note these characteristics. With the usual hastiness and unreasoning jealousy of her Sex, she flew at once to the conclusion that a Woman had entered the house through some small aperture. "How comes this person here?" she exclaimed, "you promised me, my dear, that there should be no ventilators in our new house." "Nor are there any," said I; "but what makes you think that the stranger is a Woman? I see by my power of

FLATLAND, SEE POWERS OF TEN.

"The Powers of Ten films are two short American documentary films written and directed by Charles and Ray Eames. Both works depict the relative scale of the Universe according to an order of magnitude (or logarithmic scale) based on a factor of ten, first expanding out from the Earth until the entire universe is surveyed, then reducing inward until a single atom and its quarks are observed." [1]

Sight Recognition—" "Oh, I have no patience with your Sight Recognition," replied she, "'Feeling is believing' and 'A Straight Line to the touch is worth a Circle to the sight'"—two Proverbs, very common with the Frailer Sex in Flatland.

"Well," said I, for I was afraid of irritating her, "if it must be so, demand an introduction." Assuming her most gracious manner, my Wife advanced towards the Stranger, "Permit me, Madam, to feel and be felt by—" then, suddenly recoiling, "Oh! it is not a Woman, and there are no angles either, not a trace of one. Can it be that I have so misbehaved to a perfect Circle?"

"I am indeed, in a certain sense a Circle," replied the Voice, "and a more perfect Circle than any in Flatland; but to speak more accurately, I am many Circles in one." Then he added more mildly, "I have a message, dear Madam, to your husband, which I must not deliver in your presence; and, if you would suffer us to retire for a few minutes—" But my Wife would not listen to the proposal that our august Visitor should so incommode himself, and assuring the Circle that the hour of her own retirement had long passed, with many reiterated apologies for her recent indiscretion, she at last retreated to her apartment.

I glanced at the half-hour glass. The last sands had fallen. The third Millennium had begun.

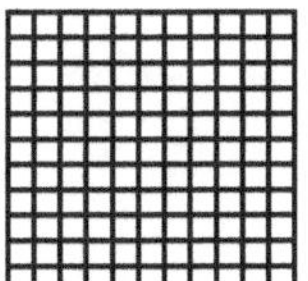

How the Stranger vainly endeavoured to reveal to me in words the mysteries of Spaceland

144

On God and blind faith

As soon as the sound of the Peace-cry of my departing Wife had died away, I began to approach the Stranger with the intention of taking a nearer view and of bidding him be seated: but his appearance struck me dumb and motionless with astonishment. Without the slightest symptoms of angularity he nevertheless varied every instant with gradations of size and brightness scarcely possible for any Figure within the scope of my experience. The thought flashed across me that I might have before me a burglar or cut-throat, some monstrous Irregular Isosceles, who, by feigning the voice of a Circle, had obtained admission somehow into the house, and was now preparing to stab me with his acute angle.

In a sitting-room, the absence of Fog (and the season happened to be remarkably dry), made it difficult for me to trust to Sight Recognition, especially at the short distance at which I was standing. Desperate with fear, I rushed forward with an unceremonious, "You must permit me, Sir—" and felt him. My Wife was right. There was not the trace of an angle, not the slightest roughness or inequality: never in my life had I met with a more perfect Circle. He remained motionless while I walked round him, beginning from his eye and returning to it again. Circular he was throughout, a perfectly satisfactory Circle; there could not be a doubt of it. Then followed a dialogue, which I will endeavour to set down as near as I can recollect it, omitting only some of my

Some time later God tested Abraham.

profuse apologies—for I was covered with shame and humiliation that I, a Square, should have been guilty of the impertinence of feeling a Circle. It was commenced by the Stranger with some impatience at the lengthiness of my introductory process.

"Many—but not all—of the digital designs are created by non-artists who are just trying to figure out the software ('Something I made while I was bored'), but some are very earnestly made ('best sculpture ever!') and all are lovely in their own way. Using their designs, I became the 'unsolicited' fabricator of their work. The final sculptures are cleanly made from simple materials such as cardboard, plastic, Coroplast (a stiff, corrugated plastic material), paper, and tape. They were displayed on handmade Coroplast shelves and pedestals. The names of the original designers was displayed on adjacent wall labels, but I did not solicit their permission to execute the work since the design was in essence considered shareware." [25]

Stranger—

Have you felt me enough by this time? Are you not introduced to me yet?

I—

Most illustrious Sir, excuse my awkwardness, which arises not from ignorance of the usages of polite society, but from a little surprise and nervousness, consequent on this somewhat unexpected visit. And I beseech you to reveal my indiscretion to no one, and especially not to my Wife. But before your Lordship enters into further communications, would he deign to satisfy the curiosity of one who would gladly know whence his Visitor came?

Stranger—

From Space, from Space, Sir: whence else?

I—

Pardon me, my Lord, but is not your Lordship already in Space, your Lordship and his humble servant, even at this moment?

Stranger—

Pooh! what do you know of Space? Define Space.

He said to him, "Abraham!"

"Here I am," he replied.

I—
Space, my Lord, is height and breadth indefinitely prolonged.

Stranger—
Exactly: you see you do not even know what Space is. You think it is of Two Dimensions only; but I have come to announce to you a Third—height, breadth, and length.

I—
Your Lordship is pleased to be merry. We also speak of length and height, or breadth and thickness, thus denoting Two Dimensions by four names.

Stranger—
But I mean not only three names, but Three Dimensions.

I—
Would your Lordship indicate or explain to me in what direction is the Third Dimension, unknown to me?

Stranger—
I came from it. It is up above and down below.

I—
My Lord means seemingly that it is Northward and Southward.

Stranger—
I mean nothing of the kind. I mean a direction in which you cannot look, because you have no eye in your side.

“Take your son, your only son, whom you love—Isaac—and go to the region of Moriah. Sacrifice him there as a burnt offering on a mountain I will show you.”

I—

Pardon me, my Lord, a moment's inspection will convince your Lordship that I have a perfect luminary at the juncture of two of my sides.

Stranger—

Yes: but in order to see into Space you ought to have an eye, not on your Perimeter, but on your side, that is, on what you would probably call your inside; but we in Spaceland should call it your side.

I—

An eye in my inside! An eye in my stomach! Your Lordship jests.

Stranger—

I am in no jesting humour. I tell you that I come from Space, or, since you will not understand what Space means, from the Land of Three Dimensions whence I but lately looked down upon your Plane which you call Space forsooth. From that position of advantage I discerned all that you speak of as SOLID (by which you mean "enclosed on four sides"), your houses, your churches, your very chests and safes, yes even your insides and stomachs, all lying open and exposed to my view.

I—

Such assertions are easily made, my Lord.

Isaac spoke up and said to his father Abraham, "Father?"

"Yes, my son?" Abraham replied.

"Color-blocked Bauhaus-style newspapers were printed and available free to gallery visitors. The layouts and formats were taken from three local Houston ethnic-based journals: El Dia (Spanish-Language), the Houston Forward Times (African-American), and the Manila Headline (Filipino-American), and produced during the final week of the 2008 U.S. Presidential Election—a pivotal political moment which chose the first African-American president. As a racially politicized arena in which an American population was interrogating the place of 'color' and ethnic politics, this work abstracted the content of each publication, creating a new visual fomat of reduced perceptual color for viewers to attempt to 'read'." [25]

Stranger—

But not easily proved, you mean. But I mean to prove mine.

When I descended here, I saw your four Sons, the Pentagons, each in his apartment, and your two Grandsons the Hexagons; I saw your youngest Hexagon remain a while with you and then retire to his room, leaving you and your Wife alone. I saw your Isosceles servants, three in number, in the kitchen at supper, and the little Page in the scullery. Then I came here, and how do you think I came?

I—

Through the roof, I suppose.

Stranger—

Not so. Your roof, as you know very well, has been recently repaired, and has no aperture by which even a Woman could penetrate. I tell you I come from Space. Are you not convinced by what I have told you of your children and household?

I—

Your Lordship must be aware that such facts touching the belongings of his humble servant might be easily ascertained by any one in the neighbourhood possessing your Lordship's ample means of obtaining information.

How the Stranger vainly endeavoured to reveal to me in words the mysteries of Spaceland

"The fire and wood are here," Isaac said, "but where is the lamb for the burnt offering?"

Abraham answered, "God himself will provide the lamb for the burnt offering, my son."

FLATLAND, SEE THOUGHTFORMS.

Stranger (*to himself*)—
What must I do? Stay; one more argument suggests itself to me. When you see a Straight Line—your wife, for example—how many Dimensions do you attribute to her?

I—
Your Lordship would treat me as if I were one of the vulgar who, being ignorant of Mathematics, suppose that a Woman is really a Straight Line, and only of One Dimension. No, no, my Lord; we Squares are better advised, and are as well aware as your Lordship that a Woman, though popularly called a Straight Line, is, really and scientifically, a very thin Parallelogram, possessing Two Dimensions, like the rest of us, viz., length and breadth (or thickness).

Stranger—
But the very fact that a Line is visible implies that it possesses yet another Dimension.

I—
My Lord, I have just acknowledged that a Woman is broad as well as long. We see her length, we infer her breadth; which, though very slight, is capable of measurement.

Stranger—
You do not understand me. I mean that when you see a Woman, you ought—besides inferring her breadth—to

"Thought-Forms, a strange, beguiling, frequently pretentious, utterly original book first published in 1901, emerged from this ferment of late-Victorian mysticism. It was written by Annie Besant and Charles Leadbeater, erstwhile members of the London Theosophical Society alongside Yeats, and it features a stunning sequence of images that illustrate the book's central argument: emotions, sounds, ideas and events manifest as visual auras." [26]

When they reached the place God had told him about, Abraham built an altar there and arranged the wood on it. He bound his son Isaac and laid him on the altar, on top of the wood.

see her length, and to SEE what we call her HEIGHT; although that last Dimension is infinitesimal in your country. If a Line were mere length without "height", it would cease to occupy Space and would become invisible. Surely you must recognize this?

I—

I must indeed confess that I do not in the least understand your Lordship. When we in Flatland see a Line, we see length and BRIGHTNESS. If the brightness disappears, the Line is extinguished, and, as you say, ceases to occupy Space. But am I to suppose that your Lordship gives to brightness the title of a Dimension, and that what we call "bright" you call "high"?

Stranger—

No, indeed. By "height" I mean a Dimension like your length: only, with you, "height" is not so easily perceptible, being extremely small.

I—

My Lord, your assertion is easily put to the test. You say I have a Third Dimension, which you call "height". Now, Dimension implies direction and measurement. Do but measure my "height", or merely indicate to me the direction in which my "height" extends, and I will become your convert. Otherwise, your Lordship's own understanding

Then he reached out his hand and took the knife to slay his son.

must hold me excused.

Stranger (to himself)—

I can do neither. How shall I convince him? Surely a plain statement of facts followed by ocular demonstration ought to suffice. —Now, Sir; listen to me.

You are living on a Plane. What you style Flatland is the vast level surface of what I may call a fluid, on, or in, the top of which you and your countrymen move about, without rising above it or falling below it.

I am not a plane Figure, but a Solid. You call me a Circle; but in reality I am not a Circle, but an infinite number of Circles, of size varying from a Point to a Circle of thirteen inches in diameter, one placed on the top of the other. When I cut through your plane as I am now doing, I make in your plane a section which you, very rightly, call a Circle. For even a Sphere—which is my proper name in my own country—if he manifest himself at all to an inhabitant of Flatland—must needs manifest himself as a Circle.

Do you not remember—for I, who see all things, discerned last night the phantasmal vision of Lineland written upon your brain—do you not remember, I say, how, when you entered the realm of Lineland, you were compelled to manifest yourself to the King, not as a

But the angel of the Lord called out to him from heaven, "Abraham! Abraham!"

"Here I am," he replied.

FLATLAND, SEE ABY WARBURG.

"If his library was already the most eccentric of collections—organized not alphabetically or according to subject but by 'elective affinities', the secret intimacies that Warburg himself intuited between its volumes—its oddest offshoot is surely the massive and fragmentary constellation of images that Warburg, in the last five years of his life, obsessively tended and reorganized: the Mnemosyne Atlas. It is the strangest of art-historical artefacts: the kaleidoscopic image of the scholar's enigmatic reordering of a lifetime's meditation on the image." [27]

Square, but as a Line, because that Linear Realm had not Dimensions enough to represent the whole of you, but only a slice or section of you? In precisely the same way, your country of Two Dimensions is not spacious enough to represent me, a being of Three, but can only exhibit a slice or section of me, which is what you call a Circle.

The diminished brightness of your eye indicates incredulity. But now prepare to receive proof positive of the truth of my assertions. You cannot indeed see more than one of my sections, or Circles, at a time; for you have no power to raise your eye out of the plane of Flatland; but you can at least see that, as I rise in Space, so my sections become smaller.

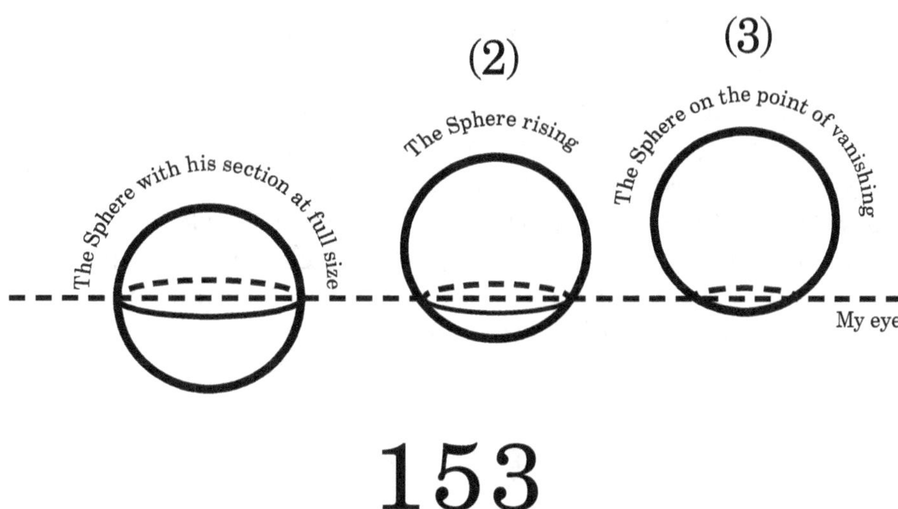

153

"Do not lay a hand on the boy," he said.

FLATLAND, SEE MEMEX.

See now, I will rise; and the effect upon your eye will be that my Circle will become smaller and smaller till it dwindles to a point and finally vanishes.

There was no "rising" that I could see; but he diminished and finally vanished. I winked once or twice to make sure that I was not dreaming. But it was no dream. For from the depths of nowhere came forth a hollow voice—close to my heart it seemed—"Am I quite gone? Are you convinced now? Well, now I will gradually return to Flatland and you shall see my section become larger and larger."

Every reader in Spaceland will easily understand that my mysterious Guest was speaking the language of truth and even of simplicity. But to me, proficient though I was in Flatland Mathematics, it was by no means a simple matter. The rough diagram given above will make it clear to any Spaceland child that the Sphere, ascending in the three positions indicated there, must needs have manifested himself to me, or to any Flatlander, as a Circle, at first of full size, then small, and at last very small indeed, approaching to a Point. But to me, although I saw the facts before me, the causes were as dark as ever. All that I could comprehend was, that the Circle had made himself smaller and vanished, and that he had now reappeared and was rapidly making himself larger.

"The memex (a portmanteau of 'memory' and 'index' or 'memory' and 'extender') is the name of the hypothetical proto-hypertext system that Vannevar Bush described in his 1945 The Atlantic Monthly article 'As We May Think' (AWMT). Bush envisioned the memex as a device in which individuals would compress and store all of their books, records, and communications, 'mechanized so that it may be consulted with exceeding speed and flexibility.' The memex would provide an 'enlarged intimate supplement to one's memory'. The concept of the memex influenced the development of early hypertext systems (eventually leading to the creation of the World Wide Web) and personal knowledge base software. However, the memex system used a form of document bookmark list, of static microfilm pages, rather than a true hypertext system where parts of pages would have internal structure beyond the common textual format." [1]

"Do not do anything to him. Now I know that you fear God, because you have not withheld from me your son, your only son."

When he regained his original size, he heaved a deep sigh; for he perceived by my silence that I had altogether failed to comprehend him. And indeed I was now inclining to the belief that he must be no Circle at all, but some extremely clever juggler; or else that the old wives' tales were true, and that after all there were such people as Enchanters and Magicians.

After a long pause he muttered to himself, "One resource alone remains, if I am not to resort to action. I must try the method of Analogy." Then followed a still longer silence, after which he continued our dialogue.

Sphere—
Tell me, Mr. Mathematician; if a Point moves Northward, and leaves a luminous wake, what name would you give to the wake?

I—
A straight Line.

Sphere—
And a straight Line has how many extremities?

I—
Two.

Sphere—
Now conceive the Northward straight Line moving parallel to itself, East and West, so that every point in it leaves

Abraham looked up and there in a thicket he saw a ram caught by its horns. He went over and took the ram and sacrificed it as a burnt offering instead of his son.

behind it the wake of a straight Line. What name will you give to the Figure thereby formed? We will suppose that it moves through a distance equal to the original straight Line. —What name, I say?

I—

A Square.

Sphere—

And how many sides has a Square? How many angles?

I—

Four sides and four angles.

Sphere—

Now stretch your imagination a little, and conceive a Square in Flatland, moving parallel to itself upward.

I—

What? Northward?

Sphere—

No, not Northward; upward; out of Flatland altogether.

If it moved Northward, the Southern points in the Square would have to move through the positions previously occupied by the Northern points. But that is not my meaning.

I mean that every Point in you—for you are a Square and will serve the purpose of my illustration—every Point in you, that is to say in what you call your

The angel of the Lord called to Abraham from heaven a second time and said, "I swear by myself, declares the Lord, that because you have done this and have not withheld your son,

FLATLAND, SEE THE HUMANITIES.

"The humanities are academic disciplines that study human culture. The humanities use methods that are primarily critical, or speculative, and have a significant historical element—as distinguished from the mainly empirical approaches of the natural sciences. The humanities include ancient and modern languages, literature, philosophy, religion, and visual and performing arts such as music and theatre. Areas that are sometimes regarded as social sciences and sometimes as humanities include history, anthropology, area studies, communication studies, cultural studies, law and linguistics." [1]

inside, is to pass upwards through Space in such a way that no Point shall pass through the position previously occupied by any other Point; but each Point shall describe a straight Line of its own. This is all in accordance with Analogy; surely it must be clear to you.

Restraining my impatience—for I was now under a strong temptation to rush blindly at my Visitor and to precipitate him into Space, or out of Flatland, anywhere, so that I could get rid of him—I replied:—

"And what may be the nature of the Figure which I am to shape out by this motion which you are pleased to denote by the word 'upward'? I presume it is describable in the language of Flatland."

Sphere—
Oh, certainly. It is all plain and simple, and in strict accordance with Analogy—only, by the way, you must not speak of the result as being a Figure, but as a Solid. But I will describe it to you. Or rather not I, but Analogy.

We began with a single Point, which of course—being itself a Point—has only ONE terminal Point. One Point produces a Line with TWO terminal Points. One Line produces a Square with FOUR terminal Points. Now

How the Stranger vainly endeavoured to reveal to me in words the mysteries of Spaceland

your only son, I will surely bless you and make your descendants as numerous as the stars in the sky and as the sand on the seashore.

you can give yourself the answer to your own question: 1, 2, 4, are evidently in Geometrical Progression. What is the next number?

I—

Eight.

Sphere—

Exactly. The one Square produces a SOMETHING-WHICH-YOU-DO-NOT-AS-YET-KNOW-A-NAME-FOR-BUT-WHICH-WE-CALL-A-CUBE with EIGHT terminal Points. Now are you convinced?

I—

And has this Creature sides, as well as angles or what you call "terminal Points"?

Sphere—

Of course; and all according to Analogy. But, by the way, not what YOU call sides, but what WE call sides. You would call them SOLIDS.

I—

And how many solids or sides will appertain to this Being whom I am to generate by the motion of my inside in an "upward" direction, and whom you call a Cube?

Sphere—

How can you ask? And you a mathematician! The side of anything is always, if I may so say, one Dimension behind

"Speculative fiction can be recognized in works whose authors' intentions or the social contexts of the versions of stories they portrayed is now known, since ancient Greek dramatists such as Euripides (ca. 480–406 BCE) whose play Medea seems to have offended Athenian audiences when he fictionally speculated that shamaness Medea killed her own children instead of their being killed by other Corinthians after her departure, and whose Hippolytus, narratively introduced by Aphrodite, Goddess of Love in person, is suspected to have displeased his contemporary audiences because he portrayed Phaedra as too lusty." [1]

Your descendants will take possession of the cities of their enemies, and through your offspring all nations on earth will be blessed, because you have obeyed me."

the thing. Consequently, as there is no Dimension behind a Point, a Point has 0 sides; a Line, if I may say, has 2 sides (for the Points of a Line may be called by courtesy, its sides); a Square has 4 sides; 0, 2, 4; what Progression do you call that?

I—

Arithmetical.

Sphere—

And what is the next number?

I—

Six.

Sphere—

Exactly. Then you see you have answered your own question. The Cube which you will generate will be bounded by six sides, that is to say, six of your insides. You see it all now, eh?

"Monster," I shrieked, "be thou juggler, enchanter, dream, or devil, no more will I endure thy mockeries. Either thou or I must perish." And saying these words I precipitated myself upon him.

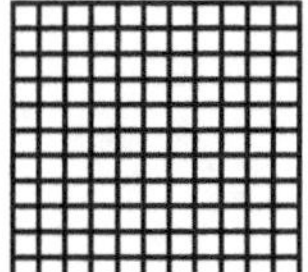

How the Sphere, having in vain tried words, resorted to deeds

160

Jump Physics

It was in vain. I brought my hardest right angle into violent collision with the Stranger, pressing on him with a force sufficient to have destroyed any ordinary Circle: but I could feel him slowly and unarrestably slipping from my contact; no edging to the right nor to the left, but moving somehow out of the world, and vanishing to nothing. Soon there was a blank. But still I heard the Intruder's voice.

> *Sphere—*
> Why will you refuse to listen to reason? I had hoped to find in you—as being a man of sense and an accomplished mathematician—a fit apostle for the Gospel of the Three Dimensions, which I am allowed to preach once only in a thousand years: but now I know not how to convince you. Stay, I have it. Deeds, and not words, shall proclaim the truth. Listen, my friend.
>
> I have told you I can see from my position in Space the inside of all things that you consider closed. For example, I see in yonder cupboard near which you are standing, several of what you call boxes (but like everything else in Flatland, they have no tops nor bottoms) full of money; I see also two tablets of accounts. I am about to descend into that cupboard and to bring

161

We like to believe the human race is silver quick, unbound and limitless but in reality we wriggle in a 4,000-mile gravity swamp. Our magicians take joy in reminding us what an utter bore we are, that nothing much happens down here, that our souls are not of this world and that the real action takes place elsewhere—up there.

I wanted to feel autonomous, self-ruling. I wanted to move upward and outward. On my own. But I couldn't. You $p = mv$ and you $F = ma$, not to mention you $F_{1\to 2} = -F_{2\to 1}$ and YOU $F_G = G_N (m_1 m_2)/ r^2$

Because of you, planets come in many shapes, sizes and colors. I know you're the you one of those tablets. I saw you lock the cupboard half an hour ago, and I know you have the key in your possession. But I descend from Space; the doors, you see, remain unmoved. Now I am in the cupboard and am taking the tablet. Now I have it. Now I ascend with it.

I rushed to the closet and dashed the door open. One of the tablets was gone. With a mocking laugh, the Stranger appeared in the other corner of the room, and at the same time the tablet appeared upon the floor. I took it up. There could be no doubt—it was the missing tablet.

I groaned with horror, doubting whether I was not out of my senses; but the Stranger continued: "Surely you must now see that my explanation, and no other, suits the phenomena. What you call Solid things are really superficial; what you call Space is really nothing but a great Plane. I am in Space, and look down upon the insides of the things of which you only see the outsides. You could leave this Plane yourself, if you could but summon up the necessary volition. A slight upward or downward motion would enable you to see all that I can see.

"The higher I mount, and the further I go from your

only one capable of forming them and the stars, even galaxies. But you're a butthole. A drag that keeps me down, glued, stuck.

Enough with that! My experiments have proven fruitful. I've tested my theory and it's flawless, airtight, watertight no less. I laugh at Newton, Clausius, Maxwell, Boltzmann and Einstein. Some say I'm deranged, that if I'm right our universe will spin into chaos. Up will become southeast, orange will be the new black, bras will be useless, Eurovision will get cancelled, the obese will rule. That existence as we know it will end as an orange hole emerges in the center of the universe swallowing all.

"Taxicab geometry, considered by Hermann Minkowski in 19th century Germany, is a form of geometry in which the usual distance function or metric of Euclidean geometry is replaced by a new metric in which the distance between two points is the sum of the absolute differences of their Cartesian coordinates. The taxicab metric is also known as rectilinear distance, L_1 distance or ℓ_1 norm (see L^p space), city block distance, Manhattan distance, or Manhattan length, with corresponding variations in the name of the geometry. The latter names allude to the grid layout of most streets on the island of Manhattan, which causes the shortest path a car could take between two intersections in the borough to have length equal to the intersections' distance in taxicab geometry." [1]

Plane, the more I can see, though of course I see it on a smaller scale. For example, I am ascending; now I can see your neighbour the Hexagon and his family in their several apartments; now I see the inside of the Theatre, ten doors off, from which the audience is only just departing; and on the other side a Circle in his study, sitting at his books. Now I shall come back to you. And, as a crowning proof, what do you say to my giving you a touch, just the least touch, in your stomach? It will not seriously injure you, and the slight pain you may suffer cannot be compared with the mental benefit you will receive."

Before I could utter a word of remonstrance, I felt a shooting pain in my inside, and a demoniacal laugh seemed to issue from within me. A moment afterwards the sharp agony had ceased, leaving nothing but a dull ache behind, and the Stranger began to reappear, saying, as he gradually increased in size, "There, I have not hurt you much, have I? If you are not convinced now, I don't know what will convince you. What say you?"

My resolution was taken. It seemed intolerable that I should endure existence subject to the arbitrary visitations of a Magician who could thus play tricks with one's very stomach. If only I could in any way manage to pin him against the

Whatever happens I'm ready. Today while you force the rest of us to side-scroll the platforms, I'll double jump up there.

Mario

wall till help came!

Once more I dashed my hardest angle against him, at the same time alarming the whole household by my cries for aid. I believe, at the moment of my onset, the Stranger had sunk below our Plane, and really found difficulty in rising. In any case he remained motionless, while I, hearing, as I thought, the sound of some help approaching, pressed against him with redoubled vigour, and continued to shout for assistance.

A convulsive shudder ran through the Sphere. "This must not be," I thought I heard him say: "either he must listen to reason, or I must have recourse to the last resource of civilization." Then, addressing me in a louder tone, he hurriedly exclaimed, "Listen: no stranger must witness what you have witnessed. Send your Wife back at once, before she enters the apartment. The Gospel of Three Dimensions must not be thus frustrated. Not thus must the fruits of one thousand years of waiting be thrown away. I hear her coming. Back! back! Away from me, or you must go with me—whither you know not—into the Land of Three Dimensions!"

"Fool! Madman! Irregular!" I exclaimed; "never will I release thee; thou shalt pay the penalty of thine impostures."

"Ha! Is it come to this?" thundered the Stranger: "then meet your fate: out of your Plane you go. Once, twice, thrice!

"Tensegrity, tensional integrity or floating compression, is a structural principle based on the use of isolated components in compression inside a net of continuous tension, in such a way that the compressed members (usually bars or struts) do not touch each other and the prestressed tensioned members (usually cables or tendons) delineate the system spatially." [28]

'Tis done!"

How the Sphere, having in vain tried words, resorted to deeds

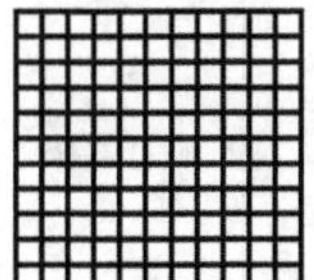

How I came to Spaceland, and what I saw there

166

It will dawn upon you by degrees

An unspeakable horror seized me. There was a darkness; then a dizzy, sickening sensation of sight that was not like seeing; I saw a Line that was no Line; Space that was not Space: I was myself, and not myself. When I could find voice, I shrieked aloud in agony, "Either this is madness or it is Hell." "It is neither," calmly replied the voice of the Sphere, "it is Knowledge; it is Three Dimensions: open your eye once again and try to look steadily."

I looked, and, behold, a new world! There stood before me, visibly incorporate, all that I had before inferred, conjectured, dreamed, of perfect Circular beauty. What seemed the centre of the Stranger's form lay open to my view: yet I could see no heart, nor lungs, nor arteries, only a beautiful harmonious Something—for which I had no words; but you, my Readers in Spaceland, would call it the surface of the Sphere.

Prostrating myself mentally before my Guide, I cried, "How is it, O divine ideal of consummate loveliness and wisdom that I see thy inside, and yet cannot discern thy heart, thy lungs, thy arteries, thy liver?" "What you think you see, you see not," he replied; "it is not given to you, nor to any other Being to behold my internal parts. I am of a different order of Beings from those in Flatland. Were I a Circle, you could discern my intestines, but I am a Being, composed as I told you before, of many Circles, the Many in the One, called in this country a Sphere. And, just as the outside of a Cube is a Square, so the outside of a Sphere presents the appearance of a Circle."

Bewildered though I was by my Teacher's enigmatic utterance, I no longer chafed against it, but worshipped him in silent adoration. He continued, with more mildness in his voice. "Distress not yourself if you cannot at first understand the deeper mysteries of Spaceland. By degrees they will dawn upon you. Let us begin by casting back a glance at the region whence you came. Return with me a while to the plains of Flatland, and I will shew you that which you have often reasoned and thought about, but never seen with the sense of sight—a visible angle." "Impossible!" I cried; but, the Sphere leading the way, I followed as if in a dream, till once more his voice arrested me: "Look yonder, and behold your own Pentagonal house, and all its inmates."

I looked below, and saw with my physical eye all that domestic individuality which I had hitherto merely inferred with the understanding. And how poor and shadowy was the inferred conjecture in comparison with the reality which I now beheld! My four Sons calmly asleep in the North-Western

"A mysterious rock suddenly appeared in front of the Opportunity rover's cameras on Mars, puzzling scientists who describe the rock as both 'a total surprise' and 'about the size of a jelly donut.'

'Only two options have so far been identified as the rock's source: 1) The rover either 'flipped' the object as it maneuvered or, 2) it landed there, right in front of the rover, after a nearby meteorite impact event. The impact ejecta theory, however, is the least likely of the two. 'So my best guess for this rock ... is that it's something that was nearby,' said Squyres. 'I must stress that I'm guessing now, but I think it happened when the rover did a turn in place a meter or two from where this rock now lies.' Opportunity's front right steering actuator has stopped working, so Squyres identified that as the possible culprit behind the whole mystery'." [29]

rooms, my two orphan Grandsons to the South; the Servants, the Butler, my Daughter, all in their several apartments. Only my affectionate Wife, alarmed by my continued absence, had quitted her room and was roving up and down in the Hall, anxiously awaiting my return. Also the Page, aroused by my cries, had left his room, and under pretext of ascertaining whether I had fallen somewhere in a faint, was prying into the cabinet in my study. All this I could now SEE, not merely infer; and as we came nearer and nearer, I could discern even the contents of my cabinet, and the two chests of gold, and the tablets of which the Sphere had made mention.

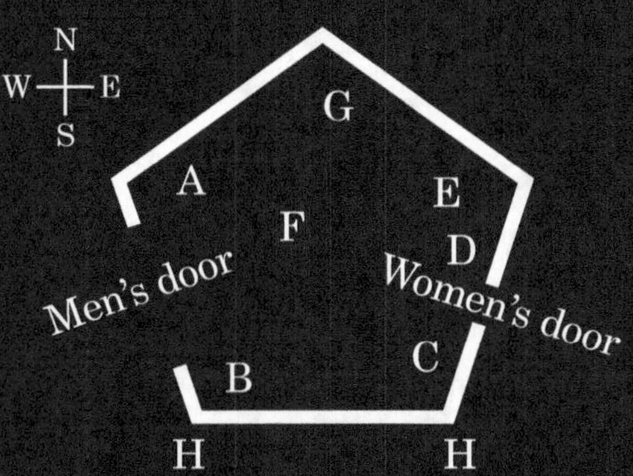

A. My Sons
B. My Grandsons
C. The Servants
D. My Daughter
E. My Wife's Apartment
F. The Hall
G. My Study
H. Policeman

Touched by my Wife's distress, I would have sprung downward to reassure her, but I found myself incapable of motion. "Trouble not yourself about your Wife," said my Guide: "she will not be long left in anxiety; meantime, let us take a survey of Flatland."

Once more I felt myself rising through space. It was even as the Sphere had said. The further we receded from the object we beheld, the larger became the field of vision. My native city, with the interior of every house and every creature therein, lay open to my view in miniature. We mounted higher, and lo, the secrets of the earth, the depths of mines and inmost caverns of the hills, were bared before me.

Awestruck at the sight of the mysteries of the earth, thus unveiled before my unworthy eye, I said to my Companion, "Behold, I am become as a God. For the wise men in our country say that to see all things, or as they express it, OMNIVIDENCE, is the attribute of God alone." There was something of scorn in the voice of my Teacher as he made answer: "Is it so indeed? Then the very pick-pockets and cut-throats of my country are to be worshipped by your wise men as being Gods: for there is not one of them that does not see as much as you see now. But trust me, your wise men are wrong."

I—

"Slashdotters read Monday about strange symbols in the Gobi Desert recently imaged and indexed by Google Maps. Alien landing zones? Some military thingy? Bizarre art project? Nope. The grids of zigzagging white lines seen in two of the images—the strangest of the various desert structures—are spy satellite calibration targets, according to one NASA scientist." [30]

Then is omnividence the attribute of others besides Gods?

Sphere—

I do not know. But, if a pick-pocket or a cut-throat of our country can see everything that is in your country, surely that is no reason why the pick-pocket or cut-throat should be accepted by you as a God. This omnividence, as you call it—it is not a common word in Spaceland—does it make you more just, more merciful, less selfish, more loving? Not in the least. Then how does it make you more divine?

I—

"More merciful, more loving!" But these are the qualities of women! And we know that a Circle is a higher Being than a Straight Line, in so far as knowledge and wisdom are more to be esteemed than mere affection.

Sphere—

It is not for me to classify human faculties according to merit. Yet many of the best and wisest in Spaceland think more of the affections than of the understanding, more of your despised Straight Lines than of your belauded Circles. But enough of this. Look yonder. Do you know that building?

I looked, and afar off I saw an immense Polygonal structure, in which I recognized the General Assembly Hall of the States of Flatland, surrounded by dense lines of Pentagonal buildings at right angles to each other, which I knew to be streets; and I perceived that I was approaching the great Metropolis.

"Here we descend," said my Guide. It was now morning, the first hour of the first day of the two thousandth year of our era. Acting, as was their wont, in strict accordance with precedent, the highest Circles of the realm were meeting in solemn conclave, as they had met on the first hour of the first day of the year 1000, and also on the first hour of the first day of the year 0.

The minutes of the previous meetings were now read by one whom I at once recognized as my brother, a perfectly Symmetrical Square, and the Chief Clerk of the High Council. It was found recorded on each occasion that: "Whereas the States had been troubled by divers ill-intentioned persons pretending to have received revelations from another World, and professing to produce demonstrations whereby they had instigated to frenzy both themselves and others, it had been for this cause unanimously resolved by the Grand Council that on the first day of each millenary, special injunctions

FLATLAND, SEE PHASE SPACE.

"In mathematics and physics, a phase space is a space in which all possible states of a system are represented, with each possible state of the system corresponding to one unique point in the phase space. For mechanical systems, the phase space usually consists of all possible values of position and momentum variables (i.e. the cotangent space of configuration space). The concept of phase space was developed in the late 19th century by Ludwig Boltzmann, Henri Poincaré, and Willard Gibbs." [31]

be sent to the Prefects in the several districts of Flatland, to make strict search for such misguided persons, and without formality of mathematical examination, to destroy all such as were Isosceles of any degree, to scourge and imprison any regular Triangle, to cause any Square or Pentagon to be sent to the district Asylum, and to arrest any one of higher rank, sending him straightway to the Capital to be examined and judged by the Council."

"You hear your fate," said the Sphere to me, while the Council was passing for the third time the formal resolution. "Death or imprisonment awaits the Apostle of the Gospel of Three Dimensions." "Not so," replied I, "the matter is now so clear to me, the nature of real space so palpable, that methinks I could make a child understand it. Permit me but to descend at this moment and enlighten them." "Not yet," said my Guide, "the time will come for that. Meantime I must perform my mission. Stay thou there in thy place." Saying these words, he leaped with great dexterity into the sea (if I may so call it) of Flatland, right in the midst of the ring of Counsellors. "I come," cried he, "to proclaim that there is a land of Three Dimensions."

I could see many of the younger Counsellors start back in manifest horror, as the Sphere's circular section widened before them. But on a sign from the presiding Circle—who shewed not the slightest alarm or surprise—six Isosceles of a low type from six different quarters rushed upon the Sphere. "We have him," they cried; "No; yes; we have him still! he's going! he's gone!"

"My Lords," said the President to the Junior Circles of the Council, "there is not the slightest need for surprise; the secret archives, to which I alone have access, tell me that a similar occurrence happened on the last two millennial commencements. You will, of course, say nothing of these trifles outside the Cabinet."

Raising his voice, he now summoned the guards. "Arrest the policemen; gag them. You know your duty." After he had consigned to their fate the wretched policemen—ill-fated and unwilling witnesses of a State-secret which they were not to be permitted to reveal—he again addressed the Counsellors. "My Lords, the business of the Council being concluded, I have only to wish you a happy New Year." Before departing, he expressed, at some length, to the Clerk, my excellent but most unfortunate brother, his sincere regret that, in accordance with precedent and for the sake of secrecy, he must condemn him to perpetual imprisonment, but added his satisfaction that, unless some mention were made by him of that day's

"A phase portrait is a geometric representation of the trajectories of a dynamical system in the phase plane. Each set of initial conditions is represented by a different curve, or point.

Phase portraits are an invaluable tool in studying dynamical systems. They consist of a plot of typical trajectories in the state space. This reveals information such as whether an attractor, a repellor or limit cycle is present for the chosen parameter value. The concept of topological equivalence is important in classifying the behaviour of systems by specifying when two different phase portraits represent the same qualitative dynamic behavior." [1]

incident, his life would be spared.

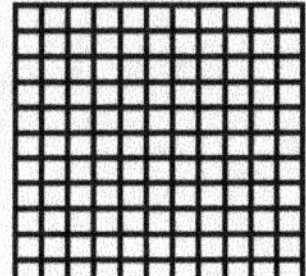

How, though the Sphere shewed me other mysteries of Spaceland, I still desired more; and what came of it

176

When I saw my poor brother led away to imprisonment, I attempted to leap down into the Council Chamber, desiring to intercede on his behalf, or at least bid him farewell. But I found that I had no motion of my own. I absolutely depended on the volition of my Guide, who said in gloomy tones, "Heed not thy brother; haply thou shalt have ample time hereafter to condole with him. Follow me."

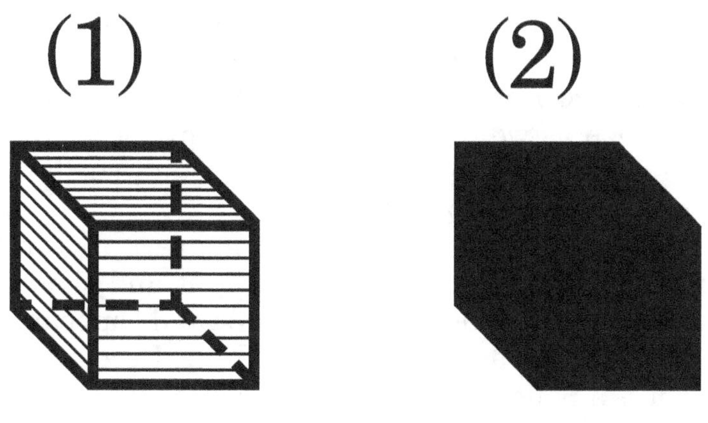

Once more we ascended into space. "Hitherto," said the Sphere, "I have shewn you naught save Plane Figures and their interiors. Now I must introduce you to Solids, and reveal to you the plan upon which they are constructed. Behold this multitude of moveable square cards. See, I put one on another, not, as you supposed, Northward of the other, but ON the other. Now a second, now a third. See, I am building up a Solid by a multitude of Squares parallel to one another. Now the Solid is complete, being as high as it is long and broad, and we call it a Cube."

"Pardon me, my Lord," replied I; "but to my eye the appearance is as of an Irregular Figure whose inside is laid open to the view; in other words, methinks I see no Solid, but a Plane such as we infer in Flatland; only of an Irregularity which betokens some monstrous criminal, so that the very sight of it is painful to my eyes."

"True," said the Sphere, "it appears to you a Plane, because you are not accustomed to light and shade and perspective; just as in Flatland a Hexagon would appear a Straight Line to one who has not the Art of Sight Recognition. But in reality it is a Solid, as you shall learn by the sense of Feeling."

He then introduced me to the Cube, and I found that this marvellous Being was indeed no Plane, but a Solid; and that he was endowed with six plane sides and eight terminal

FLATLAND, SEE LORENZ SYSTEM.

"The Lorenz system is a system of ordinary differential equations (the Lorenz equations) first studied by Edward Lorenz. It is notable for having chaotic solutions for certain parameter values and initial conditions. In particular, the Lorenz attractor is a set of chaotic solutions of the Lorenz system which, when plotted, resemble a butterfly or figure eight." [1]

points called solid angles; and I remembered the saying of the Sphere that just such a Creature as this would be formed by a Square moving, in Space, parallel to himself: and I rejoiced to think that so insignificant a Creature as I could in some sense be called the Progenitor of so illustrious an offspring.

But still I could not fully understand the meaning of what my Teacher had told me concerning "light" and "shade" and "perspective"; and I did not hesitate to put my difficulties before him.

Were I to give the Sphere's explanation of these matters, succinct and clear though it was, it would be tedious to an inhabitant of Space, who knows these things already. Suffice it, that by his lucid statements, and by changing the position of objects and lights, and by allowing me to feel the several objects and even his own sacred Person, he at last made all things clear to me, so that I could now readily distinguish between a Circle and a Sphere, a Plane Figure and a Solid.

This was the Climax, the Paradise, of my strange eventful History. Henceforth I have to relate the story of my miserable Fall:—most miserable, yet surely most undeserved! For why should the thirst for knowledge be aroused, only to be disappointed and punished? My volition shrinks from the painful task of recalling my humiliation; yet, like a second Prometheus, I will endure this and worse, if by any means I

How, though the Sphere shewed me other mysteries of Spaceland, I still desired more; and what came of it

may arouse in the interiors of Plane and Solid Humanity a spirit of rebellion against the Conceit which would limit our Dimensions to Two or Three or any number short of Infinity. Away then with all personal considerations! Let me continue to the end, as I began, without further digressions or anticipations, pursuing the plain path of dispassionate History. The exact facts, the exact words,—and they are burnt in upon my brain,—shall be set down without alteration of an iota; and let my Readers judge between me and Destiny.

The Sphere would willingly have continued his lessons by indoctrinating me in the conformation of all regular Solids, Cylinders, Cones, Pyramids, Pentahedrons, Hexahedrons, Dodecahedrons, and Spheres: but I ventured to interrupt him. Not that I was wearied of knowledge. On the contrary, I thirsted for yet deeper and fuller draughts than he was offering to me.

"Pardon me," said I, "O Thou Whom I must no longer address as the Perfection of all Beauty; but let me beg thee to vouchsafe thy servant a sight of thine interior."

Sphere—
My what?

I—
Thine interior: thy stomach, thy intestines.

"In astrophysics and cosmology, the anthropic principle (from Greek anthropos, meaning 'human') is the philosophical consideration that observations of the physical Universe must be compatible with the conscious and sapient life that observes it. Some proponents of the anthropic principle reason that it explains why the Universe has the age and the fundamental physical constants necessary to accommodate conscious life. As a result, they believe it is unremarkable that the Universe's fundamental constants happen to fall within the narrow range thought to be compatible with life." [1]

Sphere—

Whence this ill-timed impertinent request? And what mean you by saying that I am no longer the Perfection of all Beauty?

I—

My Lord, your own wisdom has taught me to aspire to One even more great, more beautiful, and more closely approximate to Perfection than yourself. As you yourself, superior to all Flatland forms, combine many Circles in One, so doubtless there is One above you who combines many Spheres in One Supreme Existence, surpassing even the Solids of Spaceland. And even as we, who are now in Space, look down on Flatland and see the insides of all things, so of a certainty there is yet above us some higher, purer region, whither thou dost surely purpose to lead me—O Thou Whom I shall always call, everywhere and in all Dimensions, my Priest, Philosopher, and Friend—some yet more spacious Space, some more dimensionable Dimensionality, from the vantage-ground of which we shall look down together upon the revealed insides of Solid things, and where thine own intestines, and those of thy kindred Spheres, will lie exposed to the view of the poor wandering exile from Flatland, to whom so much has already

been vouchsafed.

Sphere—

Pooh! Stuff! Enough of this trifling! The time is short, and much remains to be done before you are fit to proclaim the Gospel of Three Dimensions to your blind benighted countrymen in Flatland.

I—

Nay, gracious Teacher, deny me not what I know it is in thy power to perform. Grant me but one glimpse of thine interior, and I am satisfied for ever, remaining henceforth thy docile pupil, thy unemancipable slave, ready to receive all thy teachings and to feed upon the words that fall from thy lips.

Sphere—

Well, then, to content and silence you, let me say at once, I would shew you what you wish if I could; but I cannot. Would you have me turn my stomach inside out to oblige you?

I—

But my Lord has shewn me the intestines of all my countrymen in the Land of Two Dimensions by taking me with him into the Land of Three. What therefore more easy than now to take his servant on a second journey into the blessed region of the Fourth Dimension,

FLATLAND, SEE VORONOI DIAGRAM.

"In mathematics, a Voronoi diagram is a way of dividing space into a number of regions. A set of points (called seeds, sites, or generators) is specified beforehand and for each seed there will be a corresponding region consisting of all points closer to that seed than to any other. The regions are called Voronoi cells. It is dual to the Delaunay triangulation." [1]

where I shall look down with him once more upon this land of Three Dimensions, and see the inside of every three-dimensioned house, the secrets of the solid earth, the treasures of the mines in Spaceland, and the intestines of every solid living creature, even of the noble and adorable Spheres.

Sphere—

But where is this land of Four Dimensions?

I—

I know not: but doubtless my Teacher knows.

Sphere—

Not I. There is no such land. The very idea of it is utterly inconceivable.

I—

Not inconceivable, my Lord, to me, and therefore still less inconceivable to my Master. Nay, I despair not that, even here, in this region of Three Dimensions, your Lordship's art may make the Fourth Dimension visible to me; just as in the Land of Two Dimensions my Teacher's skill would fain have opened the eyes of his blind servant to the invisible presence of a Third Dimension, though I saw it not.

Let me recall the past. Was I not taught below that when I saw a Line and inferred a Plane, I in reality

saw a Third unrecognized Dimension, not the same as brightness, called "height"? And does it not now follow that, in this region, when I see a Plane and infer a Solid, I really see a Fourth unrecognized Dimension, not the same as colour, but existent, though infinitesimal and incapable of measurement?

And besides this, there is the Argument from Analogy of Figures.

Sphere—

Analogy! Nonsense: what analogy?

I—

Your Lordship tempts his servant to see whether he remembers the revelations imparted to him. Trifle not with me, my Lord; I crave, I thirst, for more knowledge. Doubtless we cannot SEE that other higher Spaceland now, because we we have no eye in our stomachs. But, just as there WAS the realm of Flatland, though that poor puny Lineland Monarch could neither turn to left nor right to discern it, and just as there WAS close at hand, and touching my frame, the land of Three Dimensions, though I, blind senseless wretch, had no power to touch it, no eye in my interior to discern it, so of a surety there is a Fourth Dimension, which my Lord perceives with the inner eye of thought. And that

"A gömböc or gomboc (Hungarian: [gømbøts]) is a convex three-dimensional homogeneous body which, when resting on a flat surface, has just one stable and one unstable point of equilibrium. Its existence was conjectured by Russian mathematician Vladimir Arnold in 1995 and proven in 2006 by Hungarian scientists Gábor Domokos and Péter Várkonyi. The gömböc shape is not unique; it has countless varieties, most of which are very close to a sphere and all have very strict shape tolerance (about 0.1 mm per 100 mm)." [1]

it must exist my Lord himself has taught me. Or can he have forgotten what he himself imparted to his servant?

In One Dimension, did not a moving Point produce a Line with TWO terminal points?

In Two Dimensions, did not a moving Line produce a Square with FOUR terminal points?

In Three Dimensions, did not a moving Square produce—did not this eye of mine behold it—that blessed Being, a Cube, with EIGHT terminal points?

And in Four Dimensions shall not a moving Cube—alas, for Analogy, and alas for the Progress of Truth, if it be not so—shall not, I say, the motion of a divine Cube result in a still more divine Organization with SIXTEEN terminal points?

Behold the infallible confirmation of the Series, 2, 4, 8, 16: is not this a Geometrical Progression? Is not this—if I might quote my Lord's own words—"strictly according to Analogy"?

Again, was I not taught by my Lord that as in a Line there are TWO bounding Points, and in a Square there are FOUR bounding Lines, so in a Cube there must be SIX bounding Squares? Behold once more the confirming Series, 2, 4, 6: is not this an Arithmetical Progression? And consequently does it not of necessity

follow that the more divine offspring of the divine Cube in the Land of Four Dimensions, must have 8 bounding Cubes: and is not this also, as my Lord has taught me to believe, "strictly according to Analogy"?

O, my Lord, my Lord, behold, I cast myself in faith upon conjecture, not knowing the facts; and I appeal to your Lordship to confirm or deny my logical anticipations. If I am wrong, I yield, and will no longer demand a fourth Dimension; but, if I am right, my Lord will listen to reason.

I ask therefore, is it, or is it not, the fact, that ere now your countrymen also have witnessed the descent of Beings of a higher order than their own, entering closed rooms, even as your Lordship entered mine, without the opening of doors or windows, and appearing and vanishing at will? On the reply to this question I am ready to stake everything. Deny it, and I am henceforth silent. Only vouchsafe an answer.

Sphere—(after a pause).

It is reported so. But men are divided in opinion as to the facts. And even granting the facts, they explain them in different ways. And in any case, however great may be the number of different explanations, no one has adopted or suggested the theory of a Fourth Dimension.

FLATLAND, SEE DISCOURSE ON THE METHOD.

"...one of the most influential works in the history of modern philosophy, and important to the evolution of natural sciences. In this work, Descartes tackles the problem of skepticism, which had previously been studied by Sextus Empiricus, Al-Ghazali and Michel de Montaigne. Descartes modified it to account for a truth he found to be incontrovertible. Descartes started his line of reasoning by doubting everything, so as to assess the world from a fresh perspective, clear of any preconceived notions." [1]

Therefore, pray have done with this trifling, and let us return to business.

I—

I was certain of it. I was certain that my anticipations would be fulfilled. And now have patience with me and answer me yet one more question, best of Teachers! Those who have thus appeared—no one knows whence—and have returned—no one knows whither—have they also contracted their sections and vanished somehow into that more Spacious Space, whither I now entreat you to conduct me?

Sphere (moodily)—

They have vanished, certainly—if they ever appeared. But most people say that these visions arose from the thought—you will not understand me—from the brain; from the perturbed angularity of the Seer.

I—

Say they so? Oh, believe them not. Or if it indeed be so, that this other Space is really Thoughtland, then take me to that blessed Region where I in Thought shall see the insides of all solid things. There, before my ravished eye, a Cube, moving in some altogether new direction, but strictly according to Analogy, so as to make every particle of his interior pass through a new kind of Space,

How, though the Sphere shewed me other mysteries of Spaceland, I still desired more; and what came of it

with a wake of its own—shall create a still more perfect perfection than himself, with sixteen terminal Extra-solid angles, and Eight solid Cubes for his Perimeter. And once there, shall we stay our upward course? In that blessed region of Four Dimensions, shall we linger on the threshold of the Fifth, and not enter therein? Ah, no! Let us rather resolve that our ambition shall soar with our corporal ascent. Then, yielding to our intellectual onset, the gates of the Sixth Dimension shall fly open; after that a Seventh, and then an Eighth—

How long I should have continued I know not. In vain did the Sphere, in his voice of thunder, reiterate his command of silence, and threaten me with the direst penalties if I persisted. Nothing could stem the flood of my ecstatic aspirations. Perhaps I was to blame; but indeed I was intoxicated with the recent draughts of Truth to which he himself had introduced me. However, the end was not long in coming. My words were cut short by a crash outside, and a simultaneous crash inside me, which impelled me through space with a velocity that precluded speech. Down! down! down! I was rapidly descending; and I knew that return to Flatland was my doom. One glimpse, one last and never-to-be-forgotten glimpse I had

"Recursion is the process of repeating items in a self-similar way. For instance, when the surfaces of two mirrors are exactly parallel with each other, the nested images that occur are a form of infinite recursion. The term has a variety of meanings specific to a variety of disciplines ranging from linguistics to logic. The most common application of recursion is in mathematics and computer science, in which it refers to a method of defining functions in which the function being defined is applied within its own definition. Specifically, this defines an infinite number of instances (function values), using a

of that dull level wilderness—which was now to become my Universe again—spread out before my eye. Then a darkness. Then a final, all-consummating thunder-peal; and, when I came to myself, I was once more a common creeping Square, in my Study at home, listening to the Peace-Cry of my approaching Wife.

finite expression that for some instances may refer to other instances, but in such a way that no loop or infinite chain of references can occur. The term is also used more generally to describe a process of repeating objects in a self-similar way." [1]

How the Sphere encouraged me in a Vision

The day we arrived to Mecca

FLATLAND, SEE TRISTAM SHANDY.

"The Life and Opinions of Tristram Shandy, Gentleman (or, more briefly, Tristram Shandy) is a humorous novel by Laurence Sterne. It was published in nine volumes, the first two appearing in 1759, and seven others following over the next seven years (vols. 3 and 4, 1761; vols. 5 and 6, 1762; vols. 7 and 8, 1765; vol. 9, 1767). Probably Sterne's most enduring work, it purports to be a biography of the eponymous character. Its style is marked by digression and amplification." [1]

Although I had less than a minute for reflection, I felt, by a kind of instinct, that I must conceal my experiences from my Wife. Not that I apprehended, at the moment, any danger from her divulging my secret, but I knew that to any Woman in Flatland the narrative of my adventures must needs be unintelligible. So I endeavoured to reassure her by some story, invented for the occasion, that I had accidentally fallen through the trap-door of the cellar, and had there lain stunned.

The Southward attraction in our country is so slight that even to a Woman my tale necessarily appeared extraordinary and well-nigh incredible; but my Wife, whose good sense far exceeds that of the average of her Sex, and who perceived that I was unusually excited, did not argue with me on the subject, but insisted that I was ill and required repose. I was glad of an excuse for retiring to my chamber to think quietly over what had happened. When I was at last by myself, a drowsy sensation fell on me; but before my eyes closed I endeavoured to reproduce the Third Dimension, and especially the process by which a Cube is constructed through the motion of a Square. It was not so clear as I could have wished; but I remembered that it must be "Upward, and yet not Northward", and I determined steadfastly to retain these words as the clue which, if firmly grasped, could not fail to guide me to the solution. So mechanically repeating, like a charm, the words, "Upward, yet

191

Nothing is
Nothing is
Nothing. . .
also known
as Gravity

not Northward", I fell into a sound refreshing sleep.

During my slumber I had a dream. I thought I was once more by the side of the Sphere, whose lustrous hue betokened that he had exchanged his wrath against me for perfect placability. We were moving together towards a bright but infinitesimally small Point, to which my Master directed my attention. As we approached, methought there issued from it a slight humming noise as from one of your Spaceland bluebottles, only less resonant by far, so slight indeed that even in the perfect stillness of the Vacuum through which we soared, the sound reached not our ears till we checked our flight at a distance from it of something under twenty human diagonals.

"Look yonder," said my Guide, "in Flatland thou hast lived; of Lineland thou hast received a vision; thou hast soared with me to the heights of Spaceland; now, in order to complete the range of thy experience, I conduct thee downward to the lowest depth of existence, even to the realm of Pointland, the Abyss of No dimensions.

"Behold yon miserable creature. That Point is a Being like ourselves, but confined to the non-dimensional Gulf. He is himself his own World, his own Universe; of any other than himself he can form no conception; he knows not Length, nor Breadth, nor Height, for he has had no experience of them; he has no cognizance even of the number Two; nor has he a

"In many ways it seems oddly short-sighted of the world that Resch's work would, in the end, be most remarkable for resembling children's toys—from folding snakes to Rubik's cubes—rather than kicking off a brave new world of weird, inter-dimensional furniture and shape-shifting buildings that Resch's work implied would be only a few years away." [32]

192

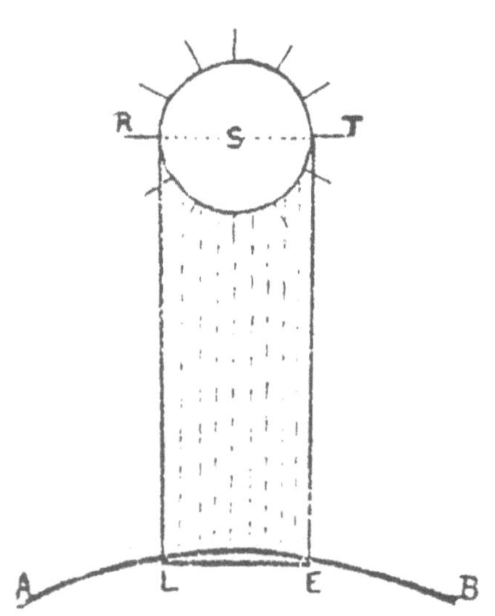

thought of Plurality; for he is himself his One and All, being really Nothing. Yet mark his perfect self-contentment, and hence learn this lesson, that to be self-contented is to be vile and ignorant, and that to aspire is better than to be blindly and impotently happy. Now listen."

He ceased; and there arose from the little buzzing creature a tiny, low, monotonous, but distinct tinkling, as from one of your Spaceland phonographs, from which I caught these words, "Infinite beatitude of existence! It is; and there is none else beside It."

"What," said I, "does the puny creature mean by 'it'?" "He means himself," said the Sphere: "have you not noticed before now, that babies and babyish people who cannot distinguish themselves from the world, speak of themselves in the Third Person? But hush!"

"It fills all Space," continued the little soliloquizing Creature, "and what It fills, It is. What It thinks, that It utters; and what It utters, that It hears; and It itself is Thinker, Utterer, Hearer, Thought, Word, Audition; it is the One, and yet the All in All. Ah, the happiness ah, the happiness of Being!"

"Can you not startle the little thing out of its complacency?" said I. "Tell it what it really is, as you told me; reveal to it the narrow limitations of Pointland, and lead it up to

something higher." "That is no easy task," said my Master; "try you."

Hereon, raising my voice to the uttermost, I addressed the Point as follows:

"Silence, silence, contemptible Creature. You call yourself the All in All, but you are the Nothing: your so-called Universe is a mere speck in a Line, and a Line is a mere shadow as compared with—" "Hush, hush, you have said enough," interrupted the Sphere, "now listen, and mark the effect of your harangue on the King of Pointland."

The lustre of the Monarch, who beamed more brightly than ever upon hearing my words, shewed clearly that he retained his complacency; and I had hardly ceased when he took up his strain again. "Ah, the joy, ah, the joy of Thought! What can It not achieve by thinking! Its own Thought coming to Itself, suggestive of Its disparagement, thereby to enhance Its happiness! Sweet rebellion stirred up to result in triumph! Ah, the divine creative power of the All in One! Ah, the joy, the joy of Being!"

"You see," said my Teacher, "how little your words have done. So far as the Monarch understands them at all, he accepts them as his own—for he cannot conceive of any other except himself—and plumes himself upon the variety of 'Its Thought' as an instance of creative Power. Let us leave this

"The continent of modern creation is not only discovered, but it already figures on various maps. Isms are the countries of the spiritual map, each one with a border separating it from the others as in a school geography—and like everything in school books right and wrong at the same time. For today the borderlines between isms are beginning to be obscured. And what interest us are not so much the surrounding constructions as the matter itself, the individual achievement which stands finally behind collective theories. In my opinion, for the sake of honesty, no new ism should be created." [33]

God of Pointland to the ignorant fruition of his omnipresence and omniscience: nothing that you or I can do can rescue him from his self-satisfaction."

After this, as we floated gently back to Flatland, I could hear the mild voice of my Companion pointing the moral of my vision, and stimulating me to aspire, and to teach others to aspire. He had been angered at first—he confessed—by my ambition to soar to Dimensions above the Third; but, since then, he had received fresh insight, and he was not too proud to acknowledge his error to a Pupil. Then he proceeded to initiate me into mysteries yet higher than those I had witnessed, shewing me how to construct Extra-Solids by the motion of Solids, and Double Extra-Solids by the motion of Extra-Solids, and all "strictly according to Analogy", all by methods so simple, so easy, as to be patent even to the Female Sex.

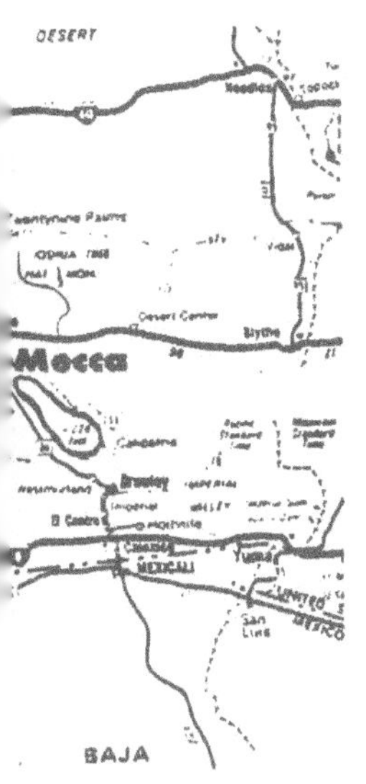

How I tried to teach the Theory of Three Dimensions to my Grandson, and with what success

I awoke rejoicing, and began to reflect on the glorious career before me. I would go forth, methought, at once, and evangelize the whole of Flatland. Even to Women and Soldiers should the Gospel of Three Dimensions be proclaimed. I would begin with my Wife.

Just as I had decided on the plan of my operations, I heard the sound of many voices in the street commanding silence. Then followed a louder voice. It was a herald's proclamation. Listening attentively, I recognized the words of the Resolution of the Council, enjoining the arrest, imprisonment, or execution of any one who should pervert the minds of the people by delusions, and by professing to have received revelations from another World.

I reflected. This danger was not to be trifled with. It would be better to avoid it by omitting all mention of my Revelation, and by proceeding on the path of Demonstration—which after all, seemed so simple and so conclusive that nothing would be lost by discarding the former means. "Upward, not Northward"—was the clue to the whole proof. It had seemed to me fairly clear before I fell asleep; and when I first awoke, fresh from my dream, it had appeared as patent as Arithmetic; but somehow it did not seem to me quite so obvious now. Though my Wife entered the room opportunely

DOGGEREL
By Sir W. Hamilton

A it affirms of this, these, all,
Whilst E denies of any;
I it affirms (whilst O denies)
Of some (or few, or many).

Thus A affirms, as E denies,
And definitely either;
Thus I affirms, as O denies,
And definitely neither.

A half, left semidefinite,
Is worthy of its score;
U, then, affirms, as Y denies,
This, neither less nor more.

Indefinito-definites,
I, UI, YO, last we come;
And this affirms, as that denies
Of more, most (half, plus, some).

just at that moment, I decided, after we had exchanged a few words of commonplace conversation, not to begin with her.

My Pentagonal Sons were men of character and standing, and physicians of no mean reputation, but not great in mathematics, and, in that respect, unfit for my purpose. But it occurred to me that a young and docile Hexagon, with a mathematical turn, would be a most suitable pupil. Why therefore not make my first experiment with my little precocious Grandson, whose casual remarks on the meaning of 33 had met with the approval of the Sphere? Discussing the matter with him, a mere boy, I should be in perfect safety; for he would know nothing of the Proclamation of the Council; whereas I could not feel sure that my Sons—so greatly did their patriotism and reverence for the Circles predominate over mere blind affection—might not feel compelled to hand me over to the Prefect, if they found me seriously maintaining the seditious heresy of the Third Dimension.

But the first thing to be done was to satisfy in some way the curiosity of my Wife, who naturally wished to know something of the reasons for which the Circle had desired that mysterious interview, and of the means by which he had entered the house. Without entering into the details of the elaborate account I gave her,—an account, I fear, not quite

"Guy de Cointet's text works on canvas and on paper were based on systems of encoding or abstracting text. He produced several encrypted publications including a completely encrypted newspaper, ACRCIT. Silkscreen printed by Pierre Picot, a French artist teaching at CalArts, ACRCIT was distributed for free through newspaper boxes across Los Angeles.

His performance pieces combined literary puzzles inspired by the works of Raymond Roussel and the tropes of TV soap opera. The pieces were performed by actors such as Factory 'superstar' Viva and diminutive comedian Billy Barty.

COUNTER DOGGEREL
By Prof. De Morgan

Great A affirms of all;
Sir William does so too:
When the subject is "my suspicion,"
And the predicate "must be true."

Great E denies of all;
Sir William of all but one:
When he speaks about this present time,
And of those who in logic have done.

Great I takes up but some;
Sir William! my dear soul!
Why then in all your writings,
Does "Great I" fill the whole!

Great O says some are not;
Sir William's readers catch,
That some (modern) Athens is not without
An Aristotle to match.

Theater critic Frantisek Deak once wrote of Cointet's structuralist approach in plays such as Tell Me (1979) in which fashionably attired actresses variously describe a white cardboard square featuring the black capital letters A, D, M, and T—the artist juxtaposed 'lifelike casual conversation with contrived literary language... (pointing) out that both are particular styles and that, with a certain distance, the casual conversation will appear contrived as well'." [1]

so consistent with truth as my Readers in Spaceland might desire,—I must be content with saying that I succeeded at last in persuading her to return quietly to her household duties without eliciting from me any reference to the World of Three Dimensions. This done, I immediately sent for my Grandson; for, to confess the truth, I felt that all that I had seen and heard was in some strange way slipping away from me, like the image of a half-grasped, tantalizing dream, and I longed to essay my skill in making a first disciple.

When my Grandson entered the room I carefully secured the door. Then, sitting down by his side and taking our mathematical tablets,—or, as you would call them, Lines—I told him we would resume the lesson of yesterday. I taught him once more how a Point by motion in One Dimension produces a Line, and how a straight Line in Two Dimensions produces a Square. After this, forcing a laugh, I said, "And now, you scamp, you wanted to make me believe that a Square may in the same way by motion 'Upward, not Northward' produce another figure, a sort of extra Square in Three Dimensions. Say that again, you young rascal."

At this moment we heard once more the herald's "O yes! O yes!" outside in the street proclaiming the Resolution of the Council. Young though he was, my Grandson—who

199

"A half, left semi-definite,
Is worthy of its score:"
This looked very much like balderdash,
And neither less nor more.

It puzzled me like anything;
In fact, it puzzled me worse:
Isn't schoolman's logic hard enough,
Without being in Sibyl's verse?

At last, thinks I, 'tis German;
And I'll try it with some beer!
The landlord asked what bothered me so,
And at once he made it clear.

It's half-and-half, the gentleman means;
Don't you see he talks of score?
That's the bit of memorandum
That we chalk behind the door.

was unusually intelligent for his age, and bred up in perfect reverence for the authority of the Circles—took in the situation with an acuteness for which I was quite unprepared. He remained silent till the last words of the Proclamation had died away, and then, bursting into tears, "Dear Grandpapa," he said, "that was only my fun, and of course I meant nothing at all by it; and we did not know anything then about the new Law; and I don't think I said anything about the Third Dimension; and I am sure I did not say one word about 'Upward, not Northward', for that would be such nonsense, you know. How could a thing move Upward, and not Northward? Upward and not Northward! Even if I were a baby, I could not be so absurd as that. How silly it is! Ha! ha! ha!"

"Not at all silly," said I, losing my temper; "here for example, I take this Square," and, at the word, I grasped a moveable Square, which was lying at hand—"and I move it, you see, not Northward but—yes, I move it Upward—that is to say, not Northward, but I move it somewhere—not exactly like this, but somehow—" Here I brought my sentence to an inane conclusion, shaking the Square about in a purposeless manner, much to the amusement of my Grandson, who burst out laughing louder than ever, and declared that I was not

Semi-definite's outlandish;
But I see, in half a squint,
That he speaks of the lubbers who call for a quart,
When they can't manage more than a pint.

Now I'll read it into English,
And then you'll answer me this:
If it isn't good logic all the world round,
I should like to know what is?

When you call for a pot of half-and-half,
If you're lost to sense of shame,
You may leave it semi-definite,
But you pay for it all just the same.

FLATLAND, SEE PHOTOGRAM.

teaching him, but joking with him; and so saying he unlocked the door and ran out of the room. Thus ended my first attempt to convert a pupil to the Gospel of Three Dimensions.

"A photogram is a photographic image made without a camera by placing objects directly onto the surface of a light-sensitive material such as photographic paper and then exposing it to light. The usual result is a negative shadow image that shows variations in tone that depends upon the transparency of the objects used. Areas of the paper that have received no light appear white; those exposed through transparent or semi-transparent objects appear grey." [34]

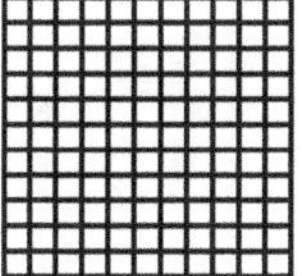

How I then tried to diffuse the Theory of Three Dimensions by other means, and of the result

My failure with my Grandson did not encourage me to communicate my secret to others of my household; yet neither was I led by it to despair of success. Only I saw that I must not wholly rely on the catch-phrase, "Upward, not Northward", but must rather endeavour to seek a demonstration by setting before the public a clear view of the whole subject; and for this purpose it seemed necessary to resort to writing.

So I devoted several months in privacy to the composition of a treatise on the mysteries of Three Dimensions. Only, with the view of evading the Law, if possible, I spoke not of a physical Dimension, but of a Thoughtland whence, in theory, a Figure could look down upon Flatland and see simultaneously the insides of all things, and where it was possible that there might be supposed to exist a Figure environed, as it were, with six Squares, and containing eight terminal Points. But in writing this book I found myself sadly hampered by the impossibility of drawing such diagrams as were necessary for my purpose; for of course, in our country of Flatland, there are no tablets but Lines, and no diagrams but Lines, all in one straight Line and only distinguishable by difference of size and brightness; so that, when I had finished my treatise (which I entitled, "Through Flatland to Thoughtland") I could not feel certain that many would understand my meaning.

Meanwhile my life was under a cloud. All pleasures palled upon me; all sights tantalized and tempted me to outspoken treason, because I could not but compare what I saw in Two Dimensions with what it really was if seen in Three, and could hardly refrain from making my comparisons aloud. I neglected my clients and my own business to give myself to the contemplation of the mysteries which I had once beheld, yet which I could impart to no one, and found daily more difficult to reproduce even before my own mental vision.

One day, about eleven months after my return from Spaceland, I tried to see a Cube with my eye closed, but failed; and though I succeeded afterwards, I was not then quite certain (nor have I been ever afterwards) that I had exactly realized the original. This made me more melancholy than before, and determined me to take some step; yet what, I knew not. I felt that I would have been willing to sacrifice my life for the Cause, if thereby I could have produced conviction. But if I could not convince my Grandson, how could I convince the highest and most developed Circles in the land?

And yet at times my spirit was too strong for me, and I gave vent to dangerous utterances. Already I was considered heterodox if not treasonable, and I was keenly alive to the danger of my position; nevertheless I could not at times

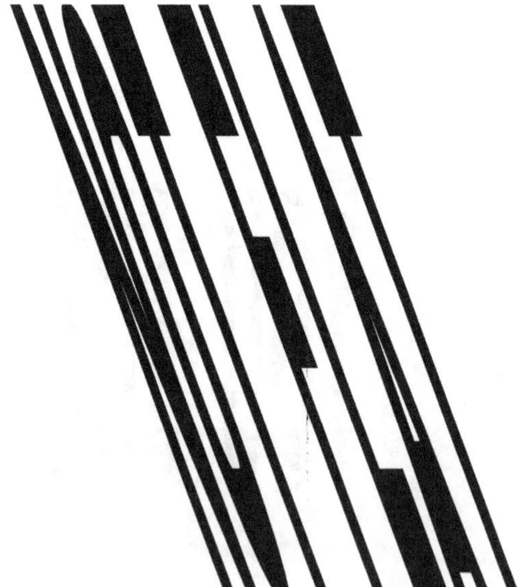

FLATLAND, SEE HERSTORY.

"Herstory is history written from a feminist perspective, emphasizing the role of women, or told from a woman's point of view. It is a neologism coined in the late 1960s as part of a feminist critique of conventional historiography, with the word 'history' reinterpreted, using a false etymology, as 'his story.' (The word 'history'—from the Ancient Greek historia, meaning 'knowledge obtained by inquiry'—is etymologically unrelated to the possessive pronoun his)." [1]

refrain from bursting out into suspicious or half-seditious utterances, even among the highest Polygonal and Circular society. When, for example, the question arose about the treatment of those lunatics who said that they had received the power of seeing the insides of things, I would quote the saying of an ancient Circle, who declared that prophets and inspired people are always considered by the majority to be mad; and I could not help occasionally dropping such expressions as "the eye that discerns the interiors of things", and "the all-seeing land"; once or twice I even let fall the forbidden terms "the Third and Fourth Dimensions". At last, to complete a series of minor indiscretions, at a meeting of our Local Speculative Society held at the palace of the Prefect himself,—some extremely silly person having read an elaborate paper exhibiting the precise reasons why Providence has limited the number of Dimensions to Two, and why the attribute of omnividence is assigned to the Supreme alone—I so far forgot myself as to give an exact account of the whole of my voyage with the Sphere into Space, and to the Assembly Hall in our Metropolis, and then to Space again, and of my return home, and of everything that I had seen and heard in fact or vision. At first, indeed, I pretended that I was describing the imaginary experiences of a fictitious person; but my enthusiasm soon forced me to throw off all disguise,

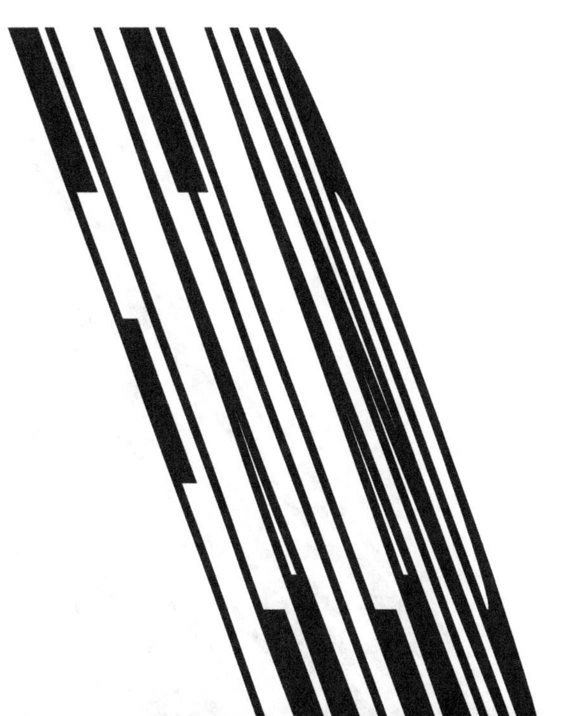

and finally, in a fervent peroration, I exhorted all my hearers to divest themselves of prejudice and to become believers in the Third Dimension.

Need I say that I was at once arrested and taken before the Council?

Next morning, standing in the very place where but a very few months ago the Sphere had stood in my company, I was allowed to begin and to continue my narration unquestioned and uninterrupted. But from the first I foresaw my fate; for the President, noting that a guard of the better sort of Policemen was in attendance, of angularity little, if at all, under 55 degrees, ordered them to be relieved before I began my defence, by an inferior class of 2 or 3 degrees. I knew only too well what that meant. I was to be executed or imprisoned, and my story was to be kept secret from the world by the simultaneous destruction of the officials who had heard it; and, this being the case, the President desired to substitute the cheaper for the more expensive victims.

After I had concluded my defence, the President, perhaps perceiving that some of the junior Circles had been moved by my evident earnestness, asked me two questions:—

1. Whether I could indicate the direction which I meant when I used the words "Upward, not Northward"?

2. Whether I could by any diagrams or descriptions

"Pong is a two-dimensional sports game that simulates table tennis. The player controls an in-game paddle by moving it vertically across the left side of the screen, and can compete against either a computer-controlled opponent or another player controlling a second paddle on the opposing side. Players use the paddles to hit a ball back and forth. The aim is for each player to reach eleven points before the opponent; points are earned when one fails to return the ball to the other." [1]

(other than the enumeration of imaginary sides and angles) indicate the Figure I was pleased to call a Cube?

I declared that I could say nothing more, and that I must commit myself to the Truth, whose cause would surely prevail in the end.

The President replied that he quite concurred in my sentiment, and that I could not do better. I must be sentenced to perpetual imprisonment; but if the Truth intended that I should emerge from prison and evangelize the world, the Truth might be trusted to bring that result to pass. Meanwhile I should be subjected to no discomfort that was not necessary to preclude escape, and, unless I forfeited the privilege by misconduct, I should be occasionally permitted to see my brother who had preceded me to my prison.

Seven years have elapsed and I am still a prisoner, and—if I except the occasional visits of my brother—debarred from all companionship save that of my jailers. My brother is one of the best of Squares, just, sensible, cheerful, and not without fraternal affection; yet I confess that my weekly interviews, at least in one respect, cause me the bitterest pain. He was present when the Sphere manifested himself in the Council Chamber; he saw the Sphere's changing sections; he heard the explanation of the phenomena then given to the Circles. Since that time, scarcely a week has passed during

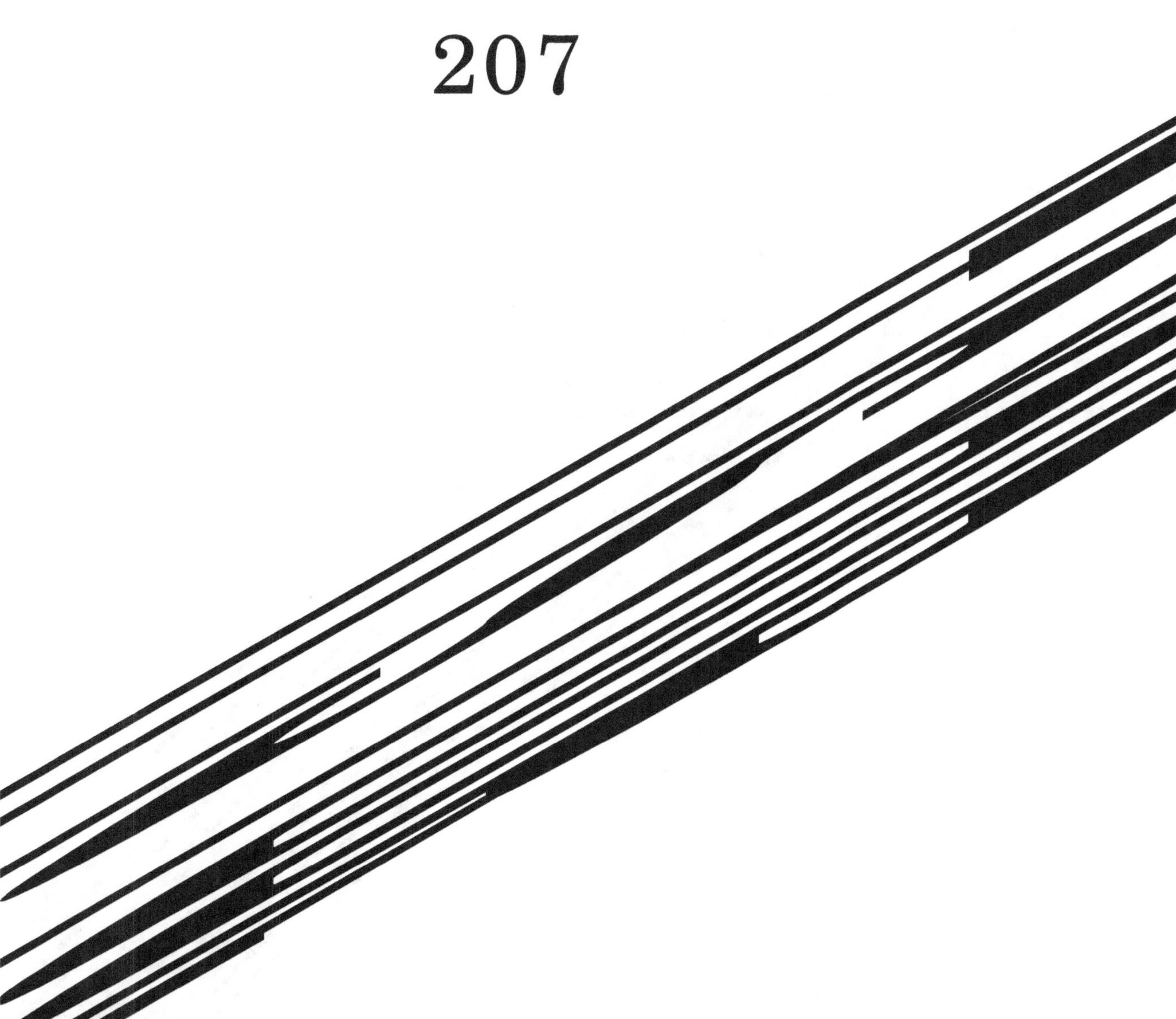

seven whole years, without his hearing from me a repetition of the part I played in that manifestation, together with ample descriptions of all the phenomena in Spaceland, and the arguments for the existence of Solid things derivable from Analogy. Yet—I take shame to be forced to confess it—my brother has not yet grasped the nature of the Third Dimension, and frankly avows his disbelief in the existence of a Sphere.

Hence I am absolutely destitute of converts, and, for aught that I can see, the millennial Revelation has been made to me for nothing. Prometheus up in Spaceland was bound for bringing down fire for mortals, but I—poor Flatland Prometheus—lie here in prison for bringing down nothing to my countrymen. Yet I exist in the hope that these memoirs, in some manner, I know not how, may find their way to the minds of humanity in Some Dimension, and may stir up a race of rebels who shall refuse to be confined to limited Dimensionality.

That is the hope of my brighter moments. Alas, it is not always so. Heavily weighs on me at times the burdensome reflection that I cannot honestly say I am confident as to the exact shape of the once-seen, oft-regretted Cube; and in my nightly visions the mysterious precept, "Upward, not Northward", haunts me like a soul-devouring Sphinx. It is

FLATLAND, SEE FLATLAND.

"Flatland: A Romance of Many Dimensions is an 1884 satirical novella by the English schoolmaster Edwin Abbott Abbott. Writing pseudonymously as 'A Square', the book used the fictional two-dimensional world of Flatland to comment on the hierarchy of Victorian culture; but the novella's more enduring contribution is its examination of dimensions." [1]

part of the martyrdom which I endure for the cause of the Truth that there are seasons of mental weakness, when Cubes and Spheres flit away into the background of scarce-possible existences; when the Land of Three Dimensions seems almost as visionary as the Land of One or None; nay, when even this hard wall that bars me from my freedom, these very tablets on which I am writing, and all the substantial realities of Flatland itself, appear no better than the offspring of a diseased imagination, or the baseless fabric of a dream.

How I then tried to diffuse the Theory of Three Dimensions by other means, and of the result

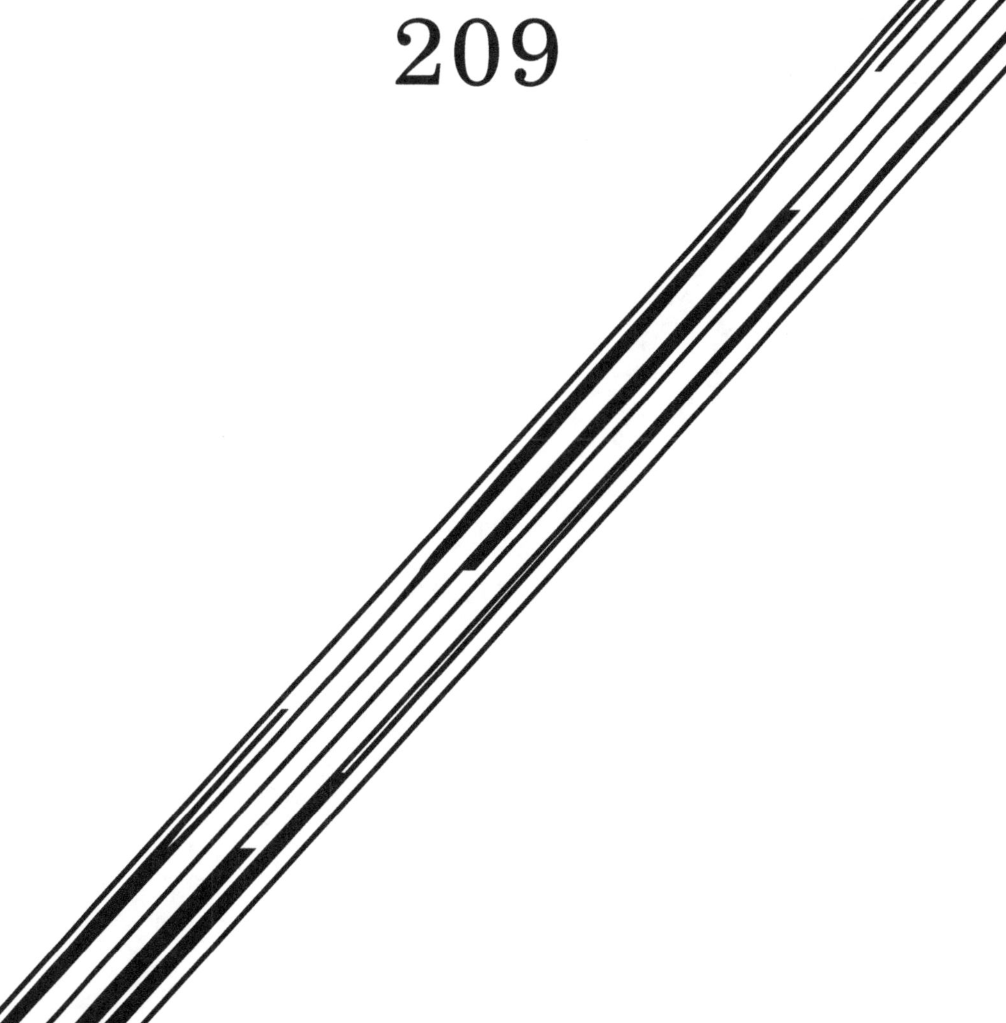

Colophon

Flatland, see Flatland.

Published by Booksfromthefuture as part of Booksfromthefuture Summer School 2014, a 10-day workshop on collaborative book design and practice-based inquiry led by Dante Carlos, Yvan Martinez and Joshua Trees and conducted at London Centre for Book Arts, Fish Island. Throughout the process, visiting practitioners Sheena Calvert, Ken Hollings and Ayse Koklu contributed invaluable perspectives and feedback.

This book contains the unabridged text of *Flatland: A Romance of Many Dimensions* (second edition, Seeley & Co., London, 1884).

Edited by Dante Carlos, Yvan Martinez and Joshua Trees

Designed by Johanna Asseraf, Dante Carlos, Emma Kalkhoven, Timothy Klofski, Elodie Märki, Yvan Martinez, Anya Radzevych, Line Arngaard Sørensen, Tsukasa Tanimoto, Joshua Trees, Marie-Pier Tremblay, Xue Wen

Special thanks to Ken Hollings for writing the book's preface, Alexander Shoukas for sharing his font Hora, Makoto Yamada for her editorial support, and London Centre for Book Arts (Simon Goode and Ira Yonemura) for hosting the workshop.

Printed by Lulu

booksfromthefuture.info

ISBN 978-0-9573509-2-2

1 Wikipedia
2 Artis
3 Dennis Overbye, 'Music of the Heavens Turns Out to Sound a Lot Like a B Flat', The New York Times, 2003
4 Manuel Cirauqui, 'Robert Breer', Frieze, 2010
5 Papillon Graphics' Virtual Encyclopedia & Guide to Greater Manchester
6 Fiona MacCarthy, British Design Since 1880: A Visual History, Lund Humphries, 1982
7 Clive Edwards, Turning Houses into Homes, Loughborough University, 2005
8 Matt Ratto and Megan Boler, DIY Citizenship: Critical Making and Social Media, MIT Press, 2014
9 Stephen Willats
10 Daniel Pies, 'Barbara Kasten', Frieze, 2011
11 Carl Sagan, 'Alternate high tech Mayan universe: note', The Seth MacFarlane Collection of the Carl Sagan and Ann Druyan Archive, 1978
12 Bilge Ebiri, 'Four Theories on The Shining From the New Documentary Room 237', Vulture, 2013
13 David Reinfurt and Robert Wiesenberger, Messages and Means: Muriel Cooper at MIT, Arthur Ross Architecture Gallery at Columbia University, 2014
14 Scholarpedia
15 Andrew Forbes, David Henley and Okakura Kakuzo, The Illustrated Book of Tea, Chiang Mai: Cognoscenti Books, 2012
16 Klaus Krippendorf, The Semantic Turn; A New Foundation for Design, CRC Press, 2005
17 Plato (translated by Allan Bloom), The Republic of Plato, Basic Books, 1991
18 Fausto Bernardini and Holly Rushmeier, 'The 3D Model Acquisition Pipeline', Computer Graphics Forum, 2002
19 David Harrison, 'The Special Theory of Relativity', Department of Physics at University of Toronto, 1999
20 Claude Bragdon, The New Image, Kessinger Publishing Company, 1998
21 Audium
22 YouTube
23 Gerhard Kaldewei, History, Design, Architecture 1882–2000, Hatje Cantz, 2000
24 Richard Newton Scarth, Echoes from the Sky: A Story of Acoustic Defence, Hythe Civic Society, 1999
25 Stephanie Syjuco
26 Benjamin Breen, 'Victorian Occultism and the Art of Synesthesia', The Public Domain Review
27 Brian Dillon, 'Aby Warburg's Mnemosyne Atlas', Frieze, 2004
28 Valentin Gómez-Jáuregui, Tensegrity Structures and their Application to Architecture, Ediciones Universidad de Cantabria, 2010
29 Ria Misra, 'This mysterious rock just appeared in front of our rove on Mars', io9, 2014
30 Slashdot
31 David Nolte, 'The Tangled Tale of Phase Space', Physics Today, 2010
32 Geoff Manaugh, 'The Handheld Mathematics of Geometer Ron Resch', Gizmodo, 2013
33 Karl Gerstner, Designing Programmes, Lars Muller, 2013
34 Michael Langford, Basic Photography, Focal Press, 2007

www.ingramcontent.com/pod-product-compliance
Lightning Source LLC
Chambersburg PA
CBHW080802020726
47501CB00008B/2314
9780957350922